Also by Jackie Ashenden

Right Where We Belong

JACKIE ASHENDEN

sourcebooks
casablanca

Published by Sourcebooks Casablanca, an imprint of Sourcebooks
P.O. Box 4410, Naperville, Illinois 60567–4410
(630) 961-3900
sourcebooks.com

Printed and bound in the United States of America.
OPM 10 9 8 7 6 5 4 3 2 1

*To Paul, who decided that all wētās
should be called Wally.*

Chapter 1

INDIGO JAMESON DIDN'T TRUST PEOPLE AS A general rule.

Especially men.

Especially the one currently sitting at her kitchen table looking like butter wouldn't melt in his mouth.

He'd disposed of a massive spiky insect she'd found on the floor of her living room not five minutes before. It was apparently a native New Zealand insect called a wētā, but since it looked like something out of a prehistoric nightmare—all spiky carapace and thorny, spindly legs—Indigo didn't want it in her house. Levi had picked it up in his bare hands—*his bare hands!*—and taken it outside, muttering something about being nice to "Wally." So, she shouldn't be too upset with him. It wasn't as if the broom she'd been holding in front of her would have been any protection if the wētā suddenly took it into its head to leap on her and eat her face, or something equally horrific.

Then again, she *was* in her pajamas, her hair a complete mess, and she'd been a total wuss about the wētā. While he was…

Well, he was gorgeous. That was the problem.

Her grandmother had always warned her about gorgeous men, about handsome men, about men who looked too good to be true, because they always were. You couldn't trust them an inch.

Her grandmother could have been talking about Levi King, since he was the prime example of everything Grandma Tilly had warned her about.

Not only could he pick up scary insects in his bare hands, but his shaggy hair was dark brown shot through with gold, and his hazel eyes had glints of gold in them too. His skin was smooth and tanned and, in the sunlight, looked deep gold as well.

His face was fallen-angel beautiful—high cheekbones, straight nose, strong jaw, beautifully carved mouth—and he was tall, six three at least. His shoulders were wide, his chest broad, hard, and muscled, his waist lean, his legs long and powerful.

He looked like he'd been chiseled out of marble by some master sculptor and then given a scattering of gold dust for good measure.

Not that she'd been looking or anything.

No, she hadn't spent the last two months seemingly incapable of noticing anything else but him, and she definitely wasn't annoyed about it.

She definitely wasn't annoyed about her apparent fascination with him in general, because she could ignore him at any time.

Completely and utterly ignore him.

After all, she'd come to Brightwater Valley, in New Zealand's South Island, to start a new business along with her friends Isabella Montgomery and Bethany Grant, and she did not have time to be distracted by handsome men.

The three of them had come from Deep River, Alaska—oh, okay, so only Beth and she were from Deep River; Izzy was from Texas—following a call from Brightwater Valley for entrepreneurs to start new businesses here as a way of reviving the town. Brightwater Valley was Deep River's sister town, and since both of them were small and isolated, they had a certain kinship.

Indigo had made the trek to New Zealand along with Beth and Izzy, and the three of them had opened a gallery called Brightwater Dreams. It stocked jewelry and local arts and crafts, gourmet foods and handmade soaps and skin care, plus a widening range of other products.

Indigo's specialty was yarn. She'd learned all about knitting and fiber arts at her grandmother's knee, and what she particularly liked was dyeing. She was fascinated with color and loved nothing better than messing around with dye pots and discovering different colorways.

What she did not love were handsome men sitting at the kitchen table of the farmhouse where she was living, spreading a whole lot of brochures out on said table, and presenting them to her as if they were new.

Because they weren't new. She'd seen them before. She'd been poring over them for the past couple of weeks, ever since Beth had fallen for and then moved in with Finn Kelly, and Indigo had realized she would need to find a more permanent place to stay.

The real question, though, was how did Levi King know she'd been looking at brochures? How had he gotten his own? And perhaps most important, why did he think her living situation had anything to do with him?

"Come on, Indy," Levi said, using the nickname he'd given her that she told everyone she hated— but secretly adored because no one had ever given her a nickname before. "Forget about the wētā and sit down."

"How can I forget about the wētā? You called it Wally!" This seemed important. That he'd named the wētā.

He only shrugged. "All wētās are Wally."

Indigo stared at him blankly. "What?"

"They just are." He raised his hands. "Sorry, I don't make the rules."

"But—"

"Don't worry about Wally. He's fine. Let's talk about your housing problem."

Indigo was not worried about Wally.

After dealing with the insect, Levi had come back into the house to tell her he had a solution to the issue of housing, and did she want to hear it?

She did not.

It had been her experience that handsome men were even more suspicious when they told her they had the answer to all her problems, because that generally turned out not to be the case. Generally, it was the handsome men who were the problem.

"No, thank you. Don't you have important guiding work to do?"

Levi was part owner of an outdoor adventure company called Pure Adventure New Zealand that was based in Brightwater Valley. Brothers Chase and Finn Kelly were co-owners, and the three men ran guided hikes, horseback riding, kayaking, boat tours, heli-skiing, and other adventure activities.

Indigo wasn't into adventure activities.

And she definitely wasn't into this man being in her house.

"No," Levi said patiently. "It's evening, in case you haven't noticed."

She had noticed actually. That's why she was in her pajamas. "Then don't you have a home to go to?"

Levi ignored her and picked up a brochure. "Look. The answer to all your housing dreams."

Indigo pulled the hand-knit shawl she'd wrapped around herself to cover the fact she wasn't wearing a bra tighter around her shoulders and glared at him, because sadly, it *was* the answer to her housing dreams, and she was annoyed that he'd found out about it.

She'd thought she'd been quite careful about not telling a soul she'd been looking into tiny houses and whether she had the option of building one in Brightwater Valley. Now it seemed someone had talked.

She *might* have mentioned it in passing to Izzy, being not at all specific, but since Izzy was Chase Kelly's fiancée, Izzy must have talked to Chase, and of course Chase, being the pain in the butt that he was, would have likely mentioned it to Finn, and no doubt then Levi would have found out.

Secrets could not be kept in a small town, which she should have known since she came from a small town herself.

Not that her housing plan was actually a secret. She just liked keeping her cards close to her vest.

"Who told you that I wanted that?" She gestured to the brochure, on which was pictured the most adorable tiny house with lavender out front and a little vegetable garden.

Levi, irritatingly, again ignored her. "I can build you one of these easily. And it wouldn't take me very long. In fact, given no issues with suppliers, you could be in by winter."

Which was in three months.

And she had to be out of the farmhouse soon, because Finn had finally hired someone to permanently manage the stables that were attached to the farmhouse. Pure Adventure NZ ran horse trekking, and Clint, who used to own and manage the stables, had moved to the city a month earlier, which had left the Pure Adventure team without a permanent stable manager. But now that Finn had found one, Indigo was going to have to move because accommodation in the farmhouse was part of the job package.

She didn't mind moving, and Finn had given her plenty of alternatives to the farmhouse. But the tiny house option was one she'd been especially fantasizing about. A tiny home of her own, with perhaps a dyeing shed out back and lots of lovely flowers and herbs. Maybe even a cat.

She didn't need a lot of space. She liked small and cozy. The house she'd grown up in had been like that. Small and cluttered and homey. It had been fairly isolated from the rest of the Deep River community, but she hadn't minded that.

Her grandmother had always told her that the outside world was a dangerous place, and after the stroke, she'd become even more paranoid.

Indigo couldn't blame her. Indigo's parents had split up just before Indigo had been born, her mother returning to her own mother's house to live. Then seven years later, Indigo's father had reentered the picture.

Indigo had been thrilled. Her mother had told her stories about her handsome, charming dad, and indeed, he was everything she'd thought he'd be. So, when he'd told her that he and her mother were moving to Anchorage, and that once they were all set up, they'd come back for her, she'd accepted it. Indigo loved her grandmother and didn't mind staying with her in the meantime. Her dad had promised that she'd join him and her mother eventually, and Indigo had believed him.

And she'd carried on believing it as months went by and more promises were given. Soon, her father had said. Soon, she'd join them. By her birthday, her mom had said during one phone call. By Christmas. But then the calls had stopped, the birthday cards and letters had become sporadic, and then there was nothing at all.

Indigo had stopped believing in promises then, and she stopped trusting that people would do what they said. There were only two people worthy of her trust: one of them was dead and the other was *not* Levi King.

"No, thank you," she repeated, wondering how many times she'd have to say it before he stopped talking about it. Levi was like a sandfly, the irritatingly persistent biting insects that were a curse when you lived by any body of water in New Zealand's South Island. No amount of clothing would stop them, and only tropical-strength insect repellent could repel them.

What she needed was Levi repellent, and sadly, she didn't have any.

True to form, Levi didn't collect his brochures

and get his ass out of her kitchen. He put his elbows on the table and gave her the wicked grin that turned all her insides into a quivering wreck. Not that she'd ever let him know that.

"Are we ever going to talk about it?" he asked.

A long shaft of sunset light speared through the window and illuminated Levi where he sat, dipping him in gold.

And oh man, she hated it when the sun did that. She could see the gold threads in his hair and in his eyelashes. The gold flecks deep in his eyes. That smile of his was mesmerizing, as were his strong forearms and the large capable hands he'd clasped in front of him. His fingers were long and blunt and extremely dexterous. She knew they were, because she'd watched him fix any kind of machine you'd care to name, as well as gently gripping the elbow of a client to steady them on a trek. Or lifting someone into the saddle of a horse. Or manipulating the controls of the helicopter the crew of Pure Adventure NZ owned. Or carrying a scary insect gently outside.

You should not be so fixated on his hands.

No, she shouldn't. She shouldn't be so fixated on him, period.

Men had always seemed deeply suspicious to her, so she'd missed the schoolgirl-crush stage when she'd been a teenager. Not that she'd ever met guys anyway, since her grandmother hadn't liked her to leave their house for too long. And even if she had left the house, if she'd seen a hot man, she'd have avoided him like the plague.

So, it was disconcerting to find her mouth had gone dry. In fact, all her physical reactions to Levi were disconcerting, not to mention unwelcome.

He would go if she asked him and was utterly serious about it. She knew that. But something inside her wouldn't let her dismiss him quite yet. That tiny house was just...beautiful.

Indigo gripped her shawl tighter and gave him a mistrustful look. "Talk about what?"

"About why you don't like me."

Great. So, they were going to have *that* discussion, were they?

Over the past two and a half months she'd been in Brightwater, she and Levi had been at each other's throats. Or rather, she'd been at Levi's while he'd simply let her chew at him. Initially he'd flirted outrageously with her. Mostly, she'd decided, because she didn't want him to, and there was nothing Levi liked better than annoying someone.

So, she'd told him to stop, and to give credit where credit was due, he had. Unfortunately, much to her chagrin, she didn't like that either. In fact, she often found herself in his vicinity, surrounded by clouds of irritation, mainly at herself for being in his vicinity, and yet unable to leave him alone.

She didn't know why she found him so fascinating. He was everything she should have hated. He flirted outrageously with everyone and everything, obviously thinking himself God's gift. He always had a comeback, never seemed to get angry when people snapped at him, and could both create tense situations by being a dick and also defuse them with sincerity and honesty that left people speechless.

He was one of those intensely charismatic, engaging assholes, with a surface so slick you'd always find yourself sliding off it.

Indigo had wondered sometimes if there was anything beneath that surface—and it *was* a surface. She could tell. But he'd never given her even a hint of the substance beneath it. If there *was*, in fact, any substance.

Maybe that was why she found him so fascinating. She was curious and she didn't want to be.

"I like you fine." It sounded unconvincing even to her own ears.

Wordlessly, Levi raised one dark-shot-with-gold brow.

Indigo glared. "Okay, no, I don't like you."

He didn't seem to find this a problem, which only irritated her more. "Why not?"

Many reasons. The main one being that her father had been one of those charismatic assholes, and while Levi wasn't exactly like her father, there were enough similarities that Indigo couldn't find it in herself to trust him.

But she wasn't going to tell him that. The

wētā incident had put her off-balance, and Levi bringing brochures containing her fondest dreams and spreading them all over the kitchen table, even more so. It was as if he'd seen the contents of her soul and was pawing through it for his own pleasure.

A tad dramatic, maybe?

Not at all. Frank Jameson had known how much Indigo adored him and wanted to go with him and her mother, Claire, to Anchorage to live. He'd known and he'd used it to convince Indigo's initially reluctant mother. Claire, starry-eyed at his return, had believed him too, swallowed all his lies, hook, line, and sinker.

Indigo had never forgotten her mother's betrayal either.

People couldn't be trusted, period. In fact, there was now only one person she trusted completely, and that was herself. Though since Levi was here, she might as well listen to what he had to say about this house idea. Then she'd take the info and do her own thing.

Indigo fussed with her shawl, then reached for one of the kitchen chairs, pulled it out, and sat down opposite her hated enemy. "I don't want to talk about that," she said flatly. "Let's talk about my house instead."

RIGHT WHERE WE BELONG

Levi knew that needling Indigo was a bad idea. But bad ideas were his catnip and he absolutely couldn't resist them.

It had always been that way, ever since he could remember. If something was dangerous or mad, or simply stupid, he had to do it. Sometimes it worked out well; sometimes it didn't.

The numerous social workers who'd managed his life back when he'd been a kid in the foster system had made copious notes and had intense discussions about his poor impulse control and perhaps undiagnosed ADHD. But all the notes and discussions had remained just that: notes and discussions. No one had actually done anything, which was kind of the story of his life.

He didn't mind. He'd figured it out himself and worked out ways to manage his many and often suicidal impulses.

Probably having this discussion with Indigo was suicidal, in which case he needed to handle himself and talk about the tiny-house brain wave he'd had earlier like she'd said.

Except...

She sat across from him, her small form swathed in a giant shawl knit in various shades of blue. Her long, dark brown hair was tangled over her shoulders, her sky-blue eyes narrowed, her delicate, precise features set in stern, no-nonsense lines.

She was judgmental, prickly as a hedgehog,

apparently had no sense of humor, and he wished he found that as off-putting as it sounded.

But the fact was that he didn't.

Because she was also pretty as hell, cute as a button, and sexy as all get-out, and he was still suffering from the wētā incident not five minutes earlier.

Not from the wētā itself—he liked wētās—but from the sight of her with a broom raised above her head, brown hair tangled in a wild skein down her back, and wearing the cutest pair of pajama pants he'd ever seen. They had little hedgehogs all over them, which suited her down to the ground. Though even those had paled in comparison to the light blue, loose T-shirt she was also wearing. The fabric was silky and soft-looking and rather clinging, so he'd known in an instant she didn't have a bra on underneath it.

She'd grabbed a shawl to put around her shoulders as they'd come into the kitchen, and thank God, because he wasn't sure his body could stand being in close proximity to the vision that was Indigo Jameson's perfect round breasts.

The past couple of months of her being everywhere he looked had been hard enough—in more ways than one—let alone sitting across the table from her.

Riling her up didn't help, of course, but as with most things concerning Indigo, he couldn't seem to help himself.

"You didn't answer my question," he said.

"You're one of those boys, aren't you?" Her little

chin jutted, her blue gaze spitting sparks at him. "The ones that pull girls' hair in school because 'you like them.'" Her hands came up to give the words exaggerated quotation marks. "You know what that is in reality though, don't you?" She leaned forward slightly. "Toxic masculinity."

Dammit. Maybe he was like that. Certainly he couldn't seem to resist pulling her pigtails, even if that was only metaphorically. And if that made him a damn cliché, then he was a damn cliché.

"No one's ever found my masculinity toxic before—or at least they didn't tell me if they did," he said and grinned. "You could be the first though. Shall we discuss in greater detail?"

Indigo's expression got very set. "No, we shall not. Who told you I've been thinking about a tiny house?"

He gazed at her a second, noting the tension in her chin and jaw, her neck and shoulders. It was probably better if he didn't push her.

He could control himself. He'd been doing it for the past two months after all.

Being in the army had given him the structure and discipline his early life had lacked, and had taught him how to keep his impulses in check. He'd learned early on that throwing himself into dangerous missions and situations helped with his excess energy, as did focusing on tasks such as fixing engines or anything else mechanical.

However, when there wasn't a dangerous or overly physical thing to do or an engine to fix, he had to rely on his own self-control. Luckily, being around Chase and Finn helped with that, since the two of them were such control freaks in their own way, and he'd learned how to keep himself locked down.

"Who told me?" He gave her a curious look. "Why? Does it matter?" It had been Chase who'd mentioned it in passing a few weeks earlier, and he'd likely heard it from Izzy, his pretty Texan fiancée.

Levi wouldn't mind telling Indigo he'd heard it from Chase, but something in her expression told him that she wouldn't be pleased about it.

"I never told anyone but Izzy." Indigo was looking very annoyed. "And I didn't want her to tell anyone else."

"Why? Is it a big secret?"

Her expression darkened and she glanced away. "No, I just…" Her voice trailed off; then after a moment she glanced back at him. "Look, all of this has got nothing to do with you, okay? I appreciate you getting rid of the wētā for me, but I don't need you involving yourself in my housing issues."

"Wally," Levi felt compelled to point out. "The wētā's name is Wally."

Indigo just looked at him as if he was speaking Greek.

"And as for the housing issue," he went on. "You haven't heard my solution yet."

"Thanks, but I already have a solution."

"Have you?"

Her mouth, which he'd tried not to notice, was of the delicious rosebud variety, and it compressed. "Yes."

"And what is it?"

"None of your business."

He grinned. "You don't have one, do you?"

She stared crossly at him, which of course meant that she didn't.

Really, she was such a prickly little thing, and he wasn't sure why he found that quite so fascinating. Perhaps it was because women generally weren't prickly with him. In fact, they liked him and he liked them. A lot. He never had to work for their attention, and he was always appreciative of it. And if, on the rare occasion it happened, a woman wasn't into him, he didn't mind. There were plenty of others who were.

Then again, it had been a *long* time since a woman had taken against him quite as fully as Indigo Jameson had, and the basic male in him was curious as to why. Especially since her dislike had been apparent from the moment they'd met.

But no. He'd already made the decision that he wasn't going there with Indigo Jameson. She didn't like him, and no matter how sexy and interesting he found her, he wasn't going to push himself where he wasn't wanted.

No, what he was going to do was find a solution to her accommodation crisis. Initially, there had been plans for the three Deep River ladies to move into a currently vacant house near the township, but those had fallen through when the house was determined to be unsafe and its owner, who was overseas, couldn't be contacted. By that stage, Izzy and Chase had fallen in love and she'd moved in with him. Beth and Indigo, who'd been living at the Rose, Brightwater's hotel, had moved into the farmhouse after Clint, who'd owned the stables, had sold it to Finn and gone to Christchurch to live.

But then Finn and Beth had gotten together, and Finn had found a permanent stable manager. Since the house came with the job, that left Indigo with nowhere to go.

Free houses were at a premium in Brightwater Valley and since there were none to be had currently, Indigo's only alternative seemed to be going back to live at the Rose. Then Chase had mentioned something about tiny houses to Levi, and a fantastic idea had been born. Not only would it solve Indigo's problem, but it would also, hopefully, cast him in a more positive light.

He was getting tired of being viewed as an enemy.

You could, of course, just stop being a dick around her.

Yeah, that too. But he was trying not to be one, as he hoped she'd see with this idea of his.

"So," he said when she didn't speak, "here's what I've been thinking. I've got some land here in Brightwater. I haven't built anything on it yet. It's just bush at the moment. But there's a great spot that wouldn't require too much clearing where we could build something like one of those tiny houses." He gestured at the brochures. "Any one of those would fit, and it would take me probably...well, without help, three to four months. With help from Chase and Finn, probably two to three. You could be in there by winter if we don't run into too many issues."

Indigo's chin had gotten a mulish cast to it, and there was a stony expression on her face. "That's great and all, Levi. But I don't have any money for a tiny house, let alone for the land to build it on." She leaned forward all of a sudden and began to gather all the brochures up. "So if you could just take these and—"

"I haven't finished," he interrupted.

She let out an annoyed-sounding breath. "I don't know what—"

"I'm not asking for money." He met her irritated gaze and for once didn't smile, so she would know he was serious. "I don't want you to give me a cent. The land is mine, and I can do what I want with it, plus tiny houses are cheap to build."

She blinked. "What? You mean you won't charge me for it? At all?"

He grinned. "That's what I said."

Indigo stared at him for a long moment, and he let himself enjoy her surprise, waiting for the happiness and gratitude that would no doubt follow. Oh, she'd probably protest and might want to insist on some kind of payment, but he'd gently refuse. He had plenty of money and he never spent it, so this would be no skin off his nose. And he liked building things. Building one of those tiny houses would be a great project to keep him occupied for the next couple of months or so.

Except there was no happiness or gratitude on Indigo's face. Only a glare that threatened to melt him on the spot.

"No," she said flatly. "Absolutely not."

This time it was his turn to blink. "What do you mean, 'Absolutely not'?"

"I mean no, I don't want you building me a house."

Levi didn't get angry. Anger wasn't a useful emotion, and it didn't get you what you wanted anyway, so what was the point? Yet he felt an undeniable flicker of irritation coiling through him now.

He'd thought about this house stuff carefully, and it wasn't some off-the-cuff offer he'd make to just anyone. He wanted to do it for her.

Two of her friends now had partners and were starting families, but Indigo had no one. She wasn't a local here. She was a newcomer and that set her apart. She was on her own, and he knew what that was like. Even though he'd been here for over five years, he was still thought of as a newcomer himself, and that was isolating.

The thought made some deep, protective instinct he hadn't known he possessed stir to life inside him.

"Why not?" An edge crept into his voice even though he tried not to let it. "You need a place to stay and you like tiny houses. This is the perfect solution."

She scowled. "So, what? I just let you build me a house? For free?"

"Yeah, that's what I said. And what's wrong with it being for free? I don't need money. I've got plenty of it."

"How nice for you," she snapped. "But I don't need or want any charity. I don't need a pity house. And I'm certainly not going to live in one that *you* built that sits on *your* land. Because seriously, how does that make it mine?"

Okay, she had a point there.

"Fine," he said patiently. "Then I'll subdivide my property and you can have some of it. I'll gift it to you."

"You absolutely will not."

"Really? What's wrong with that? It would be yours and in your name."

"Yes, and you still would have given it to me."

He couldn't see the issue. He had land, and

she needed some but had no money for it. Why shouldn't he give her a part of it? "So? I'm not using it. Seriously, I bought the place a few years ago and haven't done anything with it."

Indigo continued to glare, her white teeth sunk into her soft-looking bottom lip. With her shawl wrapped around her, her dark hair falling everywhere, and her summer-blue eyes stormy with annoyance, she reminded him of a highly irritated kitten. All sharp little teeth and sharp little claws.

It made him want to stroke her ruffled fur to soothe her.

"I don't care if you haven't done anything with it. It's still your land, and if you're buying the materials for the house as well as building it, then it will be your house too."

"Not if it's in your name," he pointed out.

"I still don't care. It's the principle of the thing." She collected the brochures into a little stack and pushed them across the table to him. "Don't get me wrong. I appreciate the offer, Levi. But the answer is no."

Chapter 2

"WHAT DO YOU MEAN, YOU TOLD HIM NO?" Bethany Grant said as she ham-fistedly struggled with the knitting needles Indigo had given her.

Beth had decided she wanted to learn to knit and had refused the beginner baby blanket Indigo had suggested, going straight for a much more difficult pair of booties. It was for the baby she was having in about five months, and she wanted to do it herself. Apparently.

Indigo sighed, reached over, and coaxed the needles away from her, expertly reattaching some dropped stitches and fixing a hole. "I mean, I told him no."

"Why did you do that?" Izzy asked, frowning at her own knitting.

The three of them, plus Shirley, who filled in at Bill Preston's general store, and who had been helping Indigo source yarn and various other things, and, surprisingly, Jim O'Halloran, who owned the Rose Hotel, one of three buildings that comprised Brightwater Valley's tiny township.

This was the second meeting of the Brightwater Valley knitting circle, which Indigo had decided to set up after Beth had wanted to learn how to knit. Shirley had brought along her needles, then Izzy had decided she wanted to join in, and then Jim had quietly appeared, whipping out a crochet hook and making a granny square with silent competence.

It was an odd bunch of people, but then Brightwater Valley was full of odd bunches of people, which made Indigo feel right at home. Deep River, back in Alaska, was also full of odd bunches of people.

The Rose Hotel was a two-story, ramshackle old wooden building that faced Brightwater Lake with the road separating the lake foreshore from the hotel. Indigo had a fondness for it, especially the deep porch with its big shady awning and the chairs that had been set out on it. The perfect place to enjoy some late summer heat.

To the right of them was a long, low stone building that housed Bill's general store and Brightwater Dreams, the gallery space she, Beth, and Izzy had set up. And to the left was a much newer two-story wooden building that was the Pure Adventure New Zealand HQ.

It was a Saturday evening, the cicadas were still buzzing loudly in the twilight heat, and a few tourists were parked by the lake, though the big buses that came at least once a day had all left. A couple of people were paddling kayaks, which they'd hired from Pure Adventure HQ, judging from Finn

Kelly's tall form standing on the lakeshore and watching them alertly.

Surreptitiously, Indigo checked to make sure she couldn't see any other equally tall form, with shaggy dark hair shot with gold, but there was no sign of him.

"Because he was offering to give me the land and the materials to build the house," she explained, handing back the bootie to Beth. "I couldn't take them."

There were other reasons too. Reasons that had far more to do with her father than she wanted to admit, but she wasn't going to get into that right now. Anyway, her dad was long gone and so was her mom, both still living it up in Anchorage. She was over her abandonment issues.

So over them you refused Levi's help point-blank.

Yeah, she had, and she'd do it again. He might not be anything like her father, but she wasn't going to take the risk. She knew how that had turned out.

"Levi's got land here?" Izzy asked in surprise, putting the plain scarf she was knitting down in her lap.

"Yep," Jim said unexpectedly. "Bought it off me a few years back. It's up the hill."

Indigo knew enough of the inhabitants of the town by now to know that "the hill" could mean any one of a number of hills around the town, or even one of the jagged mountains that ringed Brightwater Lake. Jim was fond of understatements.

"Which hill?" Beth asked.

Jim inclined his head to the right, where the general store and the gallery were. "Over there."

She, Beth, and Izzy all looked. There was nothing but the old stone building and the bush that covered the hill directly behind it.

"You mean the hill behind the gallery?" Izzy asked.

"Yes." Shirley rearranged bits of material she was holding in her lap. She wasn't knitting today; she was sewing. "And the gallery too."

Indigo blinked in surprise. "The gallery? But doesn't Bill own that building?"

But Izzy was shaking her head. "No, Bill doesn't own it. The rent we pay goes into a company account, and I'm pretty sure it's not Bill's."

"It isn't," Shirley said. "Levi owns it."

There was a shocked silence.

Indigo looked at Beth and Izzy, because this was the first she'd heard of Levi owning anything, let alone the building their gallery was in. Did they know? But the other two looked as surprised as she was.

"Jim..." Izzy began.

Jim didn't look up from his crocheting. "Needed to sell it. Needed the money. I wanted to sell it to someone in town, but no one could pay for it. No one except Levi. He told me he'd never sell it to some bugger developer or any of that malarky, and he had cash." Jim lifted a shoulder. "So, I sold it to him. Kept his word too."

It was the longest sentence that any of them had heard from Jim, and there was a moment's silence in acknowledgment.

Then Beth muttered, "Finn has got some explaining to do."

"So has Chase," Izzy added, frowning. "He didn't tell me anything about it."

"Well, no, he wouldn't." Shirley examined the quilt square she was sewing. "Levi doesn't like people to know."

"Really?" Indigo didn't bother to hide her skepticism, because Levi not wanting people to know he owned a chunk of Brightwater Valley seemed… unlike him.

Shirley glanced up from her sewing and gave Indigo a look over the top of her glasses. She was in her late sixties, with a soft, grandmotherly face and dark eyes sharper than a pair of knitting needles. Her hair was pure white, very curly, and worn down to her shoulders. She reminded Indigo of an encouraging art teacher who could turn very stern at the drop of a hat.

"Yes." Shirley's voice held a slight edge of warning that any criticism of Levi would not be tolerated. "He's uncomfortable about it."

"Why?" Beth sounded intrigued. "That man clearly has hidden depths."

"People here don't like outsiders owning things," Jim said, not looking up from his granny square. "So, we keep it quiet."

It was clear he meant that it should stay quiet too.

Interested despite herself and not wanting to show it, Indigo leaned back in her chair and glanced down, unseeing, at the shawl she was knitting.

How weird that Levi should end up owning the building that housed the general store. It made her uncomfortable, especially because the business she and the others had started was based in that same building.

She didn't know what she thought about that. She didn't know what she thought about Levi having money either. He'd mentioned it the night before, when he'd made his offer, but she'd been so shocked and not a little incensed by the thought of him giving her a house and land that she hadn't realized he must be loaded if he could afford to just hand them over.

And now that she thought about it, it wasn't the money that bothered her. It was that she hadn't known about it. Because he never talked about it.

People hid things. They told you how special you were to them while at the same time planning on abandoning you. And when they told you how much they loved you, they were just straight out lying.

Levi didn't lie—or at least she'd never caught

him in one—but it was obvious he'd kept things hidden, which was not a point in his favor.

That made her wonder where he'd gotten his money, because he certainly couldn't have gotten it doing guiding or being in the army. And he didn't seem to spend it on anything but wild nights in Queenstown bars.

Beth had mentioned to her that he had a house in Queenstown, and that it was a pretty fancy one, but since he never seemed to live there, Indigo hadn't thought about it again.

But she was thinking about it now and she wished she wasn't. She wished she wasn't thinking about Levi King at all.

At that moment, there came the sound of footsteps on the porch, and then a deep, smooth voice said, "Is this a private party? Or can anyone join?"

Everything in Indigo went tight, the way it always did whenever Levi was around.

She looked up from her shawl.

Sure enough, leaning against one of the wooden posts that supported the awning was Levi's tall muscular form.

The late morning sun was doing its usual glorious thing with his hair, making her want to run her fingers through it to see all those beautiful golden threads, like a miner panning for gold in a stream. His hazel eyes gleamed, and she found herself mesmerized by the golden flecks in them too.

He wore a black Pure Adventure NZ T-shirt, the way all the guys did, with worn, dusty jeans, and standing there leaning casually against the post, he was the most ridiculously handsome man she'd ever seen.

"Speak of the devil," Shirley said, smiling at him, her soft spot for Levi clearly on display. Not that having a soft spot for Levi was unusual. In fact, everyone in the entire town seemed to have a soft spot for Levi, which made it very difficult when all Indigo wanted to do was complain about him.

Even more difficult that her dislike was complicated by her own inexplicable and intense physical reaction to him.

She had zero experience with men, but Indigo wasn't stupid. She knew that for some reason she was very attracted to Levi. She also knew that she hated it.

Grandma had been very specific: never let a man's good looks turn your head, because the good-looking ones were always the ones who couldn't be trusted. And Grandma hadn't been wrong about that. Indigo's father had been extremely good-looking, and he'd used it to his advantage shamelessly, having had more than one affair while married to Claire. She'd found out soon after she'd gotten pregnant with Indigo and, heartbroken, had left him.

And that would have been that if he hadn't

reappeared not long after Indigo turned seven, wanting Claire to take him back, and of course she had. She'd never been able to resist a handsome man, or so Grandma had said. Indigo had loved her father back then. He'd brought her gifts, told her stories, taken her for ice cream. She'd thought he'd hung the very moon in the sky.

Until he'd left with her mother and never returned, and she'd understood that the moon had only been a flashlight that had blinded her.

He'd kept making promises over the years—he and her mother both—that eventually they'd come back for her. But they never had. Frank just hadn't loved her enough, while Claire had loved a handsome face more than her own daughter.

Reason enough not to want to have anything to do with men, most especially the good-looking ones. She'd never believe in a man's promises again like she had with her father, and she'd certainly never be her mother, letting her head be turned by a pretty face.

She was smarter than that these days.

"It's a knitting circle," Indigo said pointedly, staring hard at her shawl and not at him. "So, if you can't knit, you can't join."

"I can't knit, and I joined," Beth said, then cursed under her breath. "I give up." She flung her bootie down on the porch floor beside her yarn. "I need a break from that damn bootie. You sit here, Levi."

She pushed herself out of her chair. "I need a word with that man of mine."

Indigo opened her mouth to protest, but Levi said, "Oh, don't mind if I do," and sat down in Beth's vacated chair. Then he grinned at everyone. "That okay with you guys?"

Shirley, predictably, beamed at him. "Of course. And you don't have to be able to knit to join. I'm sewing and Jim's crocheting."

Levi beamed back. "I can't sew or crochet either."

"Perhaps Indigo can teach you," Izzy murmured, giving Indigo a knowing look that she pretended not to see.

She didn't understand why Izzy and Beth kept encouraging her to be nice to Levi. And they weren't subtle about it either. Beth had told her that she liked seeing the "fireworks," and Izzy said that it was in the town's best interests that everyone get along.

Indigo understood and she tried to be nice, she really did. But he was just so...provoking.

He was sitting next to her now, that wicked smile of his playing along his beautiful mouth, making her feel hot and restless, and his long legs were outstretched in front of him. She couldn't take her eyes off the way the denim stretched across his powerful thighs.

This was the worst. Why was she hypnotized by a man's thighs? Especially *this* man's thighs?

"Well?" Levi gave her a look beneath dark,

gold-tipped lashes. "Teach me the way of the needles, O holy one."

Jim snorted.

Levi ignored him.

Well, great. She didn't want to teach him because he didn't really want to learn. He was only here to be a dick.

She looked up from her shawl and met his gaze head-on. "Do you really want to learn? Or are you here because I told you I didn't want you building me a house last night?"

He grinned, the way his mouth curved doing stupid things to her insides. "What would you say if I told you it's a combination of both?" Then, before she could get another word in, he added, "Actually don't tell me what you would say. I feel I know the answer to that already."

Izzy leaned forward unexpectedly, packing her knitting away in the little project bag Indigo had made for her before pushing herself to her feet. "I have to see Chase about…something," she said vaguely. "I'll see you later."

Indigo sent her a "really?" look that Izzy pretended not to see.

Shirley cleared her throat. "You know, I think I've forgotten that errand I was going to run. You were going to help me, Jim." She pulled on his arm.

He jolted slightly. "Eh?"

A minute later, Indigo found herself sitting by

herself on the porch of the Rose with a grinning Levi and a sense of betrayal sitting in her gut.

They'd left her alone on purpose, which did not improve her temper one bit. She wasn't sure if it was a bad attempt at matchmaking or because they all wanted her to be friends with him, but whatever it was, it was annoying.

Knowing that her own annoyance at herself and her fascination with him were making her so bad-tempered did nothing at all for her mood.

Levi sighed. "Put the prickles away, hedgehog. I'm not going to wind you up today."

Indigo bit her lip. "You could start by not calling me 'hedgehog.'"

"Why not? You've got a lot of needles." He gestured to her knitting needles. "Both real and figurative."

That was not...untrue.

Being grumpy with him is not going to help. And he was offering you an olive branch last night. He's not that bad. And he's not like your dad.

It was true; he wasn't. He'd stopped flirting outrageously with her when she'd asked, though that hadn't stopped him from teasing her.

You like him doing that; don't lie.

Indigo stared hard at the tumble of blue-and-purple-speckled yarn sitting in her lap, trying to wrestle her intense annoyance into submission. Being grumpy with him because he reminded her of someone who'd left years ago was stupid and petty.

Also, it wasn't his fault she was wildly attracted to him. It wasn't his fault he was handsome either, or that she had good reasons for not trusting handsome men as far as she could throw them.

It wasn't just handsome men she didn't trust. That extended to people, period, and she'd found that prickliness and grumpiness were excellent deterrents when anyone tried to get too close.

She didn't like it when people got too close.

Living in a literal cabin in the woods and being brought up by her hermit grandmother, who barely let Indigo out of her sight let alone out of the house, would do that to a person. In fact, from the age of eight on, the only human Indigo ever saw was grandmother.

Still, that was her deal, not Levi's, which meant she couldn't in good conscience keep being crappy to him. Since she'd come to Brightwater Valley, she was trying to be more open, less mistrustful.

She let out a silent breath, deciding to leave the matter of "hedgehog" out of it for the time being, and looked at him. "You really want to learn how to knit?"

"Yes, absolutely." He glanced at the shawl in her lap. "Looks hard though."

"You don't need to flatter me," she said shortly. "It's not hard."

"I'm not flattering you. That genuinely looks hard."

She gave him a stare, examining his handsome face for signs that he was, as Kiwis termed it, *taking the piss*, AKA making fun. But no, it seemed he was genuine.

"You fix engines," she said, relenting slightly. "Engines are hard. Knitting is easy. It's basically two stitches, knit and purl. That's it."

"Engines are *not* hard. An engine is—"

"Do you want to learn or not?" Indigo interrupted, not really in the mood for an explanation of what engines were.

He gave a long-suffering sigh. "Why does no one want to listen when I talk about engines? Okay, fine. Yes, I do." A spark of amusement glimmered in his eyes, making her heart flutter in her chest for absolutely no reason at all. "And while you teach me, I'll tell you about my further thoughts on your tiny house."

It was immediately obvious to Levi that Indigo did not want to hear his further thoughts on her tiny house, but hey, that was too bad.

He was obsessed with it now.

He'd spent all night turning the problem over in his head, trying to figure out why she was so opposed to it and what he could do to make her change her mind. He understood her reluctance about him paying for everything. Money was a whole thing. He'd learned early on that if you had something other people wanted and they were stronger than you, they'd take it from you whether you wanted them to or not. As a kid, his solution to that problem had been to have nothing. That way, no one bothered him.

He would have been fine with that as an adult too, because he didn't need a lot of things. But he'd learned he had a talent for making money, and because he enjoyed it, he exercised that talent often, much to the continued happiness of his bank managers.

He didn't like to talk about it though. The secretive habits of his childhood were too ingrained, and flaunting the fact that he was loaded in a place like Brightwater, where no one had a lot, was too much even for him.

But that didn't mean he couldn't use his wealth for the good of the people here when he so choose. For the good of Indigo, for example.

Except she clearly saw it as charity she didn't need and didn't want.

Who knew that such a small prickly woman would have such a streak of pride? He would have found it endearing if it hadn't been so damn annoying.

Still, that was the way she felt, and he didn't want to ride roughshod over her feelings. Which meant if he wanted to help her out, he was going to have to find a way that would allow her to keep that pride of hers intact and not make her even madder at him than she was already.

Except he had the impression that she kind of liked being mad at him as much as he kind of liked teasing her.

More than "kind of."

That was true. He liked it very much. It was just the kind of challenge he liked, and that was wrong of him. Very wrong.

She was glaring at him as if he'd said something offensive, all her sweet little prickles on show despite his urging her to put them away. Today, she was in a long-sleeved, many-tiered dress of soft-looking light blue linen almost the same shade as her pretty eyes. Her brown hair was in a ponytail down her back, exposing small ears and the silver hoop earrings in them.

There was something a little bit fey about her, something slightly magical to do with her sharp nose, determined chin, and the feline tilt of her dark eyebrows.

She wasn't anything like the women he usually went for. There was nothing fey about them, though they were in their own way magical. They were usually curvy and cheerful, flirty and fun, and they were generally up for anything. A woman who took pleasure out of life was a woman he wanted to get to know.

Indigo wasn't cheerful or flirty, and she certainly didn't like the things he thought were fun. But that made her all the more fascinating to him. It got him thinking about what would make her smile. What would make her laugh. What would make her flush with pleasure...

Yeah, perhaps stop there.

Yes. Absolutely he should stop there.

He was here to try to talk to her about this house plan, not anything else. Well, nothing bar knitting.

"What?" He lifted a brow. "Are you going to show me this knitting thing or what?"

She let out a huff of irritation, then put her own knitting down before reaching into the big patch-work style bag that sat near her chair. After a bit of rummaging, she brought out some big pink plastic knitting needles that looked very unlike the small metal ones she used.

The plastic ones looked very much like kind of needles you gave to kids—big because they were easy to use and blunt so someone wouldn't hurt themselves.

He didn't know whether to be offended or relieved.

"You can start with these," she said. "This is how you hold them." She demonstrated, then handed them over to him. Then she rummaged more in her bag and brought out some thick red yarn. "We'll start by learning the knit stitch. Can you tie a slipknot?"

That was a good start. Of course, he could. He could tie any knot she cared to name. Knots were his thing.

He demonstrated with the yarn she'd given him, feeling smug about it.

She sniffed, unimpressed. "Now we need to cast on. We'll start with a knitted cast-on."

She did something complicated with the yarn and the needles that Levi missed. Then she did it slower so he could see.

Okay, that didn't look too hard. He hadn't been kidding when he'd told her that her shawl looked difficult. He'd never been artistic, and the thought of creating something from scratch with nothing but a pair of needles and some yarn seemed like magic to him.

"I didn't know Jim crocheted," Indigo said after she'd demonstrated casting on to him a few times.

"Oh yeah." Levi frowned at the five stitches he'd managed to create. They seemed good, though holding the needles felt weird. "He's been crocheting for years. He made beer cozies for everyone for Christmas once. I've still got mine somewhere."

"Right." She watched him laboriously cast on another stitch, though he was finding it faster than the first couple. "I didn't know you owned the gallery and the general store either."

A flicker of annoyance arrowed through him, though he immediately locked it down. He'd told

Jim when he'd bought the land off him that he'd prefer if the rest of the town didn't know. He hadn't wanted to create any feelings of suspicion about outsiders coming in and taking over, not when at the time he'd been such a newcomer himself.

Over the years, people had slowly found out but it had never been a problem, not even with Bill, who was notoriously skeptical about outsiders. It helped that Levi had given responsibility for rent of the building and other details over to a real estate company and had never done anything with the land the building sat on or that stretched up into the bush behind it.

He'd never had any intention of doing anything with it either. As far as he was concerned, he'd bought the land to help Jim out and to keep it in the hands of locals who cared about that town. And while technically he wasn't a local, he cared about the town very much and wanted the same things for it that everyone else did.

At least, until Indigo Jameson had come onto the scene and he'd decided she needed a place to live.

"That's right." He kept his voice level as he added another couple of stitches. "That's the land I was talking about last night."

"The land you were just going to give to me."

"No, I was not going to just give it to you." He glanced over at her, met her gorgeous blue eyes. "There's a moderately flat bit up the hill behind the gallery building. It's a great spot for one of those little houses and it's close to the gallery, which is great for you since you don't drive." Indigo opened her mouth, but he put down one needle and raised a hand. "Wait, I haven't finished."

To her credit, Indigo waited.

"I made a promise to Jim that I wouldn't do anything with the land or sell it and that it would stay bush. Those houses have a tiny footprint, which means I won't have to do much in the way of clearing, and I don't think any of the locals will mind if you have a little house there. But I can't sell you the land or give it to you, even if I wanted to."

Indigo stared ferociously at him. "So, you'd give me the use of it?"

"Yeah, if you want to put it like that."

"What about a lease? Or rent?"

That wouldn't be happening. He had a lot of money, and he didn't need any more, and certainly not from someone like Indigo who didn't have any to spare.

What about her pride?

He shifted uneasily in his seat. He'd love to say he didn't care about her pride since, as she didn't have anywhere to live, she couldn't afford to have any. But he'd been in that situation himself, and he knew how difficult it was. And apart from anything else, he did care about her pride, and he didn't want to make her feel bad. It was an irritating conundrum.

"I don't want money," he said gruffly. "I've got enough. I don't need any from you."

Her chin came up. "And I don't care if you need it or not. I'm not going to accept someone giving me land, building me a house on it, then me living there without paying a cent. It's not right. And it wouldn't be mine. It would be a pity house you built for me because you felt sorry for me."

"I do *not* feel sorry for you," he insisted, now feeling irritated. Only for his irritation to die away as he realized that actually, he understood.

He'd had his pride too as a foster kid, and sometimes charity wasn't really all that charitable. Plus, he'd never had anything that was his and most especially not a home, and it was why he was so fiercely protective of Brightwater Valley and the people in it. This was his home, and they were his family, and he'd do anything for them. Anything at all. And that included newcomers like Indigo.

"Look," he went on, more calmly this time. "I get where you're coming from. But that house with lavender and the little garden for herbs has a cute little window seat." Yeah, he'd seen the look that had crossed her face when he'd presented her with the brochures he'd collected. Especially the one with the slightly witch-cottage look. He knew longing when he saw it, and it had been plastered all over her face the moment he'd shown her that particular brochure.

Her eyes narrowed and her chin got stubborn.

"You could push the windows open and sit on it in summer and knit. Watch the bees buzzing. Get some chickens…"

"Don't," Indigo said grumpily. "I'm going to teach you the knit stitch now."

But although she might be grumpy, he could tell she was wavering. She really did like the idea of that little house. And no wonder. She'd left her home thousands of miles away to come to New Zealand, and since she'd gotten here, she'd been staying in the Rose and then in Clint's farmhouse. She didn't have a place of her own, and everyone needed one of those.

"Here," she said, "this is how you do a knit stitch."

Obediently he paid attention, watching her long clever fingers work her metal needles. Her fingertips were stained with color from the yarn dyeing she did, all red and blue and green, and he found himself wondering how those fingers would feel on his skin. Would her touch be as deft on him as she was with those needles? Would she leave stains of color on his skin? He kind of wanted her to…

Uh, stop right there.

"Are you listening?"

He was now. "Of course."

"Show me."

Briefly he debated the merits of showing off and then decided not to. Another, much better idea slid into his subconscious before he knew what was happening.

It's also a very bad idea.

It was, but then he was the king of bad ideas. He also couldn't resist.

"Hmmm," he murmured, deliberately mucking up a stitch. "I don't think I've quite got it. Why don't you come over here and show me?"

He thought she might pick up on the slight note of flirtation in his voice, but she didn't, making a small exasperated sound instead. Putting down her knitting, she leaned over the arm of her chair in his direction.

It put her very close, the silken mass of her ponytail slipping over her shoulder and trailing over his forearm. She was warm and he was very conscious that the soft curve of one breast was pressed to his upper arm as she leaned over to grab his needles.

"It's like this." She demonstrated by knitting a stitch, then a second one, slower this time. "See?"

But he didn't see. Because he was suddenly painfully aware that the skein of dark hair lying across his forearm was full of shades of caramel, toffee, and chestnut, and that she smelled of lavender, herbs, and a soft, sweet musk that made everything male in him spring to attention.

Bad idea. Very bad idea.

Oh yeah, it really was. Yet he was in no hurry for her to move away. For over two months, he'd been irritatingly and completely physically aware of her, and he was going to take this moment while he could. A moment to drink up her warmth and inhale her sweet scent, catch a glimpse of softness beneath all her sharp prickles.

"No, I didn't quite get it," he murmured. "Show me again."

She made an irritated sound and showed him the stitch again.

Clearly, she wasn't as affected by his nearness as he was by hers, which wasn't a disappointment, not in any way. Not when he wasn't going to be doing anything about it even if she had been.

It was just a little odd, since he could have sworn that Indigo wasn't entirely indifferent to him.

Yes, she'd told him to stop flirting with her in no uncertain terms, and he had, because he wasn't a man who pushed himself on uninterested women. Why would he? When he had so many interested ones to choose from?

Yet if she'd truly been indifferent, she'd have left him alone and she hadn't. She was somehow, mysteriously, always in his vicinity, looking balefully at him as if he'd personally offended her. Which he took to mean that she was into him but was very, *very* annoyed about it.

Not that it mattered. Not when he wasn't going to touch her.

He'd asked Izzy and Beth a few surreptitious

questions about her for idle curiosity's sake—at least, that's what he'd told himself—but all they'd told him was that she'd lived with her grandmother in an isolated homestead in Alaska, and that after her grandmother's death, she'd come to Brightwater.

Nothing about any previous relationships or anything, which he didn't care about either. She might have a long-distance boyfriend and that would be okay. Yep, A-OK with him.

"There," she said. "Do you see now?"

But he was still staring down at the top of her head and thinking about whether she had a boyfriend or not. "Do another one."

This time she turned and looked up at him, her dark brows drawn down in one of her habitual ferocious frowns.

Her eyes really were the prettiest shade of blue. Light and clear, like the sky at high altitudes, up near the peaks where he took clients heli-skiing. He loved the sky when it was like that. It felt like freedom to him.

Then she blinked and he saw awareness suddenly take hold. Awareness of him and how close she was making that infinite light blue darken into deep azure. Pink flushed her cheeks and her mouth opened.

Then abruptly she dropped the needles she'd been holding into his lap and shoved herself away from him like a scalded cat.

"Well." She grabbed her knitting and stuffed it back into her patchwork project bag. "That's that. I hoped you learned something."

Levi didn't move, noting that her cheeks were still bright pink, and she was very, *very* flustered. It appeared she wasn't quite as oblivious to him as he'd thought.

Well, you're screwed.

"But you haven't taught me what the other stitch was," he said mildly, ignoring the thought. "The ruby stitch or something."

"It's a purl stitch." She got to her feet and brushed past him to the stairs. "I'll show you later."

"Indigo," he said, pitching his voice low.

She stopped at the top of the stairs that led down to the street, just as he hoped she would, but she didn't turn around. "What?"

"Think about it." He didn't elaborate. She'd know what he was talking about.

"Okay," she said woodenly, then went quickly down the stairs and was gone.

Chapter 3

Beth sat at the farmhouse kitchen table, a cup of hot chocolate at her elbow, examining the brochures that were lying on top of it. Izzy, sitting opposite with one of her favorite coffees, was also frowning at the brochures.

Indigo was at the head of the table nursing a cup of herbal tea in her favorite flavor, which was currently cinnamon. She didn't have many tea bags left, and she knew that was going to mean a trip into Queenstown at some stage. She didn't much like towns and so was trying to hoard the tea as much as possible, but dammit, talking about her living arrangements was difficult and the situation called for some cinnamon tea.

The other two had invited themselves to Clint's farmhouse so they could have a more private chat about Indigo's housing problem that didn't involve random men suddenly wanting knitting lessons.

"Honestly?" Beth gave Indigo a look. "I don't know what your problem is. This house is gorgeous." She tapped the brochure with Indigo's favorite on it.

You could push the windows open and sit on it in summer and knit. Watch the bees buzzing....

Indigo shoved Levi's deep voice from her head, along with the shiver that went with it. When he'd spoken about that little house… Well. He'd made it sound so good. Everything she hadn't realized she'd wanted.

Except that didn't change her feelings about him giving her the land and building her the house.

People promised all kinds of things and then never came through with them, and she didn't want to be put in that situation again.

She didn't want to tell the others about the real reason she couldn't take his offer, so all she said was, "It is. But if I let him pay for all the building and land and stuff, it wouldn't be mine, would it? Plus, I don't want him paying for everything just because he feels sorry for me."

"Good point," Izzy said, sipping her coffee. "No one wants a pity house."

Beth grimaced. "Okay, sure. I can see that. But what are your choices? You have to stay at the Rose and wait until Chase can get hold of that guy who owns the vacant house—and let's face it, he's been trying for months with no luck. Or you wait until something comes up." Her green eyes lit suddenly. "Or you could come and stay with Finn and me. We've got a spare—"

"No," Indigo said firmly. "I mean, thanks, Beth.

I appreciate it. But I'm not being a third wheel in your happy love nest."

Beth scowled. "We do *not* have a happy love nest."

"Also," Indigo went on, "you're pregnant and you're going to need all the room you can get once the baby's born."

"What about Chase's and my place?" Izzy asked. "If the worst comes to the worst, you could always sleep on the couch." Her friend's dark eyes were full of concern. "I don't want you to have nowhere to go."

A warm glow sat in Indigo's chest, and she tried very hard to disregard it. She was wary of people who seemed to have her best interests at heart, for the same reason she couldn't accept Levi's offer. Being brought up on a steady diet of her grandma's paranoia hadn't helped either.

Izzy and Beth were the exception to this rule. Over the past couple of months, she'd learned that they genuinely cared about her and wanted the best for her. It was strange having friends. She'd gone to school before her parents left, and presumably she'd had friends then, but she barely remembered them. Grandma had homeschooled her after her parents had gone and hadn't liked outsiders, even kids, so friends hadn't been a thing.

Indigo liked having them now though, even if that left her feeling a bit exposed.

"I know." She sighed. "I just…don't want anyone to have to have to put themselves out for me."

"But we're not—" Beth began.

Indigo held up a hand to stop her. "I really appreciate your offers and I mean that. But it's not just that I don't want to impose. I want…" She paused, because it was hard telling people what she wanted. Even all these years later, after her mom and dad had gone, it left her feeling vulnerable, as if she'd given something away she wasn't supposed to. Not that telling people how badly she wanted a little house of her own was any big secret; it was just that it meant a lot to her, and she was used to keeping those secret desires private. After all, you never knew when someone could use them against you.

They're not going to use it against you, come on. They're your friends.

That was true; they were.

"I want a home," she forced out, holding her teacup between her hands and staring down into it since it was easier to stare at the cup than it was to look at the other two. "I want to feel like I belong here, and I can't when I don't have anywhere to live."

"Of course, you do." Beth reached across the table and laid her hand gently on the tabletop in front of Indigo, a gesture of comfort. "You really need a place that's yours."

"Yes," Izzy agreed. "Absolutely you do. And not like it's a gift from some guy, right?"

She couldn't help smiling at that. They got it, her friends. They understood. She'd been distrustful of them at first, Izzy especially since she didn't come from Deep River and had turned up out of the blue at Auckland Airport, just as Indigo and Beth had arrived in the country. Izzy had told them that she was Georgie's replacement and would be joining them on their expedition. Georgie was supposed to have been the third member of their team, but she'd had to pull out for family reasons.

Indigo had viewed Izzy with some suspicion, but over the past couple of months, she'd heard Izzy's story and knew her to be a woman of strength and courage. A problem solver with a whole lot of smarts and a caring heart to match.

"Yeah, that's exactly it." Indigo bit her lip. "I mean, I'm grateful to Levi for the offer but... How did he find out about the tiny-house thing anyway?"

Izzy sighed, looking shamefaced. "Sorry, that was me. I was feeling frustrated for you and mentioned what you wanted to Chase, and he must have said something to Levi."

It wasn't anything Indigo hadn't suspected, and she knew she shouldn't get pissed off about it. After all, not wanting to give anything away to people was her own deal, not Izzy's, and besides, she hadn't told Izzy not to tell anyone.

"It's okay," she said. "It wasn't like a state secret or anything."

Izzy gave her a concerned look, then said hesitantly, "He's not a bad guy, you know. Levi, I mean. Chase wouldn't be such good friends with him if he was."

Everything in Indigo tightened. "I don't have to be friends with him if I don't want to." She tried not to snap yet knew she sounded snappy anyway. "And while I'm on the subject, leaving me alone with him on the porch of the Rose yesterday was mean."

She wasn't going to think about what that had led to. Nope, not at all. Not about how she'd leaned across the arm of his chair to help with his knitting, not thinking about how getting close to him might not be the best idea. She'd been too focused on showing him how a knit stitch was done.

Then as she'd demonstrated a couple of stitches and he'd told her he still didn't get it, a slow awareness had filtered through her. Of the way she was leaning and how she was almost in his lap. Of the long, muscular male body stretched out beneath her and how warm he felt. How she could smell something spicy and earthy that reminded her of the bush on a hot day, and that it was a delicious smell. And that he was probably lying when he'd said he didn't quite understand the stitch yet, because he was an intelligent man, and he should have picked it up.

She'd turned to look at him—probably the stupidest move ever—and met his gaze. The impact of it had stolen her breath. Because deep in the green and gold of his eyes, she'd seen sparks of heat.

Even the memory of it made her face flame, so she quickly shoved it from her head and hoped the other two hadn't noticed her blushing.

"Sorry," Beth said, not sounding sorry at all. "I'd be more sympathetic if you genuinely didn't like him and didn't want to be around him, but I don't think that's the case, is it?"

Damn Beth. The woman could read minds like nobody's business and had a sixth sense when it came to people's emotions too. And she tended toward bluntness.

It was clear she wasn't going to let Indigo get away with anything tonight.

"Beth," Izzy chided gently. "Come on."

Beth's eyes widened. "What? Anyone can see she's got the hots for him, and who can blame her? He's hot AF."

Izzy frowned. "That may be the case, but—"

"It is the case," Indigo said quietly, deciding it was high time she stopped behaving like a teenage girl about it. She was twenty-five, for God's sake. And okay, she had issues with trust, and she didn't much like men as a species, but that was all due to her upbringing. Not that Grandma hadn't had reason to distrust people and men in particular since her daughter had basically abandoned her along with Indigo for one. But Grandma was gone and so were her parents. And Indigo was in Brightwater, where it was obvious there were a whole lot of people she *could* trust. People who genuinely cared about her and who had her best interests at heart.

She was trying to be less guarded and less prickly, and snapping at her friends for telling the truth wasn't okay.

Izzy was right. Chase and Finn were good men, and they wouldn't be friends with someone who didn't deserve it, which meant that Levi was also a good man. He was a pain in the ass and persistent as all get-out, but he wasn't awful.

Yes, her attraction to him was a problem she didn't know how to handle, but really, if she could interact with him like a normal person and not a spitting fiend, that would help.

But the way he looked at you—

No. She wasn't going to think about that. She could maybe figure out how to handle her own attraction to him, but if he returned the feeling? No, that was a bridge too far.

Izzy and Beth were now staring curiously at her.

"So, you agree?" Beth asked. "That's he's hot AF?"

Indigo steeled herself. "Yes. He is."

Beth's green eyes danced. "OMG! If you and he get together, then we could—"

"No," Indigo interrupted flatly before her friend could get going. "I'm not going there. He doesn't feel the same way about me and—"

"Are you sure about that?" Beth's face was alight with excitement. "I've seen him—"

"Beth, if Indigo doesn't want to go there, she doesn't want to go there," Izzy reached across the table and laid a calming hand on Beth's. "Though, Indigo, if you want him, you should talk to him."

But even the thought of talking to Levi about how hot she found him made Indigo squirm with discomfort.

She shook her head. "No. I don't want to get into that at the moment."

"Is this an 'I don't have time for men' excuse?" Beth said. "Because seriously. There's always time for men."

"For you, maybe." Indigo frowned at her. "I just want to get a house sorted out and a place where I can do my dyeing, okay?"

Beth gave a gusty sigh. "Fair enough. I'm not trying to be an asshole. I only want you to be happy."

And it was true that while Beth could be relentless with her optimism and her honesty, she had a caring heart too, and Indigo appreciated that a lot. Like Izzy, who'd left a career in ruins and a broken engagement back in Texas to come to New Zealand, Beth's journey to Brightwater hadn't been an easy one.

She'd lost a baby back in Deep River and had fallen into a severe bout of postpartum depression and had come to Brightwater to find some relief. Which she'd found in the form of Finn Kelly, Chase's handsome, reserved brother. Of course, it had taken an accidental pregnancy and Finn's grief over the death of his first wife before they could find their happy ending, but find it they had. And Indigo couldn't be happier for her.

But her own happy ending involved a little house, a dyeing shed, lots of yarn, an herb garden, a cat, and possibly some chickens. And absolutely zero men.

"I know that." Indigo met her friend's gaze. "I really do know that."

Beth smiled. "Good. So, what do you want to do about Levi's offer then?"

"Obviously she's not going to just let him pay for everything," Izzy said. "Right?"

"Definitely not," Indigo agreed, swirling the contents of her teacup slowly as she thought. "But I'm not sure what else to do. Even if I did get him to build it for me, I don't have the money for the kit set I liked, and I don't have it to buy some land to put the house on."

"Hmmm." Izzy tapped her chin thoughtfully. "We could get Finn and Chase to help with the building, and I'm sure there are some others who would also pick up a hammer. Cait's not bad with a saw, for example. But the land question is an issue."

Indigo sighed. "Sadly, Levi's land is the most useful place to build it, since it's close to the gallery."

"Or, I don't know," Beth said. "You could learn to drive."

Indigo pulled a face. "Uh, no thank you. Machines freak me out." Which wasn't a lie. They did.

Beth shrugged. "Then you're limited to where you can go. And you're right, Levi's is perfect."

Indigo took a sip of her tea, relishing the spicy taste and trying not to think about how it reminded her of Levi's warm, musky scent. Dammit, why did he have to smell like one of her favorite spices? It wasn't fair.

It also wasn't fair that Beth was right. Levi's land *was* perfect. But she wasn't sure how she could bring herself to accept it.

She wanted the house and the land to be hers so no one could take it away from her, but it would never feel like hers if it came as a gift or charity. There was also the chance that Levi might change his mind and rescind everything, because she knew all too well how promises could be broken, and then where would she be?

"He won't take money for it either," she said, giving her tea another swirl. "I asked him if he would lease me the land or whether I could pay rent or something, but he said that he'd promised Jim he wouldn't sell it or rent it or anything else. That the land was to stay as is."

"Well, it's great that he keeps his promises and all," Beth muttered. "But that's not much good to you, is it?"

Promises… The word echoed inside Indigo uncomfortably. If he'd promised Jim he wouldn't sell it and he still held firm to that years later, then perhaps he genuinely was a guy who did what he said.

Izzy was frowning. "So…why don't you ask Jim? Get him to okay you paying rent or leasing the land, and then Levi can't argue, can he?"

Actually, that was a good idea. It would solve the issue of her being dependent on the word of a man she wasn't sure she could trust.

Why hadn't she thought of that?

"Do you think Jim would go for it?" she asked. "You know what people are like about this town, and especially about us being here."

Not all the inhabitants of Brightwater had been pleased to see the three Americans, and for the first month or so, there had been a degree of suspicion thrown their way. But over time, that suspicion had morphed into something warmer and friendlier, especially when it became clear that the gallery was a great idea and that tourists were enjoying it.

"I think he'll be fine with it." Izzy smiled. "He likes you."

Indigo felt a little jolt go through her. "How do you know that?"

"You gave him a good excuse to get out his crochet hook. Plus, I have it on good authority, AKA Chase, that he likes you because you're 'not a chatterer.'"

"Oh," said Beth, who very much was a chatterer. "I see how it is."

Izzy grinned. "He likes you too. You know that."

But Beth wasn't offended. She grinned back. "I know. He's crocheting me a baby blanket."

Indigo also had plans for a baby blanket and was a bit miffed that Jim had gotten in first. "Okay, I'll speak to him," she said. "And if he says no, I guess I'll have to figure something else out." She bit her lip, thinking. "So, if the rent is good to go, I'm still going to have to think about materials for the house. I mean, I love that kit set." She looked longingly at the brochure on the top of the pile. "But it's just too pricey."

She had a little nest egg that her grandmother had left her after she'd passed away, but she needed that for capital for the business and living expenses. There wasn't enough to cover building a tiny house too, or at least not the one in that brochure.

Then again, she didn't have to get a kit set. She could do something similar with cheaper materials maybe. Or, even better, she could use recycled stuff, which would be much better environmentally.

"Looks like you have an idea," Izzy said, looking at her.

"Actually, I do." Indigo put her teacup down, suddenly feeling energized and just a little excited. "What about using reclaimed or recycled materials?"

"Oh yes!" Beth clapped her hands together. "I

love that idea. You could find some really cute stuff that would make it much more individual."

Indigo's excitement fizzed, visions of a much more quirky, rustic little house dancing in her head. "I know, right? It could be so cool."

Izzy coughed. "Um, hate to tell you this, but if you don't get a kit set, you're going to have to get someone to design the house for you."

Argh, that was true.

"Gah," she muttered. "Architects are expensive. Does Chase have any contacts who might be able to do some drawings for me cheaply?"

"Not sure, but I'll find out for you." Izzy grinned, clearly catching her and Beth's excitement. "Hey, this is going to be so fun. I'm almost jealous I don't need a tiny house too."

Indigo didn't blame her. Because this was going to be good. And best of all, it would be hers. No more Clint's. No more hotel. She would be living in the community like her friends. A real local.

"You know," Beth said. "If you build the house on wheels, it means that if Levi is a dick and you end up not wanting to be on his land, you can move it somewhere else."

Oh, of course. She hadn't thought of that, but it was true. She could just move it.

"Okay, okay," she said, grinning. "Now all I need is a pen and paper, and I'll draw up a quick budget."

Levi stepped into the pub at the Rose that evening feeling unexpectedly grumpy. He was supposed to meet Chase and Finn there for a beer, because Finn had told him the pair of them wanted "a word."

Levi was pretty sure it wasn't going to be just one word, and he was also pretty sure he knew what that word was going to be, and quite frankly, he wasn't here for it. He wasn't in the mood for a lecture.

Because of course this was going to be about Indigo.

The pair of them had already grilled him extensively about his interactions with her, and he'd told them in no uncertain terms that he wasn't interested. And it wasn't his fault if she kept turning up wherever he was and digging at him.

Nothing had changed, not even since last evening when his body had put in another enthusiastic bid on how delightful it would be to seduce her. But while he might be the king of bad ideas, starting anything with pretty Indigo Jameson was one bad idea too far, and that wasn't happening.

Jim gave him a level look as he came into the pub and went straight up to the bar. The old man said nothing, just gave him his usual, a pint glass from the lager he had on tap—Levi didn't much care for craft beer—then nodded toward the table at the back of the room where people usually went if they wanted a private conversation, since that particular table was set apart from the rest.

The pub in the Rose was a quirky little place. The walls were festooned with what looked like the contents of someone's attic—miners' helmets and framed photos. Beer coasters and old newspaper clippings. Antlers. A raincoat. Someone's boot—and Levi had fallen in love with the place the moment he'd stepped inside it.

But you did have to be careful about what you said, because those walls also had ears in among all the clutter, and sometimes what you told someone in confidence ended up as town business in five seconds flat.

Levi nodded back, picked up his beer, then turned toward the table. Of course the two assholes were already there, no doubt rehearsing the lecture they were going to give him.

He marched up to them, put his beer down on the tabletop, then sat and gave his two friends a narrow look. "Before you say anything, it's not happening. I already told you two that." He lifted a finger. "And another thing—"

"Levi," Chase interrupted calmly. "What did you think we were going to say?"

Finn was sitting back in his chair, his arms folded across his chest, holding his beer in one hand. He didn't say anything, merely lifted one dark eyebrow. A man of few words was Finn.

Caught off guard, Levi scowled. Telling them he was anticipating a lecture about Indigo would reveal far too much, especially when he'd probably come off sounding defensive as hell.

"I don't know," he muttered. "Something about flirting with the clients." Which was true, he *did* do that. But only if the client flirted with him first and seemed into it. Which most of them did.

"Well, it's not," Chase said. "It's about Indigo—"

"I knew it. Look, I'm not—"

"And your plans to build her a tiny house," Chase went on as if Levi hadn't spoken.

Levi shut up before he incriminated himself, then took a swallow of his beer. "I see," he said evenly. "Who told you I wanted to build her a tiny house?" A redundant question since he knew full well who'd told Chase: Izzy. But still, he wanted to hear Chase say it.

"Izzy," Chase said, surprising absolutely no one. "You went round to Clint's last night and put an offer to Indigo."

A memory rose in Levi's mind—of Indigo leaning against him this morning, her dark hair falling over his arm, the scent of her skin clouding his thinking…

He shifted uncomfortably, conscious of his body's enthusiastic reception to the memory. No, it was not happening. Not happening *at all*.

"Yeah." He cleared his throat. "I did."

"Any particular reason you want to build her a house?" Finn's tone was very casual, but Levi knew the question wasn't casual in the slightest.

He got it. He was a bit of a man whore, it was true. But he owned it, and he only ever indulged himself with women who didn't want anything more than what he did, which was a couple of hours of harmless fun.

Finn might have still been a bit pissed with him about how he'd given him the hard word about Beth back when that relationship had first been starting. But hell, someone had to. Beth was such a sweetheart and didn't deserve Finn blowing hot and cold and being a dick. That he had good reason to, Levi was well aware, but still. If you were grieving your first wife, you didn't mess around with someone else's heart.

Levi had known that Chase would have been reluctant to talk to Finn, since he was hugely protective of his brother. Which was why he'd decided to have a word. And yeah, Finn hadn't been pleased, but too bad.

Anyway, the whole point was that he wasn't touching Indigo. He'd decided that right back at the beginning, when she'd first arrived. She was here to build a new business and make a new life for herself, and he wasn't about to mess with that just because baser parts of his anatomy were interested in her.

He might be a man whore, but he liked to think of himself as a man whore with ethics. An ethical man whore, if you will.

"Yeah, there's a reason." He gave Finn a direct look. "She doesn't have a place to go, and I know what that feels like."

He didn't like bringing up his past, especially not to make a point. But he didn't want Finn thinking he was only doing this to get into Indigo's pants, and quite frankly, now that he thought about it, he was pissed off that despite his continual denial that he was doing anything with her, Finn still didn't believe him.

Finn's dark gaze sparked with annoyance, and he leaned forward in his chair, his mouth opening.

"Shut it, Finn," Chase ordered, the SAS commander he'd once been clear in his tone. "I don't know what your deal is, but if Levi says he has no ulterior motive, then he has no ulterior motive, okay?"

Finn sat there a second, his jaw tight. Then abruptly he blew out a breath, put his beer on the table, and ran a distracted hand through his black hair. "Yeah, sorry. Keep worrying about Beth. This whole pregnancy thing is doing my head in."

Immediately the tension in the air eased as did Levi's own annoyance.

Beth was expecting her and Finn's first child, and Finn was a protective bastard. Of course, he'd be worried. He'd lost his first wife, so this couldn't be easy for him.

"It's okay," Levi said. "You have reason." He took another swallow of his beer, then gave both Finn and Chase a level look. "I mean it. I only want to give her a home. That's it. I've got the perfect site for what she wants, not to mention the money for the kit she really liked, so why not?" And then, because he might as well put all his cards on the table, he added, "It's not a sex thing. I want to do it for her because she's part of this town and I'd do the same for anyone here."

Two sets of eyes, one gunmetal gray, one dark brown, gave him a hard stare. But he was used to it, and he met it without complaint.

Being involved in a business with two of the most stubborn assholes he'd ever come across had been tough at first, since all three of them very much liked getting their own way and found it difficult to concede or give ground.

But they'd found a way to handle difficulties, because when all was said and done, Levi would have given his life for either of them. Chase, because when Levi had met him in the SAS, he'd discovered a kindred daredevil spirit, the brother he'd never had. And Finn, because any brother of Chase's was also a brother of his. That was just the way it worked.

"Okay then," Finn said after a moment. "We'll help, obviously."

"Yes, we most certainly will," Chase agreed. "What do you need?"

Levi folded his arms on the tabletop and leaned on them. "I need Indigo to say yes."

Finn's gaze narrowed. "What do you mean, you need her to say yes?"

"Just that. I talked to her about it and she refused."

Chase's gray gaze also narrowed. "She refused?"

"Do you guys have to keep repeating my statements and making them into questions?"

Chase rolled his eyes. "Levi—"

"Yes, she refused." He shook his head. "Gave me some bullshit about not wanting charity, and how it wouldn't feel like it was hers if I paid for everything."

Finn had picked up his beer and was sipping on it. He pointed the bottle at Levi. "She's not wrong, hate to say it."

"I realize that. I just don't know what to do about it. I made a promise to Jim I wouldn't do anything with that land when I bought it. I wouldn't sell it or lease it or receive any other financial gain apart from rent from the building. And she doesn't have any money even if I did let her lease it or whatever." He frowned, uneasy at the thought of taking Indigo's no-doubt hard-saved cash. "She's got capital for her business, I assume, but I can't take that."

Chase shrugged one massive shoulder. "Sorry, mate, but that sounds like a you problem. If giving you money would help her feel better about the house, then what's the big deal? I mean, if I was her,

I wouldn't want some guy giving me some land and building me a house without me paying a cent."

"Yeah, yeah." Levi waved an irritated hand at him. "I get it. It just…doesn't feel right." And it didn't. He had the money, money he didn't use for anything beyond nights out at the bars of Queenstown and running the charity he'd set up a couple of years back for homeless kids. No one knew about the charity, and he preferred to keep it that way. Just as he preferred to keep what he did with the rent money from the building that housed the gallery and Bill's store on the down-low. That money had paid for several "emergencies" that various inhabitants had run into and didn't have the cash to pay for. A new roof and kitchen cabinets for Shirley's cottage. Some rewiring in the Rose. A new septic tank and some fencing for a retired shepherd up the hill.

Little things to help people who couldn't afford something themselves.

Hell, it made him feel good to give back to the community that had been there for him all those years ago when he'd turned up here, following Chase because he had nowhere else to go and Chase had been as close as a brother to him.

And while the community hadn't exactly welcomed him with open arms—they were wary of strangers—he'd made it his personal mission to prove to each and every one of them that he was someone they could rely on, one of their own. And he had.

This was his home now and it always would be. He'd never leave. But he still felt crappy about taking Indigo's money.

"What's the alternative?" Finn asked. "Beth said Indigo has her heart set on one of those little-house things, with a dye shed out the back, and we don't have anything like that here now. I guess you could always ask around, see if anyone would mind you building her a house on their land—"

"No." The word was out of his mouth before he'd even had time to think about it.

Both Finn and Chase stared at him in surprise, the looks on their faces identical.

Yeah, that had sounded a bit too…vehement, hadn't it? Well, weirdly, he felt vehement about it. He didn't like the idea of Indigo's house being on anyone else's land but his, which was extremely territorial of him and no doubt one of those "toxic masculinity" things she'd talked about, but shit. He didn't like the thought of her being at anyone else's mercy. At least if she was on his land, he could make sure she was okay and not being taken advantage of.

You know how that's going to look, don't you?

Which was why he wouldn't say anything about it. Best keep any strange territorial feelings to himself.

"No?" Chase inquired delicately.

Levi let out a silent breath and leaned back in his chair, stuck one hand in the pocket of his jeans, and picked up his beer, being casual. "You know she can't drive. And who knows what kind of money anyone else will charge her? My land is perfect, especially since the gallery will only be a minute's walk, if that."

"Okay then." Finn's voice was very neutral. Too neutral. "So how are you going to get around the money aspect?"

But an idea was already forming in Levi's head, though it would involve a chat to Jim to get his agreement. In fact, he was almost tempted to go chat with him now, but no. He needed to work some things out first, get some figures, think of a good angle for his case. Going off half-cocked would risk failure, and failure in this instance was not an option.

Levi gave Finn his best "nothing to see here folks" grin. "Oh, don't you worry. I think I might have that under control."

Chapter 4

THE NEXT MORNING, AFTER BETH HAD COME TO give her a lift down into Brightwater since Clint's farmhouse was a ten-minute drive from the township, Indigo went straight into the Rose. It was too early for the pub to be open, but Jim was usually there behind the bar preparing for the afternoon, and sure enough, she spotted him as soon as she walked in.

After the chat with the girls the night before, she'd been almost too excited to sleep, so she was feeling slightly dusty this morning. But in the pocket of her loose blue-striped cotton trousers was a piece of paper with her budget all worked out. Some things were going to be tight—especially getting materials for the house, since she suspected some would be expensive—but that was a problem she'd work out when the time came.

Right now, the most important thing was getting Jim's okay on her paying rent to Levi, and then she'd take that, and her budget, to Levi himself and tell him what she wanted.

She'd get him to build it. That would be no problem, not if there were others around to help as well, so it wouldn't *all* be dependent on him.

He'd probably make some kind of big fuss, but too bad. She could be stubborn when she wanted to be. Grandma used to call her a damned stubborn cuss, but being stubborn could only be a good thing when dealing with a man like Levi King.

Jim was fiddling around underneath the bar when she walked in, and while he didn't smile—he wasn't a smiler—he did give her a nod.

Indigo gave him a determined look back and made a beeline for the bar.

Jim's eyes widened slightly. "We're closed."

"I know." Indigo put her folded arms on the bar and leaned on them. "I'm not here for a drink. I wanted to ask you something."

A wary expression tightened over his craggy features, but he didn't speak. He only gave her one of his laconic nods.

"Okay," Indigo said, taking this as permission to keep going. "So, you know I'm trying to find a more permanent place to live, right? Well, I'd really like one of those tiny houses. Levi has offered to build me one, and he suggested building it on the land he owns." She gestured in the general direction of the gallery and Bill's. "It would be really convenient for me, but the issue is that I want to pay him for it, especially some money for the land. Except he doesn't want me to."

Jim pursed his lips. "What's this got to do with me?"

"You said Levi bought the land from you. And he told me that he made you a promise not to take money for it, or to rent it out or develop it in any way."

"That's right." Jim nodded slowly. "He did."

Indigo's gut tightened with sudden anxiety. What if he wasn't going to go for it? What if he insisted that no money could change hands? That he didn't even want a tiny house on the property? Where would that leave her?

Levi was loyal to this town, she knew that. If Jim told her no, Levi would refuse too. But hell…she really wanted this house, and the position of Levi's land was just too convenient. She was going to have to tell Jim why this was so important to her, despite her wariness at giving away her secrets.

"Okay." She took a breath. "The thing is, I don't have a home here, and I…well, I really want one. I want to feel a part of this town." She swallowed, overcome by a sudden intense wave of emotion. How weird to feel all teary about a place she'd only lived in for two months. "This town has come to mean a lot to me. But I can't let Levi pay for everything. And even if you agreed to let him build a tiny house on the site, I don't want to live there and pay nothing. It's just not right. I wouldn't be pulling my own weight, if you get what I mean."

Jim grunted, his face now expressionless.

Indigo plowed on. "So, what I'm asking is this: Is it

okay if Levi builds the tiny house on that property for me? And if so, will you allow him to receive rent for it?"

Jim was silent, his blue eyes impenetrable as he gazed at her. Then abruptly he turned and reached for something underneath the bar.

It was the granny square he'd been working on yesterday, along with a couple of balls of yarn. One yellow and one green.

Indigo frowned. What on earth?

"Which one do you think I should do next?" Jim asked. "I'm not good with color."

She blinked, taken off guard by the randomness of the question. But then she realized this was a gesture. An important one. He was asking her opinion on something because he valued it. He valued her.

There was a small lump in her throat, emotion still washing around inside her, and she had to swallow past it as she gave the yarn situation serious consideration. "Is this for anything in particular?"

"Baby blanket," he said. "For Finn and Beth."

Oh, that's right. She'd forgotten that apparently everyone in the entire town was doing a blanket for Finn and Beth.

Indigo put away her slight grumpiness at being pipped at the post. "Okay, I say the green."

Jim considered the square for a long moment before nodding in agreement. Then he put the square and the yarn back beneath the bar and added, "I don't see why not."

"I think it's a good choice," Indigo said. "The green is for the bush and the—"

"This house thing. He can build it for you, and sure, you give him some rent. I'm okay with it. You're one of us and you need a place to live."

Indigo paused, her mouth still open. Then she shut it.

She was one of them. That's what he'd said. *"You're one of us."*

Her eyes prickled, a small warm glow sitting behind her breastbone. She didn't know what to say. She hadn't been expecting laconic, suspicious Jim O'Halloran, hotel owner and local skeptic, to suddenly tell her that she was one of them.

It had been a long time since she'd been one of anything, and she hadn't known she'd feel so strongly about it.

Luckily, Jim saved her from having to reply as he went on. "Just how big a house are we talking about?"

"They're called tiny houses, Jim," a deep male voice said from behind her. "And we're talking about twenty-one square meters, or at least that's the average."

Indigo went very still, her breath catching.

Damn Levi King. Of course, he'd turn up right when she didn't want him to. What was he doing here?

She didn't move as six foot three of long and

lean muscled gorgeousness propped himself casually against the bar at her elbow. Not that she could have moved even if she'd wanted to, because all she could think about was that moment on the front porch of the Rose, where she'd leaned over the arm of his chair to help him with his knitting. And she'd realized how close she was to him and how warm he was, and how good he smelled. How her whole body had hummed in awareness of him.

How, when she'd looked into his eyes, she'd seen the same awareness reflected back…

"Huh," Jim was saying. "That *is* tiny."

"Yeah, the footprint isn't large and they're pretty ecologically friendly, depending on how you build them and where you get your materials," Levi went on as if he'd personally done a lot of research himself into the matter.

He probably has. You know what those guys are like. Boy Scouts to a man.

Yes, but still. Infuriating. The tiny house had been *her* idea, not his, and now suddenly he was the expert?

Irritation wound through her, but she bit back the impulse to say something sharp. After all, he *was* offering to build her a house and on land that he owned, and him being prepared was a *good* thing. Also, hadn't she decided she was going to be *less* prickly?

It wasn't his fault she found him far too attractive for her own good and that she didn't know how to handle it.

"I was just telling Jim about *my* idea for the house," she said, unable to stop herself from emphasizing the "my" part of the sentence.

"Hi, Indigo," Levi said, amusement coloring his voice. "Nice to see you too."

She bit her lip and forced herself to look at him. Which was a big mistake since he was just as gorgeous today as he had been the day before. Not that he was ever *not* absolutely gorgeous in his usual uniform of jeans and the black Pure Adventure NZ T-shirt that all three guys normally wore.

He had one elbow on the bar top and was leaning on it, and though he wasn't close enough to her to make it uncomfortable, he was nevertheless close enough that she was painfully aware of his height and how the way he was leaning pulled tight the cotton of his T-shirt across his wide shoulders and broad, muscled chest.

Close enough that she could see how long and thick his dark lashes were and how the gold flecks in his eyes glittered like tiny sparks. It seemed he hadn't bothered to shave this morning, because there was a dark five o'clock shadow defining his strong jaw, and she could see more than a few whiskers gleaming gold.

Her heartbeat thudded hard in her ears, and she knew she should say something, but she'd completely forgotten what words even were.

Come on, pull yourself together, for God's sake. He's just a man, and men aren't to be trusted, remember?

Oh, she remembered. She could still hear the warmth in her dad's voice the day she'd met him for the first time. Claire had brought him back to Tilly's because he'd wanted to meet Indigo, and she'd been so nervous. But he'd smiled and told her what a pretty girl she was and how he'd always wanted a daughter…

Indigo shoved the memories away and dredged up her voice from somewhere. "Hello, Levi," she said with as much dignity as she could muster, hoping he wouldn't notice her suddenly flaming cheeks.

He smiled his wicked, slow-burning smile, making it obvious he *had* noticed her blushing, which only made her blush even harder. "Gidday, hedgehog," he said in his beautiful, deep voice, drawing the words out in his sexy accent, so that she almost missed the "hedgehog" part.

She was about to tell him her thoughts on it when she was suddenly aware that Jim was on the other side of the bar staring at them with some interest.

"Jim said he wouldn't mind me paying rent on the land." She hoped she sounded utterly indifferent to

Levi's "gidday, hedgehog" greeting. "Since you told me yesterday you promised you wouldn't take any money for it."

"I see." Levi flicked a look at Jim. "Funnily enough, that's why I'm here too."

Jim frowned at him. "Should have come to me first, you know."

"I know," Levi acknowledged, frowning right back. "And before I offered to build it for her on that land. Sorry 'bout that. Just wanted to make sure she was taken care of."

Indigo scowled at the assertion that she needed "taking care of." "I'm not a child, thank you very much. I can take care of myself." After all, she'd spent years living on her own after her grandmother died, and even before that, she'd been the one taking care of things when Grandma had her stroke and hadn't been able to leave the house.

"Sure you can," Levi said.

Which instantly irritated her even more, despite the fact that she'd decided she *wasn't* going to be prickly.

"Tell me," she said, unable to resist rising to the bait. "Have you ever had to deal with a bear trying to come into your house?"

Much to her annoyance, far from Levi being put in his place, his expression lit with sudden interest. "Actually, no. I haven't. What happened?"

"I said yes," Jim said flatly.

Levi threw him a grin. "Come on, Jim. Don't you want to hear about the bear story?"

"No." Jim picked up the cloth he'd been using to wipe down the bar when Indigo came in. "I got work to do. But you have my okay on the use of the property and for you to have some financial compensation."

"Yes," Indigo said, needing to get the conversation back on track. "In fact, I'm going to pay you some rent."

"Sounds good," Levi said without missing a beat.

Indigo realized her mouth was open, so she shut it. She'd been expecting an argument or a cursory protest at least, especially when he'd seemed to hate the idea of her paying him anything at all.

She gave him a suspicious look. "You're fine with it?"

Levi only grinned and pushed himself away from the bar. "Let's discuss this somewhere else so we don't interrupt Jim's day."

Instinct had her wanting to refuse, because she didn't want to go anywhere with him to discuss anything. Which was ridiculous since if she wanted her tiny house—and she did—she was going to have to have a talk to him about it.

Plus, weren't you going to be nice to him?

Oh yes, that's right. There was that.

Levi examined his fingernails. "I can't possibly

reveal who, but someone might have managed to get their hands on a couple of Bill's scones before he sold out this morning."

Bill sold various baked goods in his bakery cabinet in the general store, and every single item was loved by the inhabitants of Brightwater. In fact, they mostly sold out the moment he'd finished baking them, so if you wanted something from his cabinet, you had to get in very quickly.

Indigo loved his scones in particular, especially with a nice cup of Earl Grey.

Sneaky man. Levi *knew* she loved the scones and he'd planned for it, hadn't he?

"Scones?" she asked warily, just to be sure.

"Scones," he confirmed, looking extremely pleased with himself.

Dammit. She didn't have a good excuse not to talk to him, did she? Especially not now scones were involved. Well, she needed to get this project started, so now was as good a time as any.

Indigo let out a silent breath and braced herself for the avalanche of male charm that was no doubt going to come her way.

"Okay," she said.

———

Levi felt exceptionally smug. The scones had been a power move, and silently he thanked Finn and

Chase for setting the example of courting their partners with food.

Chase had gotten Izzy eclairs, while Finn had used sausage rolls to good effect with Beth.

Finding out that Indigo loved Bill's scones had been a simple matter of asking Bill himself what she bought from his cabinet. So now he had a couple of fluffy scones in a paper bag in the little kitchen of the Pure Adventure NZ HQ, and he knew also that Indigo loved tea, and there was certainly a lot of tea there too.

He'd wanted to have as many weapons in his arsenal as he could when it came to getting her agreement on building her a tiny house.

"So where are we going to have this chat?" she asked as they stepped outside onto the porch of the Rose.

Across the road was the lakeshore, its usual brilliant turquoise blue muted today due to the cloud cover. A chilly wind blew off the jagged mountain range in the distance, bringing with it the icy scent of snow. Definitely signs that summer was on its way out and autumn was approaching, which meant building this house ASAP if Indigo wanted to be in there by winter.

It didn't get as cold here as it did in Alaska—the lake never froze over, for example—but some winters there was snow in the township and your pipes could freeze if you weren't careful. She'd need some double-glazing and some good heating, that was for sure.

Already halfway down the porch steps, Levi paused and turned.

Indigo stood on the porch, frowning down at him. She wore a pair of loose blue cotton trousers today, with an oversized white T-shirt and a darker blue fleece thrown over the top. Clothing that screamed practical rather than sexy, yet she was super sexy all the same.

Somehow the loose, oversized nature of the clothing emphasized her petite size and her fey femininity in a way that very much appealed to him. Even with her winged brows drawn into that habitual frown of hers.

Even when her downright beautiful sky-blue eyes were giving him the sternest of looks.

"I thought HQ." He nodded his head in the direction of the building. "It's private and there's tea."

Her expression became a touch less suspicious. "Oh." She bit her lip, glanced over at HQ, frowned a bit more, then said, "I guess that's okay."

"Glad you approve." Levi turned and went the rest of the way down the steps. As he stepped onto the road, a black shape came slinking out from under the Rose's stairs and trotted over to him.

He stilled, his hands in his pockets, and let

Mystery, the stray dog that had been hanging around the town for the past few months or more, have a sniff.

No one in Brightwater had successfully managed to convince Mystery to go home with them, even though the dog had no shortage of people willing to give him a home. But the animal had his own ideas about what he wanted and had steadfastly refused all comers.

Levi had privately decided that he was going to adopt Mystery—he'd been a lost stray himself once—and had been waging a secret campaign to get the dog on his side. He hadn't been successful so far, but Mystery had seemed to warm to him. Or rather, he hoped Mystery had warmed to him.

He'd taken to carrying around treats in his pocket to give the dog whenever he spotted him, but he'd run out today and was silently cursing himself as Mystery, having sniffed his fill, sat at his feet and looked up hopefully at him.

"Sorry, boy," Levi murmured. "I don't have anything for you today."

The dog seemed to understand, giving a disgusted sneeze before turning and running off toward the lake.

"That dog," Levi pronounced as Indigo came up beside him, "will come home with me one day. I swear it."

Indigo stared after the dog. "I thought everyone was waiting until he decided who got to adopt him."

"Well, sure. And he'll decide that I'm the best option."

She glanced at him, eyes bright with curiosity. "Oh? Why? Are you a dog person?"

"I like dogs, yes. But I also know what it's like to not have a home." His background wasn't a secret, and she may as well know. It might even help his cause. "And I want to give him one."

Indigo's brow creased, but not with suspicion this time, more puzzlement. "But don't you have a home? Beth told me you've got some massive house in Queenstown."

"It's three bedrooms, which hardly counts as massive," he corrected mildly. "No, I'm talking about my previous life, before I came here."

"Oh?"

He looked down at her, into her blue eyes, a strange sense of disquiet stealing through him, which was weird. Normally he had no problems with talking about his childhood and the difficulties he'd had. True, he didn't often talk about it since everyone here knew already, but he didn't have an issue with answering people's questions.

Perhaps he was out of practice or something.

"Yeah," he said, shoving away the disquiet. "I

was a foster kid. Got bounced around the system, twenty homes in two months, that kind of thing. Ran away eventually and lived on the streets in Auckland for a while. Then joined the army, since that was preferable to sleeping rough."

There was shock in her eyes that morphed instantly into concern.

It hit him oddly. Most people when he told them greeted the story with varying degrees of pity, which he shrugged off since pity wasn't useful to him in any way, shape, or form. But concern was new, and he wasn't sure he liked it.

Concern implied that he was suffering, which was bullshit, because he definitely *wasn't* suffering. He was completely and utterly fine.

He had a home now and people who cared about him, a family, and his life was pretty damn good. There was no need for her concern.

"Oh, Levi," Indigo murmured. "I had no idea."

"It's fine," he said, deciding he was done with the conversation. "It's all good now. Brightwater is my home and everyone here is like a family to me." He turned in the direction of HQ. "Come on, let's get you a scone."

They walked along the road, gravel crunching under their feet.

Indigo kept glancing at him, her brow still furrowed.

"What?" he asked eventually.

"Oh…I just wondered…" She bit her lip again. "Has you wanting to build me a house got—?"

"Anything to do with me having been homeless?" he finished, getting in before she could because he knew exactly how this conversation was going to go. He'd had it before with people. Many times. "Probably. Homes for everyone, I say."

But she didn't smile. If anything, her gaze became even more concerned. "Levi, I've been pretty awful to you for—"

"Come on," he interrupted yet again, because that unease was still inside him and he didn't like it. And he didn't want to talk about this, at least not out on the street and not when he was feeling so uncomfortable. The last thing he needed was her feeling sorry for him. "Let's get you some tea."

Indigo's gaze narrowed, but she closed her mouth and didn't push, for which he was thankful.

Chase had just left for a two-day guided hike, and Finn was downstairs in the front desk part of the building, fiddling around with some bookings, so Levi had the upstairs to himself.

It was a small area consisting of a main lounge room with a door to a small kitchen, then a tiny hall with a bathroom and a couple of small bedrooms off it.

The lounge area had couches and a wood burner up against the wall, plus bookshelves stuffed with all kinds of different books from outdoor activity

how-tos, New Zealand guidebooks, and engine
manuals to first aid, plus a range of fiction titles
covering various genres. On the walls were photos
and posters of the activities Pure Adventure NZ
took clients on, plus other striking photos of New
Zealand landscapes.

Levi loved this room, and he spent a lot of time
in it since the guys used it as their staff room. He
pretty much based himself in HQ, the bedroom
down the hall his own bedroom. It wasn't ideal
since this place wasn't his house, but commut-
ing from Queenstown every day wasn't happening either. He'd bought his Queenstown place
as an investment, and it had come in handy on a
number of occasions. But he didn't actually want
to live there.

He wanted to be here, in Brightwater. That
was home.

"Sit down and get comfortable." He gestured to
the couches. "I'll go and put on the tea."

"What kind of tea is it?" Indigo asked, moving
over to the couch.

"Gumboot."

She frowned. "What's gumboot tea?"

"Oh, you know, bog standard tea." He went into
the little kitchen and started getting out a couple of
plates to put the scones on.

"Bog standard tea?" Indigo was now in the doorway, still frowning.

Levi sighed, and before he could think better of it, he'd gone over to where she stood and had lifted his hand, pressing his thumb gently to the crease between her brows.

Her eyes went very wide, the frown disappearing as the sweetest blush he'd ever seen stained her pale cheeks.

What the hell are you doing?

Quite frankly, he had no idea. He'd seen her frown and the impulse to smooth it away had come over him and...yeah, he'd gone over there and done it. And now that he was looking down into those beautiful sky-blue eyes of hers, watching her blush deepen from pink into rose, feeling the warmth and silkiness of her skin against his finger, noticing how all that biting had left her bottom lip looking very red and full...

Damn. He'd made a mistake. The same mistake he'd made yesterday, encouraging her to get close, because he couldn't resist. Because he liked how flustered she got around him, little realizing that it would fluster him too...

For a second neither of them moved, the shock of the contact and the strange echo it had set up inside him vibrating in the air around them, holding them fast.

Then, taking him utterly by surprise, Indigo rose suddenly on her toes and, before he could move, kissed him on the mouth.

He had no time to enjoy it. No time to even feel more than a fleeting softness and a bright burst of heat before she pulled away from him as suddenly as she'd kissed him, a look of complete horror on her face.

She was going to bolt; he knew it. Just as he also knew that if she ran, he probably wouldn't see her for another week, which would mean this house idea would go completely by the wayside.

That was *not* happening.

His hand shot out, and he grabbed her elbow just as she started to turn.

"Hey," he said softly. "Don't run away."

She stilled, half turned away, her whole body trembling. "Let me go, please."

"Only if you promise me you won't run."

"Levi…"

"Why did you kiss me?"

"Oh my God," Indigo groaned and put her free hand over her face. She made no further move to pull away from him, so he loosened his hold.

He could still feel the soft press of her lips against his, the briefest of tastes, making his heartbeat accelerate. But quite frankly he was shocked—yes, shocked. A kiss from Indigo Jameson was the very last thing he'd expected. A punch in the face? Yes. A kick in the balls? Also, yes.

A kiss? Very much in the negative.

He cleared his throat, his body deciding it was

in favor of the kiss and urging him to try for more. Which he ignored. "Indy?"

"I don't know." Her voice was muffled by her hand. "I don't know. I don't know. Can we pretend it never happened?"

No. He could never pretend it didn't happen. Not when he could still feel the impression of her perfect little rosebud of a mouth on his, the softest brush of her lips, tantalizing...

Yeah, stop right there.

Shit, yes. He had to. She was at a disadvantage here, with nowhere permanent to live, a fledgling business, and limited funds. Plus, an affair with someone also living here was always going to be a terrible idea when he wasn't in the market for anything more. Especially with someone as inexperienced as he suspected she was.

Yeah, but she sort of made the first move.

"Okay," he said mildly, ignoring that little thought. "Are you going to promise me you won't run away? I've got scones and tea, and we need to talk about your house."

She was silent a couple of moments before she finally said, "I promise."

Levi released her, half expecting her to bolt anyway. But all she did was turn and go back into the living area without a word.

This was, naturally, a terrible development.

Indigo Jameson should never ever have kissed

him. He was a certified playboy, a man whore who loved bedding women as much as he loved flying helicopters or fixing engines. A man who was not for inexperienced, prickly little hedgehogs like her, and he should be very, very concerned at this development.

Except he wasn't concerned.

He was very, *very* pleased about it instead.

Chapter 5

INDIGO SAT ON THE COUCH IN THE LIVING AREA of HQ, her hands clasped tightly in her lap, listening to Levi rattle around in the kitchen getting the tea and scones ready.

Her face was still flaming, her heartbeat racing, and she could hardly breathe through the embarrassment that was threatening to drown her.

She'd kissed him. She'd *kissed* him. She'd kissed *him*.

What the hell had she been thinking? Had she gone temporarily insane? Maybe he wasn't a simple adventure guide. Maybe he was some kind of wizard who'd put a spell on her, making her do things she'd never in a million years ordinarily do.

Things such as kissing a man she actively disliked.

You don't dislike him, come on. You'd never have kissed him if you truly didn't like him.

Indigo covered her face with her hands and screamed silently into them.

She'd been standing there innocently asking him what the hell "gumboot" tea was, when he'd come over and stroked his finger between her brows. And there had been something about his touch that had gone through her like lightning. A pulse of the most intense electricity.

All she could think about was his mouth and how it was so close and how beautiful it was. His lower lip was full and soft-looking, and she'd been seized with the most intense curiosity about how it would feel on hers, since she'd never kissed a man before.

His gaze had been warm as he'd looked down at her, those fascinating sparks of wickedness glittering in his eyes.

She'd been dazzled, part of her thinking about what he'd told her earlier after they'd come out of the Rose, of how he'd been in the foster system and then been on the streets. And she'd been shocked. He'd always seemed so…confident and sure of himself in everything he did, so charming and good with people. Not like a man who'd had a very unsettled childhood and maybe even an awful one.

Her own might have been achingly lonely and isolated, but at least she'd had her grandma who'd looked out for her.

It hurt her heart to think of him as a boy, tossed from one home to another without anyone to look out for him or care for him. Why that mattered to her, she had no idea. But it did.

And that painful ache had combined with the attraction into one unholy urge, and before she knew what she was doing, she was rising on her toes and pressing her mouth to his.

Then awareness of what was happening had fallen on her full force, and she'd pulled away, horror-struck and mortified. Only to have his fingers close around her arm, preventing her from bolting like any self-respecting idiot would have done.

More rattling came from the direction of the kitchen, and she lowered her hands and glanced warily at the doorway. But Levi didn't appear.

God. Why was she still sitting here? She should have wrenched her arm from his grip and shot out the door, but he'd said that they could pretend it never happened, and they *did* have to talk about her house. She couldn't let her own embarrassment take precedence over that, so she'd stayed where she was.

But she was second-guessing herself now.

It wouldn't take a moment to get off the couch and quickly run down the stairs. Then she would be free. Then she'd go and hide in Clint's farmhouse for the rest of her natural life.

Sure. Great plan. You'll turn into Grandma before you know it.

Poor Grandma, stuck with Indigo after Indigo's mom had decided to go to Anchorage with Frank, the pair of them leaving Indigo behind. Tilly had already distrusted him after the affair he'd had while

Claire was pregnant and had transferred that hate onto the "outside world." She only left the homestead to make supply runs every couple of weeks, bringing Indigo up on a diet of fearful stories of the world and the people in it, and how dangerous and terrible it was.

She'd lost a daughter to the outside world, and to keep her granddaughter "safe," she'd planted that same fear and mistrust deep in Indigo's psyche. For a long time, Indigo had shared her grandmother's beliefs, her trust in people already broken by her parents' abandonment. But that had changed after Tilly had a stroke and was forced to let Indigo go for supplies instead. And after Grandma died, Indigo had realized that she was in danger of becoming a crazy old hermit lady too if she wasn't careful.

So, she'd taken her courage in both hands and rejoined the outside world, forcing herself into crossing the globe on a thousands-of-miles adventure to a new country and new people in an effort to prove her bravery.

It hadn't been easy. In fact, it had been more difficult than she could possibly have imagined, but she was here. She'd survived two whole months among strangers, and now she was almost like a normal person.

She couldn't put all that personal growth aside for one ill-advised kiss.

Indigo sighed and slumped back on the couch. But no, no slumping. He'd said they could pretend it had never happened, so that's what she'd do. She'd chalk it up as a bad decision and never think of it again.

You want him to think about it though, don't you?

No, of course she didn't. She didn't want to get involved with anyone. And why would he anyway? He'd be used to fabulous kisses from fabulous women, not clumsy pecks from prickly hedgehogs.

She sat up, reaching automatically for her knitting bag, then realized she'd left it back at the farmhouse. Damn, another bad decision. Knitting helped her anxiety, which was why she did *a lot* of it.

Then, just as her thoughts were relentlessly circling back to how near the door was and how she could quickly be off before Levi realized it, he came out of the kitchen carrying a tray piled high with goodies.

Reflexively, she blushed and turned away, staring out the window at the view of the fields and bush that stretched up into the hills behind HQ.

The clouds were low today, making the sky a kind of gunmetal gray. It was pretty against the deep green of the beech forest, dotted here and there with silver and red beech. Perhaps she could do some gray skeins in various tones, silver and slate and fog. And then some green, with some gold flecks to really make it pop? Just like the gold flecks in—

"One second," Levi said.

Indigo wrenched her thoughts away before they could head happily down that path and forced herself to turn.

Levi had gone back into the kitchen, but sitting on the battered wooden coffee table in front of her was the tray, and on it were teacups and plates with Bill's perfect fluffy fresh scones on them, as well as some butter and jam, and even a small pot of whipped cream.

Indigo's mouth watered. Okay, this was worth suffering through her embarrassment for. Probably.

He came back in again, this time carrying a white china teapot and a bottle of milk.

"Sorry," he said as he put the milk and teapot down on the table. "I couldn't find anything to put the milk in. We don't tend to have high tea in HQ. Do you need sugar?"

It was a perfectly neutral question, and there was nothing in his expression but friendliness. He gave no sign that she'd kissed him not moments before.

She swallowed, her tension easing. "Yes, please," she said, her voice unexpectedly husky. Great.

But he made no comment, only turning and going back into the kitchen before coming out again with a canister of sugar.

He put it down on the table and sat down too,

making her tense up again even though he hadn't positioned himself near her. "I was hoping for sugar lumps and tongs, but sadly, we don't have any of those either." His hazel eyes danced with his usual amusement. "Shall I be mother?"

Indigo stared. "What?"

He grinned and picked up the teapot, pouring the thick black liquid into one of the teacups. "Gumboot tea." He put the pot down again. "Sorry, it's all we have."

It clearly wasn't Earl Grey, but she needed steadying and maybe gumboot tea was better than no tea.

Indigo leaned forward, put a bit of milk into the cup, stared at the color critically, then dumped a whole lot more milk into it. Then a couple of teaspoons of sugar. Then she picked up the mug. "Why do you call it gumboot tea?"

He shrugged, then unexpectedly poured some into a mug for himself. "Because it looks like it's been made out of gumboots? I've got no idea. It's just black tea."

"You drink tea?" For some reason, this came as a surprise to her.

"Yeah. Love the stuff." Levi picked up his mug. "What? Is that really so shocking?"

"You just don't look like a tea drinker."

He took a healthy swallow, drinking it without milk or sugar. "And what do tea drinkers look like?"

Indigo had a sense that this conversation could go downhill if she let it, so she said briskly, "Let's talk about the house. That's what I came for."

"Of course." An amused smile was playing around his beautiful mouth, though what he was amused about she had no idea.

Perhaps it was the kiss. That silly little peck. Perhaps he was reflecting on her ridiculousness. His lips had been so warm though, and he'd smelled so delicious. And she'd wanted to get even closer...

"So, here's my plan," he went on. "I want to—"

"Can I go first, please?" she interrupted, tearing her gaze from his mouth, because she needed to get out of here and fast before she did anything else stupid.

He didn't miss a beat. "Sure. Go ahead."

"Okay." She took a healthy sip of her tea and grimaced. The liquid was bitter and thick and definitely needed more than two sugars.

Levi frowned. "Not good?"

"No, it's fine. I usually drink Earl Grey. But really, this is great," she lied. "I'll just put some more sugar in it."

"Right." He picked up a knife and reached for a scone. "You tell me what you want while I do these scones."

Strangely, the terrible tea had steadied her, and she was able to dump a couple more spoonfuls of sugar into it, plus a third for luck, without a tremble.

"I did some budgets last night." She paused in stirring her sugar to reach into her pocket and bring out her piece of paper. It was a bit crumpled, so she put her teaspoon down and smoothed the paper out. "Because I'm not letting you pay for all of this. That's why I was at the Rose. I wanted to ask Jim whether it was okay for me to pay you rent."

Levi didn't even glance at the piece of paper. "I've got no problem with that. In fact, that's why I was at the Rose too. I wanted to ask Jim if he'd accept you paying me some kind of rent. Just a nominal amount, nothing too—"

"A nominal amount?" She tried to offer a smile so it wouldn't sound so sharp. "I don't want to pay a 'nominal amount.' I'll pay the usual market rent."

Levi's expression didn't change. "Fine. But the market rent in Brightwater Valley is not high."

"How much is it?"

He named a number that seemed ridiculously cheap to her and not at all what she'd expected.

"I can't pay that," she said, aghast. "That's practically nothing!"

Infuriatingly, he only shrugged as he buttered a scone. "I can't charge you more than the market rate since that would artificially inflate prices in the area."

Dammit. He was serious, wasn't he?

"Can't you make an exception for me?"

"What? And have everyone call me Scrooge

when they find out I'm charging you an inflated rent?" He gave her the smuggest smile she'd ever seen. "No, hedgehog, I can't."

You're really going to insist you pay more *rent? When you're barely able to afford the materials? And what about labor? Did you think about that?*

Indigo gritted her teeth and took another big swallow from her teacup, deciding to let the hedgehog thing slide this once. "The kit set's too expensive," she said, breathing through the sharp bite of the tannins. "I can't afford it."

This time Levi frowned. "But you really liked that one."

"I know. Like I said though. It's too expensive."

"I can pay for—"

"No, you can't. I want to use recycled materials."

Levi's expression was unreadable this time. He looked down at the scone he was holding and put some jam on it. "Recycled materials," he echoed. "Okay. And what about the design?"

"I'll ask Chase if he knows anyone who can do some plans for me on the cheap."

Levi carefully put the scone down on a plate, then pushed it in her direction. "I can do the plans for you."

Indigo stared at him in surprise. Surely, he couldn't do the plans for her *as well*.

"Serious question," she said. "Is there anything you can't do?"

His mouth curved in that way she found so fascinating. "Oh, lots of things. I can't cook, for one. Never learned how. And…I can't knit, obviously. I can't sing either, and I'm terrible at sitting still."

Indigo let out a breath and took a much bigger sip of her sweet, milky, incredibly strong tea. It was going to take the enamel off her teeth, but it was also bracing, she'd give it that. "This is silly. You know that, right? How is any of this going to be mine if you can do all of it for me?"

He gave her a measuring look. "Eat your scone."

"Levi, this is—"

"Eat your scone."

She muttered a curse under her breath but picked up the scone and took a bite. Then tried not to moan in delight, because Bill's scones were utter perfection.

Satisfied with her scone eating, Levi fixed her with a direct look. "How about this? I'll do the plans, get the council sign-offs, et cetera. Source the materials and build the house. You okay the final design and make the decisions as to what kind of materials you want, plus you pay me rent."

"*I* will source the materials," she insisted.

Levi's stare became narrower. "*We* will source the materials."

"But I—"

"I'm building the bloody thing so I'm going to know what I need when I need it, and I don't want to have to wait around while you decide on every nail."

She didn't want to give him any ground, but that did make sense. How irritating.

"Okay," she said grumpily.

"And I've decided on something else. You don't have the money to pay me for labor, I know, but you can pay me in other ways."

A strange jolt of electricity went through her for no apparent reason, leaving little pinpricks of static chasing over her skin.

Oh, you can think of some ways you could pay him…

No. What? What on earth was her brain suggesting?

She could feel her cheeks heat again, which was extremely annoying and utterly inexplicable. "What ways?"

His expression shifted, his eyes gleaming with a kind of wickedness that made her feel hot and restless and her skin too tight. And she found herself holding her breath, every part of her almost quivering at the thought of what he might demand of her.

"What I want, Indigo Jameson," he said, giving her a smoldering look from beneath his gold-tipped lashes, "is for you to finish teaching me to knit."

Indigo blinked.

He was being an asshole and he knew it, but as usual, he couldn't seem to stop himself from teasing her just a little.

She was so unbearably sweet sitting there on the edge of the couch, holding the giant mug of tea in one hand and her scone in the other, and being all businesslike and determined about the house.

As if she hadn't kissed him just before.

And that kiss was still burning against his mouth. It hadn't gone away. He thought it might, but it hadn't. No kiss had ever done that to him before, still less a kiss like that. It had only been the briefest touch, hardly even a kiss, and yet he couldn't stop thinking about it.

If she hadn't been who she was, he'd have deepened that kiss and seduced the hell out of her before she even knew what was happening, but since she was Indigo, seduction was right out.

Except you wouldn't stop her if she tried it again, would you?

Levi knew himself. Temptation was a problem for him, but he'd give resistance a damn good go, because he'd already told himself she was off-limits.

Teasing her using their chemistry was low, and he shouldn't be doing that either, but hell, she'd unsettled him, so why couldn't he unsettle her in return?

"That's what you want?" she asked. "To finish learning how to knit?"

"That's what I said." He lifted a brow. "Why? Did you have something else in mind in terms of payment?"

She went pink, which was gratifying since it was clear the payment she'd had in mind had involved him and was maybe sexier in nature than knitting. Though his last experience of Indigo teaching him to knit had been hella sexy if he did say so himself.

"No," she said quickly. Too quickly. "That sounds good."

"That's not all," he added, because he'd been thinking about this as he'd gotten the scones and tea ready.

Her eyes narrowed and she was all suspicion again. "What else?"

He held her gaze solemnly this time. "I want us to try and be friends."

"Friends?" She said the word like she didn't know what it meant.

"Yes, you know. Two people who enjoy each other's company." Another thing he'd thought about while he'd been preparing her tea. Because he enjoyed her prickles and her teases far too much, and he already knew the slippery slope that would lead him down. Far better to get their relationship on a friendship footing, which would make him less likely to do something he'd regret.

Plus, he did want to be her friend. He wanted

to hear more about her bear story for a start and about her life in Alaska, and she was pretty much the only person in Brightwater he hadn't completely charmed the pants off and he couldn't let her be the single holdout. That didn't work for him.

"I know what friends are," she said crossly. "Why do you want to be mine?"

"Because I think you're interesting." It was true. He did. Her with her suspicion and her prickliness that he knew from Izzy and Beth hid a very soft heart. In fact, he'd caught a glimpse of that caring heart just before, when he'd told her about how he'd been in the foster system.

It would be interesting to know why she hid that heart of hers. Why she was so suspicious and why she had all those little prickles. Maybe it was innate or maybe she'd had a tough childhood.

A tough childhood like he had.

This is a very bad plan, and you know it.

Hey, it was only friendship, nothing more.

"You think I'm interesting?" She frowned as if she found the concept strange.

"Yes, I do." Levi took another sip of his tea and only just stopped himself from grimacing. He'd lied just before when he'd said he loved the stuff. He actually hated tea, but he'd decided that if he wanted her to accept his house offer, he had to use every advantage he could. And if that meant pretending he liked tea in order to build a rapport with her, then he would.

"Why?"

She was being completely genuine, which gave him a second's pause. Because how could she think she wasn't interesting?

"Uh, well, for a start you needed me to rescue you from a very small insect, yet you told me in the Rose you scared off a bear. So that's interesting. In fact, that's downright fascinating." He stared at her over the rim of his mug. "I want to know more about that definitely."

She was still quite pink. "The wētā wasn't small."

"Bears aren't small either."

She finished her scone and dusted off her fingers before picking up her own mug again. "It wasn't a big deal. There's nothing much else that's interesting about me."

"I would disagree," Levi said. "You fight bears. You knit amazing things. You dye yarn the most incredible colors. You came all the way from Alaska to New Zealand to start up a business… Come on, what's not interesting about all those things?"

Indigo glanced down her mug as if she suddenly found the contents fascinating. She held it between her fingers, the dye on her fingertips standing out against the white of the porcelain. "So, what exactly does 'being friends' entail?"

He debated pressing her as to why she hadn't answered his question, but there was no need to make her more uncomfortable than she already was. He'd have plenty of time to find out her secrets if he built this house for her.

"You've got friends, haven't you?" He gave her a grin. "Think of me as being like Beth and Izzy."

A look of indignation crossed her face. "You are so *not* like Beth and Izzy. How could you even think that?"

He laughed. "Okay, fair. Not like Izzy and Beth. More like Chase and Finn then. They're your friends too, aren't they?"

Finally, she leaned back against the couch, still cradling her teacup. "Yes," she said slowly. "I suppose they are."

"Well, then. Think of me as one of them."

"So, teaching you to knit and being friends. That seems a really small price to pay." She bit her lip again, and he really wished she'd stop doing that. "There must be something else you want."

Did this mean that she was giving it some thought? He hoped so.

"Maybe you could teach me how to cook?" He took one last sip of the disgusting tea, put it down, and got himself a scone instead. "I don't know how, and it'd be useful to learn."

"You really can't cook anything?"

"Okay, so that's not strictly true." He gave her a knowing look. "I make a mean breakfast. Eggs, bacon, the works."

"Breakfast? Why breakfast?"

He could tell her the truth, or he could make up

some worthy lie to make his reason sound better than it was. Then again, it was probably good she knew the truth about him. Then she'd be under no illusions about what kind of man he was. Not that she didn't have any illusions already, but it would just be a solid warning should she try any of those little kisses again.

His body went hot at the thought, but he ignored it.

"Why do you think?" He gave her his very best wicked grin. "I'm a full-service one-night stand. Pleasure all night and a good breakfast in the morning before you go."

"Oh." Indigo glanced away again, going pink as she took another sip from her mug. "That... makes sense."

"It really does, doesn't it?" He shouldn't enjoy her fluster quite so much. That was what had led him to this point with her, his absolute failure to resist flustering her.

You can't resist her, full stop.

No, that was bullshit. The attraction might be stronger than he was anticipating, and his ability to resist temptation could use some work, but he'd do it. He'd resist her.

The alternative was an affair that would never go anywhere, because he didn't have what it took to give a woman forever. And that was okay. He didn't want forever anyway. He was here for a good time, not a long time, and he wanted to make sure that time was as good as humanly possible.

He already had his home and his family right here. He didn't need anything else.

"There's one other idea I've been turning over," he said, deciding that now was the perfect time for his pièce de résistance. "I'm considering putting the money you pay me into a separate account that will go toward you eventually buying that land off of me."

Her eyebrows shot skyward. "Really? But I thought Jim told you he didn't want you to sell."

"He doesn't. But I think I could talk him round. After all, that land wouldn't be going to a stranger, right? It would be going to you, and he likes you." Of course, he hadn't fully cleared it with Jim yet, but he was fairly certain the old guy wouldn't mind. "Anyway, that way the land would eventually be yours legally."

Her gaze was sharp, obviously measuring up what he'd said and looking for any loopholes by staring at his face. "Hmmm…I don't know. Why can't you sell it to me now?"

"Because you won't accept a price that you can afford and can't afford the market price. Or am I wrong?"

Her nose wrinkled. "No, you're not wrong."

"Well? What do you say? Do we have a deal?"

Indigo was silent a long moment, still staring down at her mug. Then abruptly she looked up, the endless blue of her eyes momentarily catching him off guard. "I'll think about it."

Chapter 6

"THAT'S FANTASTIC," BETH EXCLAIMED WITH her usual enthusiasm. "So, he's offered to design and build you a house, and all you have to do is pay him some rent, teach him to cook and knit, and be his friend?"

Indigo, who'd dumped a bag of freshly dyed yarn on top of the counter in the gallery and was currently unpacking it, pulled a face. "You make it sound like a lot, but it isn't. Not compared to what he's doing for me."

Sadly, those were all the concessions she'd managed to get out of Levi the day before. She'd tried to dicker around with the amount for rent, but he hadn't budged on wanting to her to pay market rates, which were tiny. The worst part was, she knew the sneaky bastard was right. He couldn't charge her a higher price without affecting other rentals in the area, plus she didn't want him to look like an asshole if other people found out he was overcharging her.

She hadn't wanted to agree about him doing the drawings either, but she couldn't think of a good enough reason to refuse. She could certainly try to find someone else to do it, but that would not only take some time, but also require money she didn't have. Plus, there was the convenience factor, since he was who'd be building the tiny house.

To cap it all off, he'd mentioned that the rent would go toward a deposit for the property so she could actually own it herself.

It had all seemed far too good to be true, which was the whole reason she was so suspicious about this. She still remembered all her father's promises: About the house in Anchorage he and her mother had bought, with a room just for her and a big yard and an apple tree. A bike for her to ride, and if she was good, they'd get a dog. She'd been so excited…

But none of those things had ever happened. The house, the tree, the bike, the dog… Those had *all* been too good to be true.

You should never have believed him. You should have known he was lying.

Maybe she should have. She'd been a child though and had thought he'd really meant all those things he'd said.

Her heart twisted with the memory of old pain, but she pushed it aside.

She couldn't let the past affect her so much. She had to start trusting people sometime, and Levi hadn't actually done anything terrible to her. The community here thought highly of him, and really, she needed to get over herself.

"Oh," Beth sighed, reaching out to grab a skein

of yarn in speckled blues and greens. "This is *gorgeous*. I love these colors."

Surreptitiously, Indigo took note of the colorway and added it to the mental list of colors she was going to knit Beth's baby blanket out of. "Yes, that's pretty. I love that one too."

Beth held up another blue skein and admired it. "Pretty. People are going to love these. I think being his friend is a giant concession," she said with no discernible change of tone, so it took Indigo a second to realize what she'd said.

"I'm not that bad," she muttered.

"Seriously? You're one giant prickle whenever he's around."

Indigo wanted to protest, but alas, she couldn't since it was true. "I'm trying not to be. I mean, we managed to sit and have tea and scones together without sniping at each other."

Except you kissed him, so there's that.

Ugh, could her brain not stop reminding her about that? What was wrong with pretending it never happened?

"But you didn't agree, did you?" Beth began arranging the skeins on the countertop. "You said you'd think about it."

"I know, I know." Indigo tried not to feel cross as she nudged her friend aside. "You're doing it wrong. I know how I want to display them."

Beth stepped aside and grinned. "You're

always so scratchy about him. You know what you need?"

"You not talking about Levi?"

"You need to sleep with him."

Indigo choked.

At that moment the door of the gallery opened, and Izzy came in carrying a big cardboard box. She frowned in Indigo's direction as she came over to the counter and put the box down on it.

"What's wrong?" Izzy asked her, looking concerned. "Are you okay?"

No. No she was not okay. Sleep with Levi? Was Beth insane?

"She's fine," Beth said blithely. "I just told her she needs to sleep with Levi."

Izzy's dark eyes widened. "What?"

Beth shrugged. "She's always so cross around him. Kind of like Finn and I were at the start. Sleeping together definitely helped, and look where we are now."

Oh yes, Indigo knew exactly what had happened there. They'd slept together and Beth had accidentally gotten pregnant. None of the aftermath of that had been easy, but it was true it had worked out perfectly for the pair of them. They were blissfully in love, engaged, and looking forward to the birth of their first child.

"I do *not* want to get pregnant," Indigo managed. "No offense."

"None taken. And okay, so the pregnancy thing wasn't the best. But it turned out okay, is what I'm saying."

"Sure," Indigo couldn't help but point out. "After he nearly broke your heart."

"I'm not advising you fall in love with him, Indy. All I said was that you should sleep with him." Her green eyes were very direct. "It's possible to sleep with someone you don't love."

"That's true," Izzy said.

Indigo looked at her. "Please don't tell me you agree."

But Izzy just looked back. "You're attracted to him, Indigo. What would be so very wrong about a night or two in bed?"

She made it sound so easy, and Indigo guessed that maybe it was. For her and Beth clearly. But it wasn't easy for her. She'd never been with a guy. She'd never even been on a date. Yes, she'd kind of broken the ice already with that kiss, but God, the awkwardness of it. And the shock on his face…

Come on, wasn't it good to shock him?

Sure, but she wasn't sure if his expression had been the "wow that was amazing" kind of shock or the "what the hell were you thinking" kind of shock.

Probably the latter, since she didn't hadn't gotten the impression from him that he was interested in her in *that* way.

Seriously? After that day on the porch of the Rose?

True, she'd seen what she thought was heat in his eyes that day, but how would she know? When she had no experience whatsoever.

"Nothing's wrong with it," she said, trying to sound breezy and casual, since continuing to protest would only make things worse. "But I don't think it's a good idea. Especially if things went bad between us."

"Yeah, but they're already bad," Beth pointed out helpfully. "So, you've kind of got nothing to lose."

"Hmmm." Izzy went around to the other side of the counter and pulled out the laptop, putting that beside her box and opening it up. "Indigo should do what she wants. If she doesn't want to sleep with him, then she shouldn't."

Beth threw her hands up. "Hey, it was only a suggestion."

Yes, it was. A suggestion that was now stuck in Indigo's head.

She looked down at the skeins arranged on the counter, absently rearranging them into a more pleasing order of color. There were a lot of blues and greens that she'd dyed to match the colors of the beech forest and the lake, some silvery grays for mountain tussock, bright yellow for the gorse that bloomed on the hillsides, but now all she could see was flecks of gold...

"I don't know if he feels the same way anyway," she heard herself mutter.

"He does," Beth said. "I've seen the looks he throws you. He's into you."

Indigo kept her attention on the yarn, feeling the softness of the wool beneath her fingers. She loved yarn, loved the smell and the feel of it. It reminded her of watching her grandmother boil yarn on the stove in the kitchen of the homestead and seeing all the colors bloom. It had been the only time Grandma had smiled and softened, her suspicion and paranoia fading away.

"I sort of...kissed him," she said without meaning to.

There was a stunned silence in the gallery that was luckily free of customers.

"You...what?" Beth asked in a slightly choked voice.

Izzy was silent.

Indigo gently squeezed the yarn. "He came over to me and put his finger just here." She touched her free hand between her brows. "And I don't know what came over me. All I could see was his mouth and I...kissed it."

"Omigod," Beth breathed. "Indigo Jameson, you are an absolute goddess. You saw that opportunity and you just went for it. I love that!"

Indigo blushed for the umpteenth time, feeling a little rush of pleasure. Because she *had* done that, hadn't she? Somehow there was a small core of courage inside her, and she'd gone for it. She'd wanted to kiss him, and she hadn't let fear or anxiety overtake her. She'd kissed him like she'd been doing it for years. And she'd shocked him.

She, Indigo Jameson, ex-hermit and anxious virgin, had unsettled the gorgeous playboy helicopter-pilot daredevil by kissing him. He hadn't been expecting that, had he? Oh no, he hadn't!

Her mouth turned up at the memory of Levi's surprised face. Perhaps kissing him had been a stupid thing to do, but now, in retrospect, it made her feel pretty damn satisfied. Especially when he'd been unsettling her since day one.

Aware of Izzy's gaze, she looked up and met her friend's warm brown eyes. Izzy was smiling too. "Well," she said. "Aren't you a dark horse?"

Indigo grinned wider. "I think I shocked him."

"Omigod, yes!" Beth came over, put an arm around her, giving her a triumphant squeeze. "I bet you blew his tiny mind!"

Indigo sighed. "Yes. And then I tried to run away."

This didn't seem to dent Beth's enthusiasm. "That's fair. I probably would have too, to be honest." A sage look crossed her face. "Perhaps all you need is more practice."

Izzy rolled her eyes. "You're incorrigible, Beth. Indigo might not want any more practice."

But Indigo was looking down at her yarn again, seeing instead those gold flecks in Levi's eyes. Feeling the warm press of his lips on hers. He'd smelled so good, and she'd felt hunger stir inside her. And she'd had the sense that if she'd only put a hand on his chest, he might have reached out and drawn her closer, and then he might have… done more…

"You know," she murmured, half to herself. "I think I actually do."

"You do what?" Izzy asked.

Indigo looked up. "Need more practice."

"Yes, queen, get it!" Beth squealed, her pretty face alight with excitement.

"What is it with you?" Izzy grinned at Beth's enthusiasm. "You seem overly invested even for you."

Beth stuck her tongue out. "You just hate to see a girl boss winning."

"That's a lie. Girl bosses should always win."

"Agreed." Beth slung an arm around Indigo's shoulders. "Look, I just want our very own girl boss here to wipe that cocky smile off that asshole's face. It's all purely self-interest."

Excitement fizzed in Indigo's blood, Beth and Izzy's light teasing and obvious pleasure making her feel good. Making her feel as if she'd joined a special and very cool club, whereas before she'd been on the outside looking in. When Izzy and Beth had been going through their burgeoning love affairs with Chase and Finn, she'd felt useless, unable to offer any kind of advice because she'd had no experience with men and very little with people in general.

But now things were different. She wasn't going to be embarking on any love affair—as if!—but she could certainly indulge in a few kisses, surely? And maybe…maybe if she was brave enough, something more.

After all, it was time, wasn't it?

Indigo glanced at Beth standing beside her. "I thought you liked Levi."

"I do." Beth's green eyes danced. "But there's no woman on the planet who doesn't like seeing a confident dude taken down a peg or two by a boss-ass lady, right?"

Indigo grinned. "Me being the boss-ass lady?"

"Hell, yeah."

"I'd feel more boss-ass if I knew what I was doing." She debated whether or not to reveal the true extent of her inexperience, then decided what the hell. Izzy and Beth had shared their heartaches and losses and failures. It wouldn't be fair to keep hers all to herself.

You trust them, remember?

Yes, she did trust them. She probably trusted them more than she'd trusted anyone in her life except her grandmother.

"I've never actually been with a guy," she said shyly.

"Sorry, but that's nothing we didn't already know." Beth was smiling. "It's just like a date where—"

"Beth," Indigo said, bracing yourself. "I don't

think you quite understand. The first man I ever saw that I wasn't actually related to was when I was fifteen, and it was Mal, at the market."

"What do you mean the first man you ever saw?" Izzy asked, puzzled. "And who's Mal?"

Beth was looking at her with very wide eyes. "You're kidding me. I mean, I knew your grandma was a hermit, but…"

It was hard seeing their shock. Hard seeing their sympathy and compassion too. Hers had been a lonely childhood. First her parents had left, and then some ten years later, her grandmother had died, and after that, she'd been even lonelier. She'd had no friends and known no one, and had no other family.

Yet she'd made the best of it. And at least she'd had someone who'd loved her, and that was more than some people.

More than Levi.

Her heart gave a sudden small ache, because yes, that was true.

"What's this?" Izzy was staring at her, then Beth, then back again.

Indigo let out a silent breath. "My mom left my dad when she was pregnant with me because he'd cheated on her. Then they got back together again when I was seven. Dad convinced Mom to come to Anchorage with him, and they left me with my grandmother." She didn't want to tell them about how she'd been left behind, discarded like a piece of furniture or an old coat no one wanted, but there didn't seem to be any way around it so she said quickly, "They ended up staying there, so my grandmother looked after me. Grandma was great, but she was a hermit, living in this really remote homestead. I wasn't allowed to leave the house until I was fifteen. She homeschooled me and everything. Then she had a stroke, and she couldn't walk, so I had to go and get supplies. I'd never left the homestead since Mom and Dad left."

"Oh my God," Izzy murmured. "Seriously?"

"Indy," Beth said. "I had no idea it was *that* bad."

"Yeah." Indigo looked away, uncomfortable with the looks on their faces and how vulnerable it made her feel. "Anyway, Mal is the owner of Mal's Market in Deep River, the general store, and he was the first man I ever saw apart from my dad."

There was a heavy silence.

"I'm fine," she added, both to herself and to them. "I'm here now and everything's great." And it was. It *was* great. She was overcoming her past and being part of a community, and she even had friends. That was more than she'd ever had before.

Beth gave her arm another comforting squeeze. "Well, as first introductions to men go, Mal's one of the good ones."

Izzy reached out abruptly and laid a hand over Indigo's as it rested on the yarn. "You're amazing," she said quietly. "Did you know that?"

Heat crept into Indigo's cheeks, her chest tightening at the praise. "I'm not really."

"Yes, you are," Izzy insisted. "You hadn't met another soul until fifteen, and now here you are, ten years later, thousands of miles across the world in a town full of strangers. It takes a lot of guts to leave behind everything you know, everything that's familiar to you, and find a new life somewhere else."

The words struck a chord within all of them, because that's what all of them had done. They'd all left behind the lives and the people they knew to come here, following their own hopes and dreams it was true, but they'd all done it regardless of the whys.

There was a bond between them now, and Indigo suddenly felt it deep inside her, powerful and strong. A tether holding her to these two women, a tie that couldn't be broken.

It was so reassuring that her discomfort faded, the tight sensation in her chest relaxing.

"Thanks, guys." She looked at the pair of them. It was hard to talk about her emotions, hard to let down her guard, but she wanted them to know how she felt about them because it was important. They were important. "I–I just want you two to know how much you both mean to me. I probably wouldn't still be here without you."

And it was true, she wouldn't.

Beth's face was alight with her usual infectious smile. "Group hug?"

"Absolutely not," Indigo said, because there were still limits and far too many feelings in the room. "But I could sure use some ideas about how I can get in some kissing practice."

"What do you mean, she said she'd think about it?" Chase asked quietly as the front desk area of Pure Adventure NZ slowly filled up with the busload of tourists that had just arrived.

The three of them shared the front-of-house duties equally, though Levi couldn't help but note that he was rostered on more often than not. It didn't bother him—he was after all, very good with people—but sometimes it was irritating. Such as now, when he had other more important things to do, such as trying to convince one prickly little hedgehog of a woman to let him build her a house.

"I mean exactly that," he responded, equally as quietly. "She wanted to think about it. Though really, what's there to think about? I gave her everything she asked for, except maybe the stupid rent she wanted to pay."

The front desk area of HQ wasn't large and was fairly utilitarian, consisting of a big front counter with lots of racks of information pamphlets on it, and a big whiteboard detailing the various activities on offer for the day, plus a daily weather report.

Some clothing racks with various items of outdoor clothing on them for sale were shoved in a corner, while another corner held a shelf with other kinds of outdoor items, also for sale. Most of the equipment people needed for the activities Pure Adventure ran was already provided, but some people liked to have their own gear.

Chase had wanted to expand their range of stock, but there wasn't room. Apparently he'd been working on Izzy to get the gallery to stock some of it, but Levi didn't know whether he'd been successful or not.

The tourists today were of the less-active variety, looking around at the posters of heli-skiing, kayaking, hiking, horse riding, and other outdoor activities, and pointing. Most of them would be here for the guided walk to Glitter Falls across the lake, which was an easy track with a beautiful waterfall at the top, and a few might want to do some kayaking.

Levi's main focus today though was going to be a couple who'd booked a sightseeing flight over the ranges. They'd picked a great day for it, with the clouds of the previous day clearing and leaving all that bright-blue sky open. Plus there'd been a healthy dumping of snow on the mountains so it was going to look beautiful.

He normally loved flying people around the mountains, but not today, not with his head full of Indigo. Man, he really needed to get a grip.

"I don't think it's the money so much as it is you," Chase muttered, smiling as a couple of people came up to the counter and started asking questions.

Levi plastered a smile on his face as more people approached, and he greeted them, all the while trying not to think about the comment, because he had the feeling that unfortunately Chase was right. Indigo's hesitation probably did have something to do with their attraction. And yes, *their* attraction since his body had decided it was all in when it came to Indigo Jameson a couple of months earlier.

A problem. A very definite problem.

She'd kissed him, and no matter how much he'd like to, he couldn't forget about it. Yet he'd also told himself he wasn't going there. He *couldn't* go there. It would be wrong on every level, especially given how embarrassed she'd been afterward. He'd only just managed to stop her from bolting.

She was clearly very inexperienced, which made an affair with him very, very wrong. And while he was terrible with temptation, he did make an effort to do the right thing, and he'd been making an effort for the past two months. He couldn't throw all of that work down the drain now.

Yet…if he was the problem and she wasn't saying yes to the house because of him, what could he do? He could get Chase and/or Finn to build it, but those guys didn't have the time, not with their new families. There were others in Brightwater who might help, but again, same problem. They had their own lives, plus then Indigo would have to charge for labor, since she wouldn't want him paying for it, and she couldn't afford it. Not that he'd trust anyone else but him to do the work properly...

No, it was going to have to be him. In which case he was going to have to find a way around this attraction issue.

You know the best way around the attraction issue.

Levi politely told his brain to piss off and stop putting ill-advised thoughts into his head.

The heli trip was a good one. The couple was a pair of chatty Australians from Sydney who loved the scenery. He took them for a buzz around Queenstown and then Mount Aoraki, New Zealand's highest mountain, a perfect ice-cream cone of whiteness in the Southern Alps.

They asked him a lot of questions about the landscape and what it was like living with no internet in a tiny, isolated town with barely any people in it.

The questions took his mind off Indigo, but he had to admit to being somewhat distracted. Which wasn't great since, in his experience, piloting helis usually meant being absolutely focused at all times.

At least the tourists didn't notice his distraction, raving about the trip as they touched back down in Brightwater after it was over.

He'd just finished the postflight checks on the machine and was walking back across the little field that they used as a helicopter pad, toward the HQ building, when he saw a familiar figure coming across the grass toward him.

The wind coming from the mountains took the length of her long brown ponytail and blew it out behind her, while at the same time pressing the fabric of her loose blue dress against her figure, outlining it to perfection.

He was a man—and a pretty simple one at that—so of course he couldn't help looking, because Indigo Jameson with her outsized clothing and her many shawls had been hiding a lush little figure beneath all that fabric.

Pert, pretty breasts and small waist, nicely rounded hips and thighs, just the kind of shape he liked, though he really liked all shapes when it came to women. He just liked women, full stop.

But Indigo…

His heartbeat had accelerated and there was a certain…tightness behind the fly of his jeans.

Mate, you are so screwed.

"Hey," Indigo said as she approached him. "Have you got a moment?"

He forced dick thoughts out of his head and his gaze up to her face, trying not to linger on her knockout figure. "For you, I have several."

"Oh, good." Her hair was blowing around her face,

and she brushed it away with an irritated-looking gesture. "So, I've been thinking about your offer."

Levi found he was holding his breath, which was just ridiculous. "Yeah?" He tried to make the word sound casual.

She lifted her hand again as she looked up at him, shading her blue eyes, vivid as the sky he'd just finished visiting, from the sun. "I think we have a deal."

A savage punch of satisfaction went through him, the intensity of it seeming completely inappropriate to the situation.

Shoving his hands into his pockets to hide the fact that they'd been clenched at his sides, Levi struggled to make his smile warm and easygoing, and not triumphant as hell. "I'm pleased to hear that."

She frowned up at him. "Are you? You don't sound it."

And suddenly all he wanted to do was reach out and grab her and pull her close, let her look into his eyes so she could see just how pleased he was. Then maybe kiss the hell out of her.

But no, God, he wasn't a savage and this was broad daylight in the middle of town. If anyone saw him kissing Indigo Jameson like that, they'd probably have his guts for garters.

He clenched his fists tighter in his pockets and forced his grin wider. "Hell, yeah, I'm pleased. You could even say I'm stoked."

She made another irritated swipe at her hair. "In

that case we should have a meeting to chat about what's involved. If you're going to do the design too, I'll have to…" Her voice broke off. "What are you doing?"

He knew he shouldn't get close to her, but that surge of emotion couldn't be resisted so he didn't even try. He closed the distance between them and stopped right in front of her. Then he gently gathered all that soft, silky brown/caramel/toffee-streaked hair into one fist, while he pulled out the elastic band he had in one of his pockets with the other. "Tying your hair back," he said. "Don't ask me why I have an elastic band in my pocket. I just do."

He wondered if she'd pull away from him, but she didn't. She stayed still, her eyes widening as he snagged the elastic band around the thick skein of her hair and pulled it tight. He didn't want to let her hair go, since it felt so soft and gave him extremely wicked thoughts about how it might feel spread across all of his bare chest, but he knew doing even this hadn't been one of his best ideas, so he made himself release her and step away.

She looked at him uncertainly. "What did you do that for?"

"Because your hair was annoying you."

"You don't think I can't tie my own hair back?"

"But you didn't though, did you? And I had a band in my pocket." And because apparently he was still a goddamn idiot, he added, "I wanted to see what your hair felt like."

Her mouth opened slightly. "Levi…"

"I know, it was a gross invasion of your privacy." He couldn't look away from her, couldn't smile about it either, or make it a joke or a tease. In fact, he'd never felt less like teasing, and what that was about he had no idea. "But I'm not sorry. I'm not sorry at all."

She turned a fiery red, making the silver-blue of her eyes stand out like sapphires, and he braced himself for a show of her fearsome prickles.

But she surprised him yet again by lifting her hand, and much to his shock, she reached up and ran long slim dye-stained fingers through his hair.

The touch was so light, a fleeting caress, yet it held him rooted to the spot. He felt as if he'd been electrocuted.

"You touch my hair, I get to touch yours," she murmured, looking him straight in the eye. "Fair's fair."

He wanted to ask if that applied to anything else he touched, in which case he could think of a few places, but his voice seemed to have vanished.

Her gaze drifted upward as she sifted her fingers through his hair again. "It feels so soft." She sounded almost wondering. "So many colors…"

Her scent was all around him, despite the breeze, lavender and herbs and a sweet feminine musk that made everything male in him sit up and beg.

Okay, now *you're screwed.*

Yeah, he totally was, and he was okay with that if only she'd keep playing with his hair. Because he couldn't recall the last time a woman had touched him like that, or if a woman had *ever* touched him like that. Then again, one-night stands didn't tend to include caresses, or at least the ones he indulged in hadn't. No one touched him for the sheer pleasure of it, not the way she was doing right now.

Levi reached for her wrist and gripped it gently, because he couldn't take much more of this. He was only human after all and not made of stone. "Stop," he ordered quietly, meeting her gaze.

She didn't look away, and if he wasn't much mistaken, there was definitely a gleam of challenge in her eyes. "Why?"

"Because otherwise I might kiss you, and since we're in the middle of town in broad daylight, that's probably not a good idea."

She blushed like a rose, but that challenge in her eyes was unmistakable, and it thrilled him down to the bone.

Did she want this now? Did she want him? Had she decided to make a move on him? Because if so, he was here for it. Totally and utterly here for it.

What were you saying about you always doing the right thing? About how resisting her was the only way to go?

Levi ignored the thought completely.

After a moment, she pulled her wrist from his grip and took a step back. And it was only sheer force of will that stopped him from going after her and pulling her into his arms.

She gave a surreptitious look around to check there were no onlookers, then glanced back at him. A strangely satisfied smile tugged the corners of her rosebud mouth. "Are you free tomorrow morning?"

His voice still wouldn't work. All he could do was nod.

"Good." She turned away. "Come and see me at the farmhouse. We can discuss everything then."

And all Levi could do was stand there, watching her walk away across the green field, her pretty hair, now in a ponytail, blowing out behind her like a flag.

Chapter 7

INDIGO WAS IN THE SHED SITUATED NEAR THE stables at the farmhouse when she heard the engine of someone's truck coming up the gravel driveway.

Beth had once used the shed as a jewelry workshop, but now it was totally given over to Indigo's dyeworks, which meant lots of buckets and basins for dye baths, and drying racks for the yarn, plus the long bench built against one wall that was now stained with dye from when she painted yarn on it. A couple of slow cookers were sitting on the bench for hot dye baths, while an old gas barbecue with big kettles on it for bigger jobs stood beside it.

She hadn't been able to sleep the night before, her head too full of the feel of stupid Levi's stupid hair, and so, the way she always did when she couldn't sleep, she'd gotten up and gone out to the shed to do some dyeing.

First, she'd done some variegated grays and then some rich deep browns. She'd left them drying so she could add more color this morning, and she'd been up first thing, fiddling about with adding some gold speckles to the gray and some gold streaks to the brown, mixing it up a little with toffee and caramel colors.

Except she was a perfectionist, and she hadn't quite been able to capture quite the same flecks of gold as she'd seen in his eyes, or the precise shades of brown and gold in his hair...

A quiver ran through her as the sound of the engine got closer. She pulled off the respirator mask that covered her face, which she wore to prevent inhaling dye particles, and scrubbed her hands over her cheeks. The mask left a mark, which was rather unfortunate. Her hair was probably a fright too, since she hadn't brushed it.

She stood there for a moment feeling ridiculous, because she never bothered with her appearance and now here she was, wanting to look a certain way for a man...

She remembered how her mother used to fuss with her appearance when Frank had reappeared on the scene, wanting to look good for him. And Indigo had fallen into the same trap, since Frank had spread his compliments around, noting whenever his daughter wore a pretty dress. She'd been so dazzled by him that she'd worn nothing but dresses whenever he visited.

Indigo had been too young to understand that Frank's charm was all on the surface. That what he'd really come back for was Claire, not the child they'd created together. She'd let herself be totally sucked in, and she never wanted to do that again.

So, she wouldn't. She wouldn't let herself be

dazzled, and she wouldn't fuss around with her appearance either. She hadn't worried about it before, and she wasn't going to worry about it now, no matter what decision she'd made about Levi King.

And she had made a decision.

In fact, after her pep talk with Izzy and Beth the day before, Indigo had decided several things. First, for reasons best known to himself, Levi did appear to be into her. He'd said he'd wanted to kiss her yesterday and she believed him. Second, that meant she could proceed with a bit of confidence about the whole kissing thing since presumably he'd be into it. Third, if she wanted "more practice" with men, he was the perfect man to get that practice with.

He was experienced, and she had to admit that, yes, he *was* a good guy despite his irritating ways. He was also extremely hot, and if anything got out of hand, both Chase and Finn would probably skin him alive. Plus, and this was the biggest plus: Indigo wanted him.

It was strange to admit that to herself, to let herself feel it. She was actually surprised by how much she wanted him. Like the day before, out by the helicopter, when she'd come across the grass to him. She hadn't expected him to gather her hair gently in his fist and tie it back for her, and she certainly hadn't expected her own powerful reaction. And it hadn't been to slap his hands away. When he'd told her that he wasn't sorry for touching it anyway, the gold in his eyes glittering, a strangely intense look on his face, she'd felt the most extraordinary sense of power fill her.

He hadn't meant to touch her hair—she could see that in his eyes—but he had. As if he hadn't been able to help himself. As if she'd made him do it. Her, the inexperienced hermit girl who not even her own parents had wanted.

So, she'd done what she'd been fantasizing about for weeks now: she'd run her fingers through his hair, touching all those golden strands, feeling it against her fingertips, thick and silky and soft.

He'd actually caught his breath. She'd heard it.

It had given her an intense thrill, as had walking away, throwing a casual invitation to come to the farmhouse out behind her. Leaving him standing there watching her leave.

Oh yes, that had felt so good.

The same burst of adrenaline filled her now as she heard his truck—and it *was* his truck—come to a stop in the gravel turnaround in front of the house.

She leaned over the bench, looking down at the skeins of dry yarn she'd spread out on the top of it to check how the dyes looked, trying to be casual. Except she didn't feel casual. Her heart was beating far too fast, and she felt breathless.

Gravel crunched under someone's boots, and she swallowed, concentrating fiercely on the yarn while every sense she had zeroed in on the man coming toward her shed.

The sounds of his footsteps stopped.

Indigo's heartbeat thumped loudly in her head.

"Hey." His deep, warm voice came from behind her. "So, this is where you hang out."

From somewhere she managed to dredge up her voice. "Just checking over some yarn."

There were footsteps behind her and then he was there, standing beside her. She was so conscious of him that it was almost painful. The warmth of his body, the spicy scent of his aftershave cutting through the acrid smell of dye and other chemicals.

"Wow." The compliment sounded genuine. "Those are great colors."

She struggled to keep her attention on the counter and not feel an instant burst of pride at his praise. "Thanks."

"What was your inspiration?"

Your eyes.

She cleared her throat. "Oh, you know. The gray mountains with little bursts of gold from sunlight."

"Fantastic." He reached over to one of the streaked brown skeins but didn't touch it, only pointed. "What about this one?"

Your hair.

"The...uh...the bush." She straightened and turned, which was clearly a bad idea because he was standing very close.

He glanced down at her, those gold flecks in his eyes glinting. There was a lot of green in them too, a deep, vibrant color like the sun shining through sea glass. His dark lashes were long and tipped with gold.

He was the most beautiful man.

And beautiful men are the worst, remember?

No, that was her grandmother talking. That was her terrible father. That wasn't Levi King, who'd bought her scones and served her tea, and offered to build her a house. Who looked at her with heat in his gaze and wanted to kiss her…

"You okay?"

Indigo blinked, realizing that he was looking at her with a touch of concern. She shoved the voice out of her head. "Of course. Why?"

"You just looked…" His voice trailed off; his hazel gaze was searching. "You don't need to be afraid of me, Indigo. I hope you know that."

Something shivered deep inside her, like the foundations of a house settling after an earthquake.

No, she wasn't scared. It wasn't fear that tugged at her, not this time. It was something else, something deeper. Something that felt almost like… longing.

She took a breath, disturbed by the intensity of the feeling. The strength of it… She'd never experienced anything like it.

"I know," she said. "Why? Should I be afraid of you?"

"Of course not. But…" He gave her a rueful look. "I shouldn't have touched you the way I did yesterday."

An odd feeling twisted inside her, like disappointment.

"Except," he went on, "I'm glad I did."

The disappointment vanished.

She gave him a shy smile. "I touched you back, remember?"

The sparks in his eyes gleamed. "Oh, I remember. I remember very well indeed."

Beth and Izzy had told her that she'd know when the moment was right to kiss someone. "When he's close and looking, you know, kind of intensely at you," Beth had said. "And if he looks at your mouth, that's the go signal."

"Or you know," Izzy had added. "You could ask him if you can kiss him."

But at the thought of asking him straight out, Indigo wavered. And even though he was looking intensely at her, he wasn't looking at her mouth. So maybe it wasn't the right time to kiss him again, not when they had to talk about the tiny house.

"What *are* you thinking about?" Levi's voice had got even deeper, all warm and liquid, like melted honey. "You look like you're planning on doing something naughty, hedgehog."

Another of those tiny thrills went through her, and she realized with a little shock that she liked him teasing her. He was never mean with it, and the way he looked at her, as if he was fascinated to see her response, made her feel warm all over.

Except she'd always wished she could tease him as much as he teased her, show him that she could fluster him too, the way she always felt flustered by him.

She did now though, didn't she? She *did* have that power. And maybe it didn't matter if the timing was right, and maybe she didn't want to ask. Maybe for her, she had to do it to surprise him. Because *that's* what she loved about their interactions. The moment when she, the poor lonely little Red Riding Hood, got to surprise the Big Bad Wolf.

"Maybe I am," she murmured. "You don't know." Then she rose up on her toes and pressed her mouth to his.

But this time he was ready for her.

One large warm hand was at the back of her head, cradling her gently, keeping her up on her toes and her mouth against his. He didn't move though, didn't try to deepen the kiss. He remained very still, as if letting her get used to the sensation and to him.

A tension Indigo hadn't realized she felt eased, and for a second every sense she had was focused on his lips on hers and how they felt. Warm and surprisingly soft and oddly familiar. As if she'd kissed him a thousand times before and knew the shape of his mouth better than she knew her own.

He was so tall, making her feel small and feminine, and even though she thought she wouldn't like that, she did. She liked it very much. She liked the broad width of his shoulders and the hard, muscled plane of his chest. It was all strength and he made her feel safe.

She was hardly even aware of lifting her hands to that hard chest of his, not until the intense heat of his body burned through the cotton of his T-shirt and into her palms.

He smelled like heaven. She wanted more.

Then as she was about to curl her fingers into his T-shirt and kiss him harder, the hand on the back of her head disappeared and his head was lifting, the kiss ending.

Her heartbeat thumped so loudly that she could barely hear, and she was conscious of a dragging ache between her legs. Her body was hungry for him.

If he'd looked smug, she would have slapped him, but he didn't. In fact, there was no smile at all on his face. He looked almost...grim, and now that she was aware of things other than his kiss, she realized his whole posture was tight, every muscle hard with tension.

"You shouldn't do that again, Indigo." The honey in his voice had all gone, leaving it rough as a gravel riverbed.

Her cheeks heated, but not from embarrassment

this time. She felt as if she'd transgressed, hurt him in some way, which hadn't been her intent at all.

"I'm sorry. I didn't mean—"

"And not because I didn't like it," he interrupted. "Because I did like it. I liked it a lot. I'm just not good at resisting temptation."

Oh. *Oh*. She was a temptation?

"I…don't mind if you want to keep kissing me," she said hesitantly, feeling very brave. "You said you wanted to yesterday."

His jaw hardened, a muscle flicking in it. "I know, and I shouldn't have. Because I don't stop at kisses. I also don't get involved with inexperienced women. I don't get involved with women who live in this town, full stop." He looked like he wanted to say something else, then stopped, turning away from her abruptly. "Come on, let's go in the house and I'll show you some of the preliminary sketches I did last night."

He didn't wait for her, striding out of the shed and over the gravel toward the farmhouse, leaving her standing there feeling like she'd done something wrong.

———

Levi was angry and it didn't help that he knew he had no one to blame but himself for it.

It wasn't Indigo's fault he had absolutely no chill when it came to her.

He had to get a grip though, because it was ridiculous to be so close to the edge of his control because of one brief kiss. He'd known she was going to do it too; he'd seen it in those gorgeous blue eyes.

He shouldn't have cradled the back of her head the way he had, holding her there, but he'd wanted to see what it felt like to have her lips on his, maybe test himself a little. Because it could be that he wasn't as turned on by her as he'd thought.

But then her hands had pressed against his chest and the chains on his control had rattled. Hard. And visions of him lifting her onto the bench and pushing down the trousers she was wearing, spreading her thighs and sinking deep inside her had filled his head. And he'd known that would be another mistake and he couldn't keep making them. He couldn't keep allowing himself to give in to temptation.

Control wasn't exactly his forte, but the best way he knew to keep hold of it was to make sure she stayed at a distance. Except that was impossible now he'd agreed to build her a house.

Great. You really screwed that one up.

He had. Because now he was going to have to be very clear with her about how things could be between them, and given the disappointment in her eyes when he'd told her not to kiss him again, that would hurt her.

Yeah, real smooth, asshole.

Behind him came the sound of her footsteps, but he didn't turn around.

He'd spoken to her quite strongly, but what else could he have done? She had to know what those kisses were doing to him, and she shouldn't be messing with him. She had to know he wasn't the kind of man who would only take a couple of bites when offered something delicious. He was the kind of man who had to have the whole damn cake. And if she wasn't prepared to give him that, then it was best she back off.

If she'd decided she wanted to act on their attraction, then they were going to have to have a little chat. Or at least more of a chat than he'd given her.

The farmhouse wasn't big, but it had two stories and a pitched roof, and there was a small porch out the front. Its red paint had seen better days, but it was a sturdy house underneath and he'd taken inspiration from it for the sketches he'd done the night before.

He climbed the small set of stairs to the front door and went in, Indigo following behind him.

When Clint, the old guy who used to own the stables, had lived here, the farmhouse had been untidy, dark, and a bit neglected, and smelled of damp parka and unwashed socks.

Now, it was neat and tidy, the wooden floors gleaming, the table in the hallway dust-free, and it smelled of lemon polish and freshly baked bread.

That was Indigo's doing. She'd made the place delightfully homey, and that tugged at something inside him. Something he thought he'd put behind him since he'd come to Brightwater. A kind of ache for something, though what he had no idea.

He ignored the feeling and continued down the hallway into the kitchen at the back of the house. It was an old kitchen, with an old stove and old cupboards and an old stainless-steel sink. But again, it was very clean, the windows above the sink and kitchen counter bright with sun.

A scrubbed wooden table sat in the middle of the room, and he headed for it, pulling out a chair and sitting down before flipping open the case of his tablet to show her the sketches he'd done the night before.

She didn't sit, standing across the table from him with her arms folded. Mercifully her dark silky hair was in a messy bun on the top of her head, and she was wearing an oversized black T-shirt and a pair of loose black cotton trousers that looked like they'd been spattered with all kinds of different paint. Except it wasn't paint, he knew, but dye.

For a change she wasn't frowning, but there was an anxious crease between her dark winged brows, and quite honestly, she'd never been sexier.

"I'm sorry," she said starkly. "I didn't think it would matter."

You did hurt her, you tool.

Regret caught at him, but he shoved it away. He'd had to stop that kiss, let her know it was a bad idea, and that was because she was so sensitive, so vulnerable beneath her prickles.

Maybe he'd hurt her, but a small hurt now was better than a mortal wound later on.

"You didn't think it would matter if you kissed me?" he asked, trying to keep his tone even.

"Yes." The crease between her brows deepened, a stricken look on her face. "I didn't know... I thought... Well, the truth is I wasn't thinking."

He let out a breath, the regret inside him tugging harder. "Don't be upset, hedgehog. It's okay. You didn't hurt me or anything. And I'm sorry, I shouldn't have spoken to you like that." He paused. "I do have to ask though. What are you wanting from me?"

She reddened. "I'm not sure. I thought we had... you know...some kind of thing... And I guess I also thought you wouldn't mind if I practiced kissing you a bit."

He blinked. Practiced kissing him? What?

Seeing his obvious puzzlement, she went on in a sudden rush. "I've never kissed anyone before. You're the first. In fact, you're the first man I've ever even wanted to kiss, and since I screwed it up the first time, I thought I could practice—"

"Wait a second. You've *never* kissed anyone before?" He stared at her, shock moving through

him, because when he'd assumed she was inexperienced, he hadn't realized she was *that* inexperienced.

Indigo bit her lip. "No."

"Seriously?" He could hardly imagine it. "But
aren't you, like, twenty-five or something?"

"Yes." She sighed. "You know I lived with my
grandmother, right? Well, she was kind of a paranoid hermit. My mom and dad left when I was really
young and my grandma brought me up. Our homestead was very isolated, and she kept me at home
as a kid and homeschooled me." Indigo paused.
"Basically, the only other person I saw between the
ages of eight and fifteen was my grandmother."

"Holy shit," Levi muttered. He hadn't realized she was *that* sheltered either. "You didn't see
anyone else?"

"No, and to be honest, I didn't want to. Grandma
used to tell me how dangerous the world was, and
men in particular were bad, so I was quite happy to
stay at home."

He frowned. "Why especially men?"

Indigo looked away for a moment. Then she
said, "My dad cheated on Mom when she was pregnant with me, so she left him. Then he came back
when I was seven and they got back together again.
He didn't like Deep River. He wanted to take Mom
to Anchorage to live, and he...he promised that
when they were settled, they would come and get
me, but..." She stopped.

But Levi didn't need her to go on. He could tell already what must have happened. Her father hadn't come to get her, had he?

Fury flickered in him at the note of hurt in her voice. It made him want to find her sorry excuse for a bloody father and pound him into the ground.

Except she didn't need his anger, so all he said was, "So what about your mom?"

She lifted a shoulder. "Mom called me once or twice after they left. But there was always some excuse why I couldn't join them yet. She never came out and said it, but I guess Dad and what he wanted were more important to her than I was."

Okay, so now he wanted to fly all the way to Alaska and give Indigo's mother a very strong piece of his mind. Yeah, he'd punch the guy and yell at her mum. That was fair.

"So what?" His voice was rougher than he'd expected. "They both just up and left you with your grandmother?"

Indigo lifted one narrow shoulder. "Yeah. I suppose they just didn't want me around and…well…" She stopped and turned toward the counter suddenly. "I'll get us some tea."

So. Her mother had left her to be brought up by her grandmother because she'd wanted to be with a guy who sounded like a complete dick more than she'd wanted her own kid.

He couldn't help it. That made him very, *very*

angry. But he forced the anger away, because he had the impression that this was something Indigo didn't share easily—yet she'd shared it with him, and that was a gift.

He didn't want to ruin that gift with his own stupid feelings, but he wanted to acknowledge it in some way, so as she went over to the sink with the electric kettle to put some water in it, he said, "I never met my mother. She was a teenage drug addict, or so I was told. I wanted to meet her when I was an adult, but she didn't want any contact. No idea who my dad was either—there's no father's name on my birth certificate."

Indigo said nothing as she switched the kettle on, but he knew she was listening, so he went on, "I'm not trying to compete with you or anything. Just wanted you to know that you're not alone in the crappy parent stakes. Not that I blame my mother, to be honest. She was fifteen and had no family support." Then she'd grown up and had another family and didn't want to hear from him.

But he didn't blame her for that either. She had a solid family life and hadn't wanted the past crashing back in on it in the shape of the kid she'd had to give away.

Indigo moved over to one of the cupboards and got a couple of teacups out. "I last saw Mom and Dad when I was eight. Dad used to tell me about how great it would be when I finally came to live with them. I'd have a big yard and a bike and maybe we'd even get a dog. And I–I believed him. I really thought that one day they'd come for me and take me away to be with them. But…they never did."

Christ, how hard for her. People made all kinds of promises and then never followed up on them. Social workers who'd promised him that this home would finally be the one he could settle in, that it was stable. Teachers who'd promised him they'd talk to the social workers about how his foster father kept drinking. Foster parents who'd promised him he'd be safe…

"I'm sorry," he said, and he was. "That really sucks."

"Oh, it was okay." She sounded resigned, but that echo of pain was still there. "Grandma took care of me, and she loved me, so I had that at least. But you know, you really can't trust anyone, can you?"

She wasn't wrong. Yet at least she'd had one person she could trust.

He hadn't had anyone, except Linda, the one foster parent who'd seemed to give a shit about him, and who'd had to give him up due to a family situation beyond her control.

But Indigo didn't need to know that. His childhood was depressing, and he didn't want to bring her down. Besides, it was over and done with—and the less said about it, the better.

"No, you can't," he said. "But I'm glad you had someone. So...are you going to tell me the bear story?"

It wasn't the most adept change of subject, but as Indigo got out a small porcelain teapot from another cupboard, he could see she was smiling, and the tension had gone from her shoulders.

"Oh, that. It was a little black bear. True, he did try to come into the house, but only because I'd left the back door open. I banged a pot at him and shouted, and he ran away."

He grinned at the image of Indigo banging a pot and shouting at a small black bear. "Terrifying. You didn't think to try that with the wētā?"

"Are you kidding?" She shot him a glance as she spooned some tea into the teapot. "Wētās are way scarier than bears."

"But you can't pick a bear up in your hand."

She gave a small, delightfully bubbling laugh. "No. And they're not called Wally either."

And he felt the oddest sense of triumph. He made people laugh all the time and never thought anything of it. But getting a laugh out of wary, guarded Indigo with a lame joke about bears made him feel as if he'd just won the lottery.

He smiled. "What do you call bears then? Smokey? Yogi?"

"We don't call bears anything except maybe 'Hey, bear.'" The kettle clicked off and she poured some water into the teapot.

He put his elbows on the table and leaned on them. "Did you know that while we might not have bears in New Zealand, we have big cats?"

She gave him a skeptical look. "You do not. Isn't the largest native land mammal you have here a bat?"

"True and well done on the research."

Her cheeks went pink. "I did some before I got here, I'll have you know."

"Right, but what I bet you didn't know, is that we've had sightings of big cats around these parts. And I'm not talking big as in a big house cat, I'm talking big as in a puma."

Indigo's eyebrows rose. "Seriously?"

"Oh yeah. People have been catching glimpses of them for fifty years." It was the truth. Big cats weren't native to New Zealand, but that apparently didn't stop people from seeing them. "Some think the gold miners in the late 1880s brought them over here, but who knows?"

A smile lurked around her lovely mouth. "I'd rather see a big cat than a wētā."

"I will not have you speak ill of Wally."

"This is a very silly conversation."

"What have you got against silly conversations?"

"Levi, the sketches."

"Okay, okay. Let me show you the sketches and you can see what you think."

Indigo brought over the teapot and the cups, some milk and some sugar, and put them on the table. He noticed that there was a slice of lemon in her cup, which was odd.

But then he forgot about that as he turned on the tablet and showed her his drawings. And he took a lot of pleasure out of the way her eyes widened and then lit up, because he'd incorporated some details from her favorite house in those brochures, and he'd hoped she like them.

"Oh, these are great," she breathed as he explained a few things and rotated the design so she could see it from different angles. "I love it."

There was no wariness to her expression now, her delicate features alight with excitement as she noted the various things he'd incorporated that he thought she might like. Shutters. A window seat that doubled as storage. Built-in shelves beneath the stairs that went up to a tiny bedroom. Skylights, including one directly above the bed.

And his sense of triumph deepened with every moment, because she was smiling, a genuine, sweet, wonderful smile that he'd seen her give other people, but never him.

Yet she was giving it to him now as she pored over his sketches. And when she held out a peremptory hand for the pencil that went with the tablet, he gave it to her and let her make some notes.

"Tell me everything you want," he said. "Anything at all and I'll see if I can put it in."

"Oh, don't worry, I will." She bent over the tablet,

scribbling down some things, her full bottom lip caught between small white teeth. "You're really good at drawing, by the way. Did you study architecture or something?"

Levi leaned back in his chair, trying very hard not to feel smug at her praise. "No. I thought I might try to be a draftsman, so I did a bit of training." Or rather, he'd sat in the local public library at the computer and taught himself from YouTube videos, since he didn't have any money to go to classes. "But then I kind of lost interest."

"Oh?" She gave him a brief glance, her gaze brilliant and blue. "How come?"

He grinned. "I'm not the greatest at sitting still, and I thought the army might be a better fit for me."

It had been the *only* fit for him. He'd loved it, finding in the forces the structure, discipline, and comradeship he'd always craved. The sense of belonging.

"And it was, I take it?" She was looking down again at the table, doing a small sketch of her own. It looked like some kind of plant.

"Yeah. The army was great, the SAS even better. I loved it."

"You didn't want to stay?"

"Well, I'd met Chase by then and he wanted out. He talked a lot about Brightwater and this business he wanted to set up, an adventure company business, and he asked me what I thought about it." He still remembered that conversation, in a tent in the middle of the desert in the Middle East, and how Chase had said to him, "What do you think? Are you in?"

And he'd realized then that Chase wasn't just telling him about this great business idea he'd had; he was also inviting him to come back to Brightwater Valley with him. A chance to have a place of his own, a place where he could put down roots. He hadn't thought twice.

"I told him it was a great idea and I wanted to be part of it."

"Were you sick of the army?" Indigo asked, squinting down at the tablet.

It didn't seem odd to talk to her about his reasons for coming here. He hadn't told many people, not because those reasons were a secret, but because it led to more questions about his past. And he didn't like bumming people out with that.

But it felt natural to tell Indigo, so he did.

"I wasn't." He leaned forward once more, putting his elbows on the table. "But army life can be fairly rootless, and I realized I wanted more than that. A place to stay, a home."

She gave him another of those piercing glances. "So why did you buy a house in Queenstown?"

Because no matter where you go, you'll always feel like you don't belong.

A threat of unease wound through him. Hell no, he didn't think that. Why would he? He'd been here over five years, and while he knew that wasn't long for many of the residents here and he was still considered "new," they'd accepted him. He wasn't the kid no one wanted anymore.

"Investment property. I rent it out as an Airbnb sometimes, plus it's useful for when I need to spend some time in civilization."

Her blue gaze narrowed, but she didn't say anything, only nodded. Then she flicked a glance at the teacup still sitting at his elbow. The teacup he hadn't touched.

"You don't really like tea, do you?"

Ah, crap. Busted. He'd forgotten that he was supposed to be pretending.

"No." He grinned. "I was only pretending to like it to impress you."

She blushed. "Impress me by drinking tea? How does that work?"

"First rule of seduction," he said, totally forgetting he wasn't supposed to be flirting with her. "Like the things the pretty girl likes. And if you don't like them, pretend."

She tilted her head. "You were going to seduce me?"

"I wanted you to say yes about the house," he clarified, even though it had never been just about the house. "Anyway, it works. Chicks love it when you have shared interests."

"But it's not real."

"Goes both ways. I had one woman tell me she loved helicopters so I tried talking to her about them, but it was clear she didn't know her tail rotor from her joystick. She just wanted to get me into bed."

Another of her quite frankly adorable blushes stole over her cheeks. "And did it work?"

"Of course. I'm a man. Doesn't take much to get me into bed."

Indigo raised one dark, skeptical brow. "I'm not sure that's true."

Heading into dangerous territory now, bro. You might want to change the subject.

That was probably a good idea.

He picked up the teacup and said quickly, "Anyway, about this tea. I'll take a sip just for you."

"Okay." She wrinkled her nose. "I was pretending too, you know."

"Pretending about what?"

"Pretending to like that horrible gumboot tea of yours."

He grinned. "I wondered. You did pull a couple of faces. The real question, though, is…" He rested one elbow on the table and lifted his teacup, making sure to stick out his pinkie. "Did you do it to impress me?"

She bit her lip again, as if she was struggling not to smile. "That depends. Were you impressed?"

He shouldn't hold her gaze like this. He should

definitely look away. "Hell yeah. That stuff could strip an engine."

She gave him that sweet smile again, making his chest feel tight. "And now we have a shared interest. We both don't like gumboot tea."

"And we both think your yarn is amazing."

She went pink. "And we both think you're an asshole at times."

He laughed. "Fair and also true."

Her gaze went to the teacup he was still holding. "Go on. Take a sip."

Was that a hint of wickedness he could see in her blue eyes? If so, it looked far too good on her.

He raised the cup and took that sip. The tea was cold, but he was surprised to find that it was drinkable. Far better than the tea he'd made her the day before.

"Well?"

"Actually, it's not bad," he admitted.

"You're not pretending just to impress me this time?"

"Hey, you're already impressed, admit it." He took another sip. "Seriously, no, I'm not pretending. Though I'm sure it's better hot."

Indigo smiled. "It's Earl Grey. And you have it with a slice of lemon. Perfect with scones."

Levi decided to file that valuable piece of information away for a later date. "I'll keep that in mind. So, do you have any other suggestions for me?"

She glanced down at the tablet, reading the notes she'd made, and then shook her head. "That's all I can think of so far."

"Okay. Do you want to go and look at the site?"

"Oh yes, I should do that, shouldn't I? Today?"

"I can't today. I'm taking some people up the river for the afternoon. But how about tomorrow morning?"

Her expression had relaxed completely, excitement glittering in her pretty eyes. "Oh yes, that would be great."

It was infectious, that excitement, and he felt an excited thrill himself, as if he couldn't think of anything better than showing her around the property.

"Excellent," he said, deciding it would be better if he ignored the feeling. "Shall I pick you up from here?"

"Oh, I've got a gallery shift. So just come there."

"Okay, great."

For a second he didn't want to leave. What he wanted was to keep sitting there with her instead, sipping her Earl Grey tea and having ridiculous conversations about bears and wētās and big cats.

But that wasn't a great idea, so he forced himself to push his chair back and get to his feet. To lean over and grab his tablet.

She didn't move, her blue eyes staring into his.

He could feel the air change around them, becoming thick and heavy with everything he wanted to do, everything he knew he absolutely shouldn't.

He wanted to reach out and brush his fingertips over the fullness of her bottom lip, to trace the line of it, feel how soft it would be. And God help him, he almost did. But at the last minute he remembered himself and got himself in hand.

He straightened. "See you tomorrow, hedgehog," he said, trying to ignore the roughness in his voice.

And the flash of disappointment in her eyes.

Chapter 8

INDIGO SMOOTHED THE SKIRTS OF HER FAVORITE blue cotton dress and tried to stop herself from fiddling with her hair. She'd put it up in a bun again to get it out of her eyes, and she thought it looked cute, but she wasn't totally sure. Normally, she wouldn't have cared whether she looked cute or not, but the fact she was worried about it now was irritating.

There were a couple of tourists in the gallery, and they were looking at Evan McCahon's painting that hung in pride of place on one of the walls. Evan was a famous New Zealand painter, and he lived in Brightwater Valley. He didn't much like tourists and kept to himself and hadn't wanted one of his paintings hanging in the gallery. His paintings were far too pricey to actually sell, but Izzy had wanted one there to draw in the tourists. Evan had refused until Finn had talked him round with a bottle of whiskey.

Since then, a couple of smaller works had appeared on the walls and Beth had told Indigo a couple of days ago that Evan's stance on the gallery had softened, and he was now thinking of providing some exclusive prints for them to sell.

It was exciting stuff. The gallery was turning out to be quite a selling point for tourists. Indigo was pretty happy with the way her yarn had been selling at least. Magic word of mouth had happened, and she'd gotten orders from yarn shops in different parts of the country. Now she was wishing she could set up an online shop that people could order directly from. A bit difficult when there was no internet service in Brightwater.

Though really, before that happened, she needed a permanent base.

At that moment, the door to the gallery opened and Izzy came in, along with Chase and Gus, Chase's thoroughly delightful twelve-year-old daughter.

Chase's tall, broad, muscled figure was in his usual T-shirt and utility pants, along with some battered hiking boots. He was obviously going to be leading a tour from the looks of things. Gus often accompanied him, and that seemed to be happening today since the girl was in a fleece.

Izzy, by contrast, was in a pair of designer jeans and a pretty red long-sleeved top that complemented her dark eyes and hair. She was clearly *not* going on any tour, which was just as well since Indigo was hoping she'd watch the gallery for her when Levi came by to show her the site.

Chase and Gus were having an argument about something, Gus looking sulky, while Izzy was obviously trying to ignore the pair of them.

"Hey," Indigo said as Izzy approached the counter. "Are you here for a bit?"

"No," Chase muttered in the background. "For the last time, you cannot drive the boat."

"Aw, why not?" Gus was scowling.

"Do I really need to tell you?"

"The tourists don't mind."

"But my insurance does."

"Yes, please," Izzy said, rolling her eyes. "It'll give me a break from those two."

"Thanks." Indigo resisted the urge to touch her hair for the umpteenth time. "Levi wants to show me the house site, and since it's just up the hill from the gallery, I won't be long."

"Oooh, exciting." Izzy glanced behind her, then leaned in toward Indigo. "And speaking of Levi, did you get any kiss practice in?"

Indigo tried not to think about what had happened the day before and her failure at the whole kiss thing, but it was difficult.

She could still feel the press of Levi's mouth on hers and the slight pressure of his palm at the back of her head. The heat of his body as she'd put her hand on his chest and the scent of him...so delicious.

Then him pulling away, looking almost angry and muttering some crap about her being too inexperienced and how he didn't have relationships with women who lived here.

He'd liked it though. She knew he had. But she

hadn't realized that he had some clear moral boundaries about this kind of thing, which made her feel slightly ashamed of herself that she hadn't even thought about that. That she hadn't even asked him if it was okay to kiss him.

In fact, she'd felt so guilty about it that she'd confessed the whole kiss practice thing and her own inexperience. Maybe that had been a bad thing. He'd certainly been shocked about it. She still wasn't sure why she'd told him about her childhood and her parents. All that stuff was so private and still painful even after all these years—yes, she could admit that—so she had no idea why she'd suddenly shared it with him, a guy she hadn't even liked until a few days ago.

But no, she knew why. It was because he'd offered her something of himself, about his own mother, how he'd never met her. And even though he'd said it kind of casually—it seemed as if Levi said the most private things casually—she would have bet money that he didn't feel casual about it.

Part of her had wanted to ask him about it, but then he'd changed the subject and that had probably been a good thing.

Still, she'd realized during that whole ridiculous conversation they'd had afterward, about bears and wētās and big cats, that kissing and attraction aside, she rather liked him a lot more than she thought she did.

Ugh. She was used to being irritated by him, not liking him. The whole thing was confusing, and she wished she'd never gone down the kissing route. Because the sad fact was that, now she'd had a taste of him, she wanted more.

Except he doesn't and he told you why.

Indigo shot a glance over Izzy's shoulder to where Chase and Gus were still arguing with each other. "I…tried again, but he wasn't…" She stopped.

Izzy's eyes widened in surprise. "What? He wasn't into it? I don't believe that for a second."

"No, it wasn't that." Indigo could feel her cheeks heating, but she made herself go on. "He said not to do it again because he wouldn't want to stop at just kisses and he doesn't get involved with women who live here. Or who are inexperienced."

"Oh," said Izzy. "I see."

"Yes." Indigo nibbled at her lip. "I felt bad about it. I hadn't thought he would care about that stuff. But it turns out, he did."

"Well," Izzy said carefully. "How do you feel about that?"

This whole conversation was making her feel embarrassed, but hell, if she couldn't talk to Izzy and/or Beth about this, then who could she talk to?

"I don't think my feelings on the subject matter. He was pretty adamant nothing was going to happen."

Izzy gave her a sympathetic look. "I'm not surprised. He's like Chase and Finn, horribly protective."

Indigo frowned in puzzlement. "But who is he being protective of? Me?"

"Oh, probably. He won't want to hurt you."

"He wouldn't hurt me. It's only sex we're talking about."

"I know, but Levi won't want to make things difficult for you here."

Indigo was mystified. "Why would it be difficult?"

"I should imagine he's trying to protect your feelings."

He's nothing like your father. Nothing at all.

Her dad had told her how important she was to him and let her believe it, then he'd turned around and shown her what a lie it all been. While Levi had been nothing but honest with her this whole time, telling her exactly where he stood and why.

Something fluttered deep inside her, and she had a horrible feeling it might have been her heart. But she couldn't let *that* happen. She wasn't going to go fluttering after Levi, regardless of how protective he was about her feelings.

Not that there were any feelings involved, just sexual attraction. And perhaps "like" too, but that was because they were friends now. That was all.

She certainly wasn't going to do anything stupid like fall in love with him, for example.

"Izzy," Chase said. "Can you come over and

explain to my daughter why driving a boatload of tourists isn't going to happen? Apparently, she won't listen to me."

At that moment, the door opened again and Levi strode in, and Indigo's heart gave another small but very definite flutter inside her chest.

His Pure Adventure NZ tee was dark green today, and it brought out the deep emerald of his eyes. He was in black utility pants that hugged his powerful thighs, and like Chase, he wore battered hiking boots. He'd obviously just come from giving some tour or other, and the sight of him looking all competent and professional and masculine made Indigo's mouth go dry.

She had a sudden and intense desire to go on a helicopter ride with him or some other thing that he did for his job so she could see him in action.

Don't go letting your head get turned. You're smarter than that, remember?

Oh yes, she remembered.

He grinned at her, making her heart flutter even harder. "Ready to go?"

Chase was frowning at him. "Where are you off to?"

"Going to show Indigo the site for the house." Levi glanced at him. "That okay with you, chief?"

Chase's frown turned into a scowl. "Don't you have—?"

"Uncle Levi!" Gus interrupted. "I'm okay to drive the boat over the lake today, aren't I? Tell Dad."

"You are not okay to drive the boat over the lake," Levi said, not missing a beat. "And especially not a boat full of paying clients."

"Aw, that's crap," Gus said sulkily, looking mulish.

"But if you play your cards right," Levi went on. "I'll take you for a spin in the heli tomorrow morning."

Gus looked marginally less sulky. "Well, okay," she said grudgingly.

Indigo came around from behind the counter, conscious of Izzy's half-frowning look from where she stood near Gus, but even more conscious of the sudden glint of gold in Levi's gaze as she approached.

She felt nervous. Which was crazy, because after their relaxed conversation of the day before, she should be feeling *less* nervous, not more.

He raised a brow at her. "Shall we?"

"Yes, let's." She gave him a smile as she walked to the door, and he came after her.

Chase said something, but whatever it was was lost as the door banged shut behind them.

"Come on," Levi said. "It's around here," and he went off around the corner of the building.

Indigo followed. She hadn't been behind the gallery before and was slightly surprised to find a small lawn out the back and a little fence marking the boundary between the lawn and the bush.

There was a small wooden gate in the middle of the fence that led onto a small track that wound through the bush and up the side of the hill.

Indigo walked behind Levi's tall figure, inhaling the rich, earthy, damp scent that she'd come to recognize was intrinsic to the New Zealand bush.

It was subalpine beech forest and beautiful, the sun shining through the bright-green leaves and dappling the dark earthy track. There were ferns and kanuka, also kowhai, which produced beautiful yellow flowers.

A green and red kea, the South Island's cheeky parrot, eyed her from a branch. Chase had told her once that they were terrors when it came to approaching humans for food, and he was very strict with tourists about not feeding them. They were so cute though.

The track was a little muddy, but it didn't take long to walk up it, and then the bush gave way, opening out into a clear space with lots of blue sky and sunlight and alpine grasses. They weren't very high up the hill, but it was enough to see over the roof of the long stone building that housed the gallery and Bill's, and out over the pristine blue of the lake to the mountains beyond.

Indigo stopped dead and grinned, joy fizzing in her blood. She could hear the birds here, and there was bush all around and plenty of flat space for a little garden. It was literally five minutes to work...

Levi walked into the middle of the flat space, long grass brushing the sides of his utility pants. "This is where I was thinking you could have the door," he said, gesturing to where the track came up. "And then you'd want your windows here, so you can face the view." He indicated the mountains and lake. "You might want to angle it slightly so you can get all-day sun, but this would be the way to place it."

She could see that. See herself, sitting in a little window seat in the sun, with the windows open and a gentle breeze blowing in.

"Oh…" she breathed, coming through the grass to stand beside him. "Oh…yes. It's perfect."

He lifted a hand and pointed. "You could have a deck to sit out on when the weather's nice. And over there…" His finger drifted slightly to the side. "You could have that garden you wanted. It should get a lot of sunlight so you can grow the stuff you like."

She could see that too, a small patch of earth where she could grow herbs and maybe some salad greens. Even plants she could use for dyeing, since she'd been toying with the idea of using natural dyes one day.

"And over there," Levi went on, pointing to another area slightly more up the hill, "you could have a custom-built dyeing shed."

Indigo's eyes went very round. She hadn't thought of that. "I don't know if I could afford—"

"I can build you a shed. That's easy and cheap. You can stock it with equipment as and when you can afford it." He glanced down at her. "What do you think?"

She met his gaze without flinching and without hesitation. "I think it's wonderful." She couldn't quite keep the slightly husky tone out of her voice. "I think it's home."

―――――――

Indigo was pretty much always serious and always direct, but there was something else in her eyes now as they looked up into his. An intensity that somehow gripped him by the throat and didn't let go.

Home. She thought this place was home.

He hadn't expected that. What he'd expected was for her to look around critically and ask questions, bite her lip and frown. Disagree with him about where to put the house and maybe argue.

But she wasn't arguing. Her sky-blue eyes had darkened with emotion, and it wasn't prickliness or irritation. It was happiness.

He hadn't seen her happy before. It suited her. She glowed.

And you were the one who could give her that.

The thought echoed through him, making his chest feel tight, an ache settling behind his breastbone. That strange sense of longing he'd felt at the farmhouse the night before.

He didn't know what to make of it, so he pasted on a smile. "You really like it?"

"Oh yes!" She turned and walked through the long grass a little way to where he'd suggested she put the deck. "I'll get a chair and sit here and knit in the sun. And then…" She walked a few steps over to where he'd indicated she might like the garden. "I can dig around for herbs and things." She glanced back at him. "I'm thinking of getting a natural dye garden going, so this is perfect."

So is she.

The thought came unbidden and unexpected as the sun shone on her dark-brown hair, picking up all the streaks of caramel and toffee running through the messy bun on top of her head. She was wearing that blue dress again, the one that the wind had pressed against her figure at the helicopter a couple of days before, and this morning, standing in full sunlight, he could see it was slightly transparent.

Her face was pink with pleasure, her eyes sparkling. His prickly little hedgehog was the most beautiful, sensual woman.

He turned away, his heart beating uncomfortably fast. This was stupid. Why was he feeling this way? Was it simply because he was denying himself? If so, maybe he shouldn't. Maybe he should indulge himself and seduce her so they could both put it behind them.

Yeah, solid plan. Not. Things haven't changed. She's

still who she is and you're still who you are. She's part of this community and that means she's off-limits, so how about you keep it in your pants?

Levi gritted his teeth.

The sound of the boat motor came drifting on the air, and out on the lake he could see the company boat heading toward Glitter Falls. He'd taken his tour up the river, but he knew he'd been distracted, his head too full of his plans for Indigo's house and Indigo herself, laughing at that crappy joke about bears.

Get it. The hell. Together.

Yeah, he really needed to. Perhaps he should head into Queenstown. Go to Paddy's down on the waterfront, one of his favorite pubs. Find a woman and take her home. Maybe if he got laid, he wouldn't be feeling these things around Indigo and wouldn't be so distracted.

A great idea if he actually wanted to go and pick up a woman, but for some reason he couldn't seem to find his usual enthusiasm. In fact, the thought left him cold.

She's getting to you.

Tension crawled through him.

The sound of grasses rustling came from behind him, and Indigo came to a stop beside him. She was looking at the lake and the boat on it, lifting a hand to shield her face from the sun. "Is that Chase out there?"

Little tendrils of brown hair curled around her ears and the nape of her neck, making her skin look very pale. Her dress had a wide scoop neck, revealing the delicate architecture of her collarbones. A few little freckles were scattered over her skin.

He wanted to touch those tendrils of hair, stroke her vulnerable nape. Trace those little freckles...

She looked up at him, frowning. "What? Is my hair coming down or something?"

"No." He cleared his throat and tried to think of an excuse that wouldn't sound like he was fantasizing about touching her. "That's a pretty dress. You wear a lot of blue."

Great comeback. Really stellar.

The pink in her cheeks deepened, and he had a sudden and very vivid vision of her beneath him in his bed in Queenstown, with the sun coming through the windows. Her dark hair spread over the pillows, her naked body pale on his white sheets. Her blue eyes would be dark with desire, and her cheeks would be a deep rose from passion. "Levi..." she'd whisper in a sweet, husky voice. "You make me feel so good..."

"I do," Indigo agreed in a sadly very normal voice, bringing him back to the present. "Because of my name, which I guess is a bit obvious. But Grandma named me. For my eyes, which she said were blue even from the moment I was born. And I guess babies' eyes aren't usually or something?

Anyway, she always dressed me in blue and told me it was my color so I should claim it."

He tried to shove the vision of a naked Indigo out of his head. "Your grandma was right. Blue is your color." He cleared his throat again. "In fact, I think you look beautiful in it."

But she wasn't listening, her brow furrowing. She pointed toward the bush near where they were standing. "Is that...?"

A familiar doggy shape came trotting out from the scrubby undergrowth, black fur covered in earth and dead leaves.

"Hey, boy," Indigo said softly as Mystery came up to them. "What are you doing here?"

Mystery gave her a sniff and then looked up hopefully at Levi.

Levi grinned. Well, he might not be able to touch the beautiful woman standing next to him, but he could give this dog a pet.

"Maybe he lives here," Levi said. "Well now, what are you looking for?" He kept his tone gentle as he held out his hand to the dog. "Think I might have a treat for you somewhere?"

Mystery took a couple of steps over to him, sniffed his hand, then sat down at his feet, brown eyes full of doggy hope.

Levi didn't move. "Where do you think they might be, hmm?" He lifted both hands. "I don't have any here, see?"

But Mystery wasn't fooled. The dog sniffed at Levi's pockets, still looking at him with big eyes.

"He knows," Indigo murmured.

"Of course he does. He's smart." Levi took the treat out of his pocket and told the dog to sit. Which the animal instantly did. Definitely a farming dog. Perhaps his owner had treated him badly and he'd run away or something. Then again, he didn't seem scared of people. Just wary.

Levi opened his palm and gave the dog the treat, murmuring praise to him and petting his silky head. The dog leaned against his leg a little and the ache in Levi's heart eased. Trust took time to build, and it seemed he was building it with Mystery.

"He likes you," Indigo said quietly.

He smiled and stroked the dog's head. "Everyone likes me."

"Yeah, they really do." Her gaze lifted from the dog to him. "I used to wonder why, but I'm not sure I wonder now. Now, I can see why."

His had been a throwaway comment, like most of the bullshit that came out of his mouth, because while people did like him, it was because he worked hard at making them like him.

He'd worked at making her like him too, and it made him feel good that she did. In fact, standing here with her, on the site of the house he was going to build for her, with the dog at his feet and her looking at him like that, he felt the most intense pleasure. Not physical, but deeper. An emotional completeness he hadn't ever experienced before.

As if this where he was supposed to be, right here on this spot. With the dog leaning against him and Indigo looking at him as if he meant something to her.

Home.

The thought drifted through his head, which was weird because he knew this was home. He'd been here for years, after all. He'd always thought of Brightwater as home.

"You like me, hmm?" He stared down into her blue gaze. "I call that progress."

A serious look crossed her face. "Levi…I–I know I haven't been very nice to you, and especially not when I first got here. I was suspicious and mistrustful, and well…I've got a lot of issues left over from my dad, and I guess I put a lot of them on you. And I'm sorry."

Ah, shit. He wished she wouldn't do things like that. Be nice to him and apologize for something she didn't need to apologize for. Make him like her even more than he did already, which was a hell of a lot.

"You don't need to apologize." He liked the dog, but he badly wanted to touch the little curls near her ears instead of Mystery's head. "I didn't exactly help matters. I was a dick to you."

"Maybe," she allowed. "But when I told you to

stop, you did. Except then I…" She hesitated, bit her lip, then went on. "Kept getting in your way. Kind of on purpose."

He shouldn't find that intriguing. He shouldn't want to know why she always seemed to be in his vicinity, though he knew the answer to that already.

Tell her it's fine and then move on. That's what you should do.

"Oh?" he asked, because apparently he had no control over his stupid mouth. "And why did you do that, hmmm?"

She gave him a look from beneath her dark lashes and then glanced away again, blushing. "I… really don't know."

"I think you do. I think you know exactly why." He tried to put more of a teasing note in his voice so she would know he wasn't being serious, except it came out sounding much lower and more seductive than he'd intended.

Her lashes lifted and she was looking up at him again, her eyes glinting. She didn't say anything, as if she was waiting for him to tell her the reason.

And because he was an idiot, he did. "I think it's because you find me absolutely irresistible."

She was doing that blushing thing again, and he was seized once more by the most insane urge to kiss her. Not those tantalizing little brushes she'd given him before, but a proper kiss. His tongue exploring her mouth and his hands in her hair.

Kissing her deeply, tasting her, learning her flavor. Pressing her sweet body against his, having her heat seeping into him...

Christ, he *wanted* it.

"I do not," she protested, but he could see the corners of her mouth lifting in a reluctant smile.

"Yeah, you do." His voice had gotten far too husky, though with any luck she wouldn't notice. "In fact, I would go so far as to say that you can't stay away."

She picked a stem of tall grass and fiddled with it. "I wouldn't mind, you know." Her voice was so quiet he almost didn't hear. "If kisses weren't enough, I mean. I could do more."

He went very still. "What do you mean, you could do more?"

Not looking at him, she began ripping the stem of grass into little pieces. "If you wanted to do more than kiss. If you wanted...you know...s-sex."

Oh shit.

What did I tell you about being screwed?

He did not need this, he really didn't. She was already one hell of a temptation and not just physically. She was so honest and up-front; there was no guile to her at all, and she was fierce too. He had the feeling that Indigo was protective when it came to those she cared about and would fight to the death for them, if need be, and hell, he admired that so much. He'd once been a soldier after all.

He'd managed to keep his distance, knowing she probably wouldn't want to have any kind of physical affair with him.

But this? Knowing she *did* want more? Yeah, he *was* screwed.

"Indy…" he murmured.

"I know that you said you didn't get involved with women who lived here," she went on hurriedly. "Or inexperienced women. I just thought that maybe a night would okay."

Bloody hell. What could he tell her? Because as much as he wanted her, he couldn't take what she was offering. Not when there were so many reasons why it was a bad idea, not the least being Chase and Finn kicking his ass all the way to Auckland if they ever found out.

He sighed. "You know I'm interested. But that doesn't change things."

She dropped the pieces of grass and picked another stem. "What things? Me living here? Me being a virgin?"

"Yeah, both."

"Do they really matter though?"

Levi let out another breath and turned to face her. The dog leaned against his legs. She continued to rip at the piece of grass.

"Indigo," he ordered gently. "Look at me."

She tossed the poor abused grass stem away and finally lifted her gaze to his. "What?"

"I like you. I like you very much. And because I like you, I don't want to make things difficult for you. And they would get difficult, hedgehog. I'm a "here for a good time, not a long time" kind of guy. Everyone in town knows it, and there are a whole lot of people here who wouldn't approve of you and me hooking up."

She was frowning now. "They don't have to know."

"Sure, but what if it ends badly between us? I've still got to build your house, and that means we'll have to stay in contact. Also, we both live and work here, so even after the house is done, we'll still see each other every day."

"Why are you assuming it'll end badly?" There was a deep crease between her brows. "A night would be fine. It doesn't have to be a big deal."

And yet here you are, turning it into one.

Yeah, because he was trying to protect her. It wasn't wrong to want to protect someone. Especially someone who didn't know what they were getting themselves into.

"But feelings have a habit of getting in the way," he said, sharper than he'd intended. "Sex changes things, and you won't really understand that until you've had it."

She scowled. "That's patronizing."

It was, and this conversation was heading downhill rapidly. But he didn't know what else to do. He couldn't sleep with her. He wouldn't.

"I'm trying to protect you." He tried to keep the exasperation out of his voice. "I don't want you to get hurt."

"Why would I be hurt?" She gave him the most irritated look. "I might be sheltered, Levi, but I'm not stupid. I'm also not looking for a relationship, not when I've got far too many other things to think about."

Well, this hole was just getting deeper and deeper, wasn't it? As was the temptation tugging at him. The temptation to just say, "Screw it," and take what he wanted, which was her.

But he was better than that. He'd worked hard to be better than that ever since he came to live here, and he wasn't messing it up just because his dick was telling him to.

Time to lay it all out for her, warts and all.

"I'm not a relationship kind of guy, Indigo," he said flatly. "You have to know that straight up. My job, this town take precedence over everything. Sex is great, but that's all it'll ever be for me. Just sex. I don't do feelings. I'm not going to be your boyfriend. What you'll get from me is a couple of nights of fun, but then I'll be moving on. So, you might want to think about that before you decide on anything else, okay?"

The deep frown on her face didn't change, her gaze searching his in a way that made him uncomfortable.

Did she not believe him? Because if that was the

case then he *definitely* couldn't go there with ...
Hurting her was the last thing he wanted to do,
and if he wasn't careful, he would. She was wildly
inexperienced—and just how inexperienced he
hadn't realized until the day before. And he wasn't.

He was experienced, hardened by years of
having no one but himself to rely on, and he didn't
want anything more than a good time.

Taking her would be criminal.

"You think I'm lying?" He let her look, let her see
the truth in his eyes. "I'm not, hedgehog. A night's
all I've got to give, and I'm not about to change my
mind about that. Not even for you."

Then he gave Mystery one last pet before
moving past her and going back down the track to
the gallery.

Chapter 9

A COUPLE OF DAYS LATER, INDIGO SAT WITH THE knitting circle in the Rose's small guest library. It was raining outside so they couldn't sit on the porch, and Jim didn't want to sit in the pub since it felt too much like work for him, so this was a happy medium.

It wasn't a big room, but it was cozy, furnished with a couple of battered armchairs, a worn couch, and a couple of mismatched wooden coffee tables. Bookcases lined the walls, stuffed full of books guests had left behind, and there were all kinds, from mysteries and thrillers, to romance and science fiction, with a couple of literary fiction tomes thrown into the mix as well, not to mention a lot of nonfiction. Guidebooks on New Zealand and a lot of other countries too—many out-of-date—lined many of the shelves.

Today it was chilly, so Cait, Jim's daughter, had lit a fire in the fireplace, and it made the room lovely and warm.

Indigo, Shirley, Beth, and Jim were there today, since Izzy had a shift at the gallery, though since there was hardly anyone around, she could have closed it up and come and knit. Then again, Indigo was starting to suspect that Izzy didn't much like knitting and had been looking for an excuse not to come.

Beth was still cursing over her bootie, while Shirley was embroidering something on an embroidery hoop and Jim crocheted away at his granny square. He was using the yarn colors she'd suggested, which was gratifying.

The others seemed engrossed in what they were doing, but Indigo was distracted. She'd left a message with Finn for Levi at the Pure Adventure NZ HQ, mentioning that she was at the Rose if he wanted to resume his knitting lessons.

Finn had stared at her in some surprise and then asked her to repeat that about the knitting lessons, which she did. He made no comment though, apart from assuring her he'd certainly pass that on to Levi when he saw him, but she had the distinct impression that Finn was amused at Levi learning to knit.

She could understand. Levi was hardly the knitting type. But he'd asked and she'd promised to teach him, since this was her way of paying him back for the tiny house.

A tiny house she'd be more excited about if it hadn't been colored by the memory of him telling her in no uncertain terms that he wouldn't be having sex with her anytime soon.

God only knew what had possessed her to broach the topic with him. She'd been excited by the thought of the little house that would be built in this perfect, perfect spot and glad that he was the one who'd made it happen.

Yes, she'd had her doubts about him, but it was clear to her now that he was nothing but genuine. He wanted to help her. He was giving up his time to build a house especially for her and not even taking any money for the labor. Plus, with one large capable hand stroking Mystery's head, the dog leaning against his legs and looking up adoringly at him, the sun gilding his skin and his hair, and catching sparks off the gold in his eyes...

He was stunningly gorgeous.

He'd deserved the apology she'd given him, and after that, the words about how she'd be okay with more than kisses had just fallen out of her mouth.

He'd been very clear at the farmhouse that he wasn't going to get involved with her, so she shouldn't have been surprised that he'd said no. And Izzy had already pointed out that he was protecting her, so the confirmation that was exactly what he was doing shouldn't have been a surprise either.

Yet despite both those things, she'd been really hoping he might say yes, and he hadn't. He'd spouted some stuff about how he didn't want relationships and one night is all he had, etc., etc. Blah, blah. He hadn't seemed to listen when she'd said she didn't want a relationship either, and then he'd been condescending about sex and feelings.

Asshole.

Perhaps she needed to give him a lecture of her own. That if he didn't want her, then he needed to stop being so damn gorgeous, because that wasn't helping.

"I hear Levi's going to build you a little house," Shirley said, breaking the silence. "How wonderful for you. He's very good at building things."

"Yes, I'm very pleased." Indigo glanced toward the door, hearing some footsteps down the hallway. But the footsteps passed by the door and went on toward the kitchens.

Not Levi then.

She told herself she wasn't disappointed.

"He built me some new kitchen cabinets after my husband died," Shirley went on. "Mine were awful, but I'd been in the middle of replacing them when Ken passed away. I didn't have the inclination to do anything about them. Half the kitchen had been ripped out, but I couldn't face having to organize someone to finish the job. Levi appeared one day, asked me how I was doing, built me some more, installed them for me, and didn't charge me a cent." She was smiling as she stabbed her needle through her hoop. "I paid him back of course, eventually, but I'll never forget what he did for me. He listened to me talk about Ken for hours. Got a good heart, that boy."

Indigo hadn't listened to Shirley's stories about how wonderful Levi was before, but now that particular story tugged at her own heart.

She didn't need any more confirmation of how great he was, how he'd seen someone in need and had turned up to help. How it was obvious he couldn't give Shirley her husband back, but he could build her a kitchen.

He was right; he *was* irresistible.

Because for a man who'd told her he didn't do feelings, he sure seemed to care about other people's. Then again, he'd also told her that this town took precedence over everything else, and it seemed that was definitely true.

"He cares about this town, doesn't he?" She didn't know why she made it a question, since it was obvious that he cared.

"Good bloke," Jim said unexpectedly. "Give you the shirt off his back."

"That I'd pay good money to see," Beth said, grinning.

Shirley gave a very youthful-sounding giggle. "Oh, I would too. He's young enough to be my son, but I don't care. A good-looking man is a good-looking man."

"Amen, Shirley," Beth said. "Amen."

Indigo glared at her friend. "Hey. Aren't you having a baby with Finn?"

"I am." Beth gave her an unrepentant look. "And you know Finn's the hottest guy in town, no question. But I've got eyes, and I'm allowed to look at things, and like Shirley said, a good-looking man is a good-looking man." She grinned. "Not getting jealous there, are we?"

Indigo opened her mouth to tell her that of course she wasn't but realized at the last moment that it was going to sound far too much like protesting. And that Shirley was giving her a certain look from over the tops of her glasses.

"You might want to be careful there, Indigo," Shirley cautioned as she peered down at her embroidery. "I'm not sure Levi is looking to settle down."

"Jealous," Beth mouthed at her and jerked her head in Shirley's direction.

Oh yes, well, that wasn't anything Indigo didn't know.

"I'm not looking to settle down either," she said, hoping she didn't sound grumpy. Because seriously, why on earth did everyone keep thinking she was after more than a night? Just because she was a virgin and sheltered didn't mean she didn't know her own mind.

Shirley looked up. "In that case you definitely shouldn't go near him."

"Oh?" Indigo asked in some surprise. "Why?"

"Because he might think he's not after a relationship and he definitely might say it, but that man is looking for a family to take care of, make no mistake."

There was a stunning silence.

"Seriously?" Beth said. "Levi?"

Shirley turned her direct look on Beth. "Of course, sweetie. Why else do you think he fixes everybody's drains and builds cabinets and offers to build houses? Why else did he take that land off Jim? He's after a home. And he's after a family to care for. It's as plain as the nose on your face."

"Hey," Beth exclaimed mildly. "My nose is not plain."

But all Indigo could think of was of Levi telling her about his childhood. About his mother who hadn't wanted any contact from him, and how he didn't know who his father had been.

"Twenty homes in two months, that kind of thing..."

He didn't blame his mother, he'd said. She'd been fifteen... And then his face as she'd told her that this town took precedence over everything else.

Her insides tightened in sympathy. Was Shirley right? Because if so...

A curious lump had risen in her throat, and she knew that all the telling herself in the world that he was an asshole wouldn't change the fact that she liked him. She liked him a lot. And the thought of him not having anyone made her feel awful.

She knew what it was like to be alone. After her grandma had died, she'd had no one. She'd been in that isolated homestead on her own. Abandoned. Terrified of the outside world, but more terrified of the loneliness that ate away at her. She'd thought she'd be okay, but she hadn't been.

And while she might find people difficult, being on her own had been more difficult still. Coming here with Beth and Izzy...it had been the best thing she'd ever done.

Had he felt that when he'd come here? A sense of place? Of home? And if he had, then why was he still looking?

"Hey."

Gradually Indigo became aware that Beth was talking to her. "Sorry, what?"

"You were zoning out." Beth waggled her pale-blond brows. "Good thoughts, I hope?"

But Indigo was too distracted to respond to the gentle tease. "I just... Speaking of Levi, he was supposed to come here for knitting lessons." She glanced at the door again, but it remained stubbornly empty. "I thought he might be here by now."

Beth stared at her in surprise. "Knitting lessons? Really?"

For some reason Jim grunted.

Indigo glanced at him, but his attention was firmly on his granny square.

"Yes, really." She looked back at Beth. "It's part

of me paying him back for his time building this house. I asked him what he wanted, and he said knitting lessons. Oh yes, and he wants me to teach him to cook too."

Jim grunted a second time.

Indigo glanced at him again, but his face was as expressionless as ever. "Are you okay, Jim?" she asked, just in case.

"He's fine." Shirley gave him a disapproving glance. "I don't know what you think is so funny, old man."

Jim only lifted a shoulder.

"Anyway," Indigo said, deciding whatever Jim was laughing about—if in fact those grunts were laughs—it probably didn't matter. "I asked Finn to pass the message on." She looked at Beth. "He *would* pass that on, wouldn't he?"

"Of course, he would." Beth frowned. "Shall I go check to see—?"

"No, it's okay," Indigo interrupted, not wanting to make a fuss. If Levi didn't want to come, he didn't want to come. She hadn't heard from him for a couple of days, not since he'd shown her the site, but that might have been because he had some tours to take. "He's probably got a lot of things to do."

You should go find him. Tell him his company is wanted.

Her heart ached at the same time as her gut

lurched. Sex was one thing, but asking him to come and knit with her as a friend was different. And if he said no to that...she wasn't sure she could take that another rejection from him.

It made her think of those few phone calls she'd had with her mother after her parents had left Deep River. Claire had made sympathetic sounds and comforting noises as Indigo had asked yet again when she could come to Anchorage to live with them, and then Claire had promptly passed the phone to Indigo's father. Who'd sounded warm and loving, making all sorts of assurances that soon she could come. Very soon.

Except soon had never come. She'd never joined them in Anchorage, because they'd never wanted her to come.

Your grandmother probably didn't want you either.

The thought sat in her gut like a piece of broken glass, hard and sharp and cutting. Her grandma had been loving and kind to her, but it was true she hadn't asked to have Indigo dumped with her.

No one wanted you. So, you can hardly blame him.

The thought made the glass cut deeper so she forced it away.

"Well," Shirley was saying. "He's a busy man. Got lots to do I should imagine."

"He's an idiot," Jim said, not looking up from his granny square.

"He is not, Jim O'Halloran." Shirley bridled at this criticism of her favorite. "Don't say that."

"He is." Jim didn't look at her. "I'll have a word with him."

But Indigo wasn't listening. Levi and his rejections were jolting that sliver of glass buried deep inside her, making her ache, making her hurt.

She didn't know why he wasn't here, but there was only one way to make it stop hurting, and that was to tell herself she didn't care. That it didn't matter if he came to knit with her or not. No skin off her nose, right?

"It's okay, Jim," she said, ignoring the pain. "His loss if he's not here. Now, I'm considering some fall colors for my next dyeing session. What do you guys think?"

━━━━━━━

Levi sat in the equipment room of HQ, sorting through a bunch of climbing helmets. Chase had signed up a small group for a guided climb—something new they were trialing—and had asked Levi to lead it. Climbing was something he loved doing, as was guiding people, so it was a no-brainer. The clients did have some climbing experience and had said they had their own equipment, but being prepared was one of the foundation stones of the Pure Adventure NZ experience, so Levi was going through the equipment just in case.

The climb was tomorrow so he had to do a quick stock take now.

Nothing whatsoever to do with avoiding Indigo and her knitting circle. Nothing at all.

Just then, Finn put his head around the door. "You're not going, are you?"

Shit.

Levi examined the helmet. "Going where?"

"Don't be a dick, bro. You know what I'm talking about. Indigo said you can come to her knitting thing for lessons."

He turned the helmet over and checked the inside. "I've got too much to do. This climb tomorrow—"

"Bullshit." Finn stepped into the room, shut the door, and leaned against it, folding his arms. He gave Levi a hard stare. "What's with you?"

"Nothing."

"Pull the other one, mate. It's got bells on."

"I really have got too much—"

"Levi, don't be a dick."

You really are.

Dammit. Yes, okay, so he'd been avoiding Indigo like the plague ever since he'd walked away from her that day at the site. Oh, he'd been working on getting some preliminary drawings together for her house as well as keeping to his guiding schedule, so that had kept him busy. And it was true that he hadn't had a lot of time, but...

Shit, the way he was feeling about her, he didn't trust himself. Which made it was easier not to be around her.

That's gonna hurt her.

It would, no getting around it. He could tell himself all he liked that she might not even notice or that if she did, she wouldn't care, but he knew she'd notice. And that she'd care. She'd apologized to him for being prickly, and she'd wanted to be his friend.

Now you're avoiding her. Nice one, mate.

He let out a breath and put the helmet down beside him on the long wooden bench he was sitting on. "Look, I'm not trying to be an active dick, okay? I just...can't be around her at the moment."

"Her being Indigo?"

"Yeah."

Finn's sharp dark eyes missed nothing. "Does she know that? Or are you stringing her along?"

"What? No." Levi scowled. "I told her it's not happening between us. I was very clear."

"Right." Anger sparked in Finn's gaze. "Levi, if you've been messing around with her, so help me, I will fuc—"

"No." Levi made the word hard and flat. "I have not been messing around with her. Bloody hell, what do you take me for? There's attraction there, can't lie, but I'm not going to do anything about it. She's way too inexperienced, and she doesn't have a home to go to or people to look out for her. So no, I'm not going to bloody do anything about it."

Finn, who never shied from difficult conversations, didn't look away. "You gave me the hard word about Beth. I'm giving you the hard word about Indigo. Also, she does have people to look out for her. She's got Beth and Izzy, and Chase and me. She's also got the rest of the damn town."

That should have been reassuring, but for some reason it wasn't. Everyone else had their own lives and their own concerns. Other people they'd put first. Indigo had no one who'd put her first, not even her own parents. He didn't know why that mattered to him, but it did.

Levi shoved himself off the bench, rising to his full height. "You can't tell anyone this, okay? But she kissed me. Twice." He shouldn't say anything to Finn, but hell. He trusted this man with his life, and he needed someone to talk to about it. Because avoiding her wasn't the answer, that was clear. Not if that caused her hurt.

He'd been a difficult kid all those years ago, but after he'd grown up, he'd resolved that he wouldn't be a difficult man. He'd make people's lives easier, not harder. At least that was the plan.

"Huh," Finn said, frowning. "She did?"

"Yes. Then she told me she wanted more than a couple of kisses. So, I told her no." He shoved a hand distractedly through his hair. "And then I told her why it wasn't a good idea. And then she said—"

"Yeah, I get it. Spare me the details." Finn held up a hand. "I still don't get why're you're ghosting her though."

Levi glared. "I'm not ghosting her."

"You're avoiding her, so same diff. What I don't get is why?"

"Why do you think?" Levi dropped his hand from his hair. "The attraction isn't all on her side. We've got…chemistry. And I'm really shit at resisting temptation."

"Ah," said Finn.

"Good word *ah*. Encapsulates the situation very well. *Shitty* also works."

Finn snorted. "Don't be dramatic. So, you want her, what's the big deal? You don't have to do anything about it."

"I'm not doing anything about it. But like I said, I'm finding it difficult being in her general vicinity and not flirting with her." He gritted his teeth. "And since flirting with a woman you've got chemistry with generally leads to sex, it's kind of a bad idea."

Finn shifted against the door. "So what? You're avoiding her because you can't help yourself?"

"You know what I'm like, Finn. Sometimes I *can't* help myself. Plus knowing she's into it just makes it worse." He shoved his hand through his hair once again, unable to see a way out of the problem. "I don't want to slip up, not with her, but I don't want to hurt her either. It's an issue."

"Yeah," Finn said slowly. "I can see that. Well, you've only got two options, haven't you? You either be completely honest with her, give it to her straight about why you can't be around her, or..."

Levi stared at him. "Or what?"

Finn stared back. "Or ask her what she wants."

"I know what she wants already." And he did, remembering the blush in her cheeks and the sparks of blue deep in her eyes. The way she'd looked at him... *If kisses weren't enough, I mean... I could do more...*" "It's not happening."

"Okay, playing devil's advocate here," Finn said and then added, "And believe me, I appreciate the irony. But I guess from what you said, she wants you too. In which case..."

"In which case nothing." He was annoyed now and didn't bother to hide it. Finn was supposed to agree with him being a better man, to help him resist, not actively encourage him. "Look, she's very sheltered. And when I mean very, I mean *very*. Hell, she's never even been on a date, let alone had a boyfriend."

"You don't go on dates either," Finn pointed out, which Levi felt was unnecessary.

"No, I know. Which is a good reason why it's a bad idea. I don't do relationships. You know that."

"Sure, but she's also an adult woman who knows her own mind. Plus this whole avoidance game you're playing isn't exactly going to *not* hurt her."

Levi kept scowling because that was *not* what he wanted Finn to say. "You know," he said, "I was expecting a lot more threats. More death and dismemberment if I went near her."

Finn shrugged. "Sure. If you break her heart, Chase and I will certainly kill you."

And what if she breaks yours?

No, that was ridiculous. No one was going to break his heart. He'd decided a long time ago that he didn't have one anymore. It was safer that way.

Levi shook his head. "No, it's easier if nothing happens between us."

"So what? You're just going to keep on avoiding her? How's that going to work with the house thing?"

"It's not going to work, is it?" Levi snapped with uncharacteristic bad temper. "I'm going to have to be honest with her, like you said. Which will end up hurting her anyway, but better a cut right now than a bullet wound later, right?"

Finn's dark gaze narrowed as if he wanted to argue. But he only shrugged again. "Okay. You'd better tell her soon then." He shoved himself away from the door, then stopped. "Wait. Why knitting lessons?"

Levi sighed. "Because she wouldn't let me pay for everything with the house stuff. And since I don't need any more money, I told her she could teach me to knit and maybe to cook as well."

Finn stared at him for a long moment. "She'll be pissed off you didn't turn up this morning then."

Yes, she would, which meant he should take Finn's advice and go and talk to her ASAP.

Still, he had to finish the equipment check, and he wanted to take a few pictures of the house site first, so he decided to call into the gallery after he'd been to the site.

It was a miserable day, raining and gray, with a chill wind coming off the mountains as if to remind everyone not to get comfortable because autumn was on the way.

Levi loved being out in the elements, and he certainly didn't care about a bit of rain. He'd been in worse conditions in the army and on various treks here on the trails around Brightwater, so standing at the house site taking a few pictures in the rain didn't bother him. The photos were only for reference anyway, so it didn't matter what the weather was doing.

It was getting on toward evening by the time he'd finished, and as he came around the side of the gallery building, he glanced inside to see if Indigo was still there. She had an afternoon shift behind the counter, and he knew because he'd memorized her schedule in case she ever needed a lift down from or up to the farmhouse in his truck.

Sure enough, the lights were on, and there she was with the laptop open on the counter, frowning at something on the screen.

He didn't want to have this conversation, because he knew it would hurt their fledgling friendship, but he didn't have any other answers.

He had to do the right thing, and the right thing was to keep her at arm's length.

Shoving a hand through his wet hair to keep it out of his eyes, Levi pushed the door open and strode in.

Indigo's head snapped up, her expression going from polite welcome to anger in seconds flat. "Oh," she said, scowling. "So, you decided to turn up after all, did you? Sorry, lessons have been canceled."

You really did hurt her, you dick.

Levi gritted his teeth, extremely pissed off with himself. But then, he knew she'd care he wasn't there. She'd made tentative steps toward friendship, and he'd done the equivalent of slamming the door in her face.

"Look," he began, grasping around for a decent apology. "I'm sorry about the lessons—"

"Oh, for God's sake," she interrupted angrily. "You're all wet." Then to his shock, she grabbed something from beneath the counter and stepped out from behind it, coming over to him. And before he could move, he found himself being very firmly swathed in an enormous shawl knit in different shades of green yarn.

Too shocked to move, he stood there motionless as she angrily wrapped him up. "What the hell are you doing?" he asked as she tucked the end of the shawl against his shoulder.

"You're wet and you'll get cold," she snapped. "And then you'll catch pneumonia and die, and it'll be all my fault because I had a shawl and didn't use it."

A painful, raw thing twisted in his gut.

She was taking care of him. Very much reluctantly and certainly angrily, yet she was. Despite how he'd treated her, despite her own anger at him, she was making sure he was okay.

No one had ever done that for him. No one except that one foster mum of his. Linda. She hadn't been affectionate in any way, but she'd always made sure he had breakfast in the morning and did his homework when he came home from school. She'd always made sure he showered regularly and brushed his teeth and knew what respectful behavior was.

She'd never stood for any nonsense, and he'd thought for the first couple of weeks that she'd hated him. It was only when her eyes had gotten suspiciously liquid as she'd told him she couldn't look after him anymore because her father had had a stroke and needed her that he'd understood.

Linda hadn't been a demonstrative woman. But all those things she'd made him do, all those rules she'd instituted, they were because she'd cared about him. Because he'd mattered to her.

He'd never mattered to anyone before, and he'd never had anyone take care of him since. Not until Indigo.

Now she was fussing around and wrapping him up in the most ridiculous shawl in the world because she didn't want him to get cold. Even after he'd been a tool to her.

"Indigo," he said, not even sure what he wanted to do or what to say, only that he had to say something.

But she ignored him, tugging at the wool around his shoulders and wrapping it tighter around his throat. "You're such an ass, Levi King," she muttered. "You think I want to get my shawl wet just so you don't die? It's only just come off the needles. I haven't even blocked it—"

Levi reached out and took her chin in his fingers, her skin soft beneath his touch, and tilted her head back.

Her eyes were even bluer than that dress she wore that he liked so much, even bluer than the far reaches of heaven, and they glittered with anger and hurt.

And suddenly it all became very clear.

He didn't want to hurt her. He *never* wanted to hurt her. And there was only one way he could think of to keep from doing that.

So, he bent his head and took her mouth.

Chapter 10

INDIGO FROZE.

Levi was kissing her. Levi was *kissing* her. Again.

Her heartbeat thumped in her head, and she didn't want to move. First, because it took her a couple of seconds to understand what was happening, and second, because she couldn't work out if this made her more furious or less.

Then she couldn't think at all, because his fingertips were warm on her chin, and he was holding her firmly, and his mouth was very hot, just as she remembered.

And she knew she was very angry with him, but she couldn't remember why. Something to do with him not turning up for her lesson and not contacting her at all over the past couple of days, and how that had hurt her far deeper than she'd expected. How angry, because anger was always better than hurt. Anger was far more powerful.

Except all that protective anger was falling away now because he was here. Kissing her.

She didn't know why he'd come through that door, rain darkening his hair and plastering the T-shirt to his broad chest, outlining all that delicious muscularity. Maybe to give her a lecture on why he'd been ghosting her, or maybe not. And maybe he had something to say about how she'd wrapped him in her shawl so (a) he wouldn't freeze to death and (b) she could cover up his chest.

But now he was kissing her and none of that mattered.

Her brain was telling her she had to stop him, that she had to push him away and demand an explanation for this behavior, but her body didn't want to. Her body wanted to stand close, just like this, and let him kiss her. Let her revel in the feel of his hot mouth on hers, let her be aware that despite his T-shirt and jeans being wet, he wasn't cold. In fact, the heat his large powerful body was putting out made her want to press herself against him, despite his wet clothes.

She trembled, caught in a battle between logic and instinct, and then his tongue gently touched the seam of her lips, and lighting struck the length of her spine, burning her logic to ashes.

A soft moan escaped her, and abruptly she was leaning into him, her fingers curled in the stupid shawl she'd wrapped around him, opening her mouth to him and letting him explore and taste.

Heat prickled all over her skin, a deep, throbbing ache pulsing between her thighs.

He smelled like rain and wet leaves, and that musky, spicy scent that was intrinsic to him, that reminded her of her favorite cinnamon tea, and she wanted more. She pressed harder against him, conscious of his height and the hard feel of his body, of the immense physical strength of him, carved out by all those activities he did. All that hiking and climbing and kayaking.

She loved how there was no give to his chest beneath her palms or to the rock-hard torso she was pressing herself against. Were all men this hard? And why did she like it so much? Why did she want to run her hands all over him to measure exactly how strong he was?

But then he'd pushed his tongue into her mouth and his taste flooded into her, and all she could do was curl her fingers tighter into the wool, because just like everything else about him, it was delicious. Chocolate and spice and mint and something else, something that had her forgetting her own inexperience and kissing him back, desperate to chase that flavor, discover what it was.

He made a deep sound in the back of his throat, and it was the most exciting thing she'd ever heard, and then his hands were in her hair, his fingers pushing into the little bun she'd put it in and hairpins flying everywhere, tendrils of hair coming down as he eased her head back, kissing her harder, deeper.

It was intense, hot, raw. She didn't know what she was doing, so she followed her instinct, exploring his mouth the way he was exploring hers, until every thought in her head was quiet and there was only him. Only the desperate need to touch him, get close to him, wrap herself around him until all his heat and strength was part of her and all the cold and hurt was gone.

She didn't know he'd been walking her backwards until the edge of the counter hit her back and then she was being pressed against it, his kiss even deeper now and passionate, almost feverish.

"Indy," he murmured against her mouth. "Christ…" Then he swore again under his breath, and his hands were out of her hair and resting on her hips instead. She found herself lifted up and placed gently on the top of the counter. Her thighs spread of their own accord, allowing him to stand between them, and when he pulled her close so the most sensitive part of her was pressed against the hard length behind the zipper of his jeans, she gasped. Lightning strikes of intense physical pleasure scattered through her, making her shudder and then press harder against him, because it felt so good. Especially when he made another of those deep, husky masculine sounds that whispered across her skin, thrilling her on some deep, feminine level.

He wanted her, that was obvious. More, he was desperate for her if this kiss was anything to go by. As desperate as she was for him.

The kiss went on and on, and she wriggled against him, rocking herself against that hot, hard ridge behind his fly, loving how good it made her feel. It wasn't enough. She wanted to touch him, to feel him. To have his bare skin against hers and his arms around her. To have him inside her, because she knew that's exactly what she wanted now. There was no doubt at all in her mind.

Levi would be the man she lost her virginity to, and she would accept absolutely no substitutes.

But then, much to her distress, his mouth lifted. She tried to follow it, reaching up to bring him back to where she wanted him, but his fingers closed around her wrists, holding on to her. "No," he murmured, his voice so deep and husky it was almost unrecognizable. "Wait."

"Don't stop." The words tumbled out of her; she couldn't keep them in. "Please, Levi. Don't stop. Don't go."

He was breathing very fast and hard, his eyes glittering with an odd intensity as he looked down at her. In fact, he looked strange and strung out, a man on the edge of a cliff wanting to jump and yet holding himself back.

"You know where we are, don't you?" He sounded almost angry. "We're in the gallery, in the middle of town, and everyone can see through these windows."

She could feel herself wanting to curl up like an

anemone around that sliver of glass deep inside her, because if he rejected her now, she didn't think she could bear it.

Yet…he hadn't let her go. He was still holding on to her wrists, and while he might have ended the kiss, he hadn't moved away. The glitter in his eyes was pronounced, an intense golden gleam that made it very obvious what he was thinking.

So, she didn't curl up or push him away. She stared right into his golden eyes and said, "I know where we are. So, let's go to the farmhouse. There's nobody there but me."

He took a sharp breath, tension making the air around them feel dense and thick. "You know I've got nothing to give you but a couple of nights. That's it. That's all it'll ever be, understand?"

"Yes." She stared back at him and opened up her heart just a little. "I…want you, Levi. I want you so much. Please don't say no."

His gaze burned fiercely as he looked down at her a moment. Then abruptly he let her wrists go and cupped her face between his palms, all traces of smiles or flirtatiousness gone.

"I should, hedgehog." His voice had roughened. "I should. I was trying do the right thing and resist you. But…you're too bloody irresistible for your own good."

She was already flushed, but that made her flush even deeper. She liked the idea of being irresistible to him. She liked it a lot. "Why is resisting me is the right thing to do?"

"Lots of reasons. But mainly because I don't want to hurt you. I told you that."

Indigo decided right then and there that she was done with him protecting her. And she didn't want to wait until they got back to the farmhouse either, because that was a fifteen-minute trip and he'd probably change his mind again.

Idiot man.

She might be inexperienced but she knew what she wanted, and what she wanted was him.

"Then don't hurt me." She pulled out of his grip and reached for the shawl, pushing it off his broad shoulders. "Have me right here in the gallery. Now."

"Indigo, that's—"

"You'll change your mind, and I don't want you to change your mind." She shoved the shawl completely off him so she could see once again his wet black T-shirt, the cotton plastered to every inch of his muscular chest. Her mouth watered and her fingers itched. She looked up at him, let him see the desire she felt burning inside her. "I want you right now."

He hesitated only a second before turning and striding to the door of the gallery. And she thought for a horrible moment that he was going to open it and go straight out, but he didn't. Instead, he flipped the sign on the door to *Closed*, locked the door itself, then hit the lights, plunging the gallery into darkness.

All she could see was his tall form coming back over to the counter, looming over her, surrounding her in heat and the scent of rain.

"I'm going to make it good for you." His voice whispered over her skin deliciously, warm and husky with desire. "I'll make it so good, I promise."

"I know you will." Her own voice sounded weirdly thick, and her racing heartbeat was loud in her ears, a strange combination of excitement and trepidation gathering inside her, making her breathless. "I hope I make it good for you too."

"Oh, hedgehog, I don't think you could do anything else." His hands settled on her hips and tugged her lightly. "Come on, off the counter. Let's get somewhere out of sight."

His reassurance made her feel good, but her nervousness was growing. Not that she wouldn't like it—she had no doubts about his abilities, not given the number of women who continually swarmed around him—but she certainly had doubts about her own, which were zero.

How could she make a man feel good when she didn't know what she was doing? Oh, she knew the mechanics—her grandmother's sex ed had left a lot to be desired, but Indigo had managed to do a few sneaky internet searches on the computer at Mal's Market, which was the only computer she had access to in Deep River. The results had been alarming, but she'd managed to find the basics, and since they'd seemed kind of gross, she'd decided she wasn't going to be having sex with anyone anytime soon. She'd been sixteen.

But she wasn't sixteen now, and the idea of sex with Levi wasn't gross but exciting, and she wished—she *really* wished—she'd had some experience so she could make it good for him.

She was trembling slightly with nerves and anticipation by the time he'd urged her behind the counter. He'd bent to pick the shawl up from the floor where she'd pushed it and was now putting it back down and spreading it out, presumably so she had something soft to lie on.

"Come here," he murmured and held out a hand.

She took it, letting him draw her close and ease her down onto the shawl.

His hand cupped her jaw, his fingers brushing the sensitive skin beneath her ear, making her shiver. Then he kissed her again, his mouth brushing softly over hers. "You let me drive, hmm?"

She swallowed. "I don't know what to do," she murmured, then instantly regretted it, because she felt vulnerable enough already.

"That's why I said let me drive." He brushed his lips across hers again, a soft butterfly of a kiss. "All you have to do is lie back and let me make you feel good."

"But I don't want it to be just about me. I want to make you feel good too."

In the darkness it was difficult to make out his expression, but she could certainly see his smile. "Indy, all you have to do to make me feel good is exist."

Her face heated, his praise making her feel ridiculously pleased. "I would like to do more than just exist, Levi."

He laughed softly. "Then I'll tell you what I want, and all you have to do is do it. How does that sound?"

That sounded…great. More than great. It meant she didn't have to think, didn't have to worry or second-guess herself. She could do what he told her, and she'd know that he'd like it.

"Okay," she said breathlessly. "But what about if there's something I don't want to do?"

"Then simply tell me no and I'll stop. In fact, do that any time you're uncomfortable, okay? My primary goal here is your pleasure."

Is this what he tells every woman he sleeps with?

The thought was surprisingly unwelcome. She hadn't cared about all the women he'd slept with before, but now…well, she kind of did.

The feeling made her uncomfortable though, so she ignored it.

"And if I…want to touch you?" she forced out. "Can I?"

"Yes. You can touch me anywhere you like."

"Really? Anywhere." Her fingers were already itching, her breath coming even faster.

"Absolutely."

"But where feels good?"

"Anywhere you touch me feels good." He was crouched in front of her and now he shifted, going down on his knees, his hands dropping to the hem of his wet T-shirt. Then he was pulling it up and off, and even in the dark, the sight of him made her breath catch. Hard.

There was enough ambient light for her see the lines of sinew and bone and hard, carved muscle. The broad width of his shoulders and chest. The distinct cut lines of his abs. The narrow span of his hips and the groove that separated hip from thigh disappearing beneath the waistband of his jeans.

Oh, Beth and Shirley had nooooo idea…

A soft sound escaped her, a cross between a sigh and a moan, and she was reaching out to him before she could stop herself. He stayed where he was, unmoving as her hands found his smooth, hot skin.

It seemed like a gift to touch him, so she did, lightly. She'd never touched a man before and he was so different. Hard where she was soft, the prickle of hair where she had none. She could feel his muscles tense under his skin as she ran her fingertips down the hard corrugations of his abs.

She looked up at him, checking his expression. Did he not like this or...?

"I like you touching me," he said as if he could read her mind. "I like it a lot. Too much, probably."

Too much? How could...oh. *Oh.*

He was holding himself back, wasn't he? That's why he was tense. A throb of heat went through her, both that he was controlling himself for her benefit and that her touch tested that control. And now all she wanted was to test him again, to see how far she could push him before he lost it altogether.

But clearly, he already knew what she was thinking because he reached for her, cupping her face between his palms and kissing her again. "Oh no," he murmured against her mouth. "We're not doing that, not yet."

He pressed her back down onto the shawl, the scent of him and rain and yarn surrounding her. The heat of his body was astonishing, making her gasp as he settled between her spread thighs. He'd shifted slightly so he wasn't lying directly on her, but she could still feel the solid weight of his body against hers. She found it tremendously exciting.

Automatically her hands went to his bare shoulders, his skin smooth as satin beneath her fingers. He kissed her again, slower this time and yet somehow hotter, exploring her mouth with a sensuality that made her heart race. Her skin felt tight. Everything felt tight. She didn't want all this material between them. She wanted his beautiful body on hers, skin to skin, being close, close as she could get.

Except he made no move to undress her, simply kissing her deep and slow and hot, making the whole world narrow until there was only his mouth on hers and the heat of it. The weight of him on her and his scent.

Her heart thundered, the ache between her thighs insistent. She kissed him back, more confident now, her hands stroking his shoulders, sliding down his spine and then up again, following the lines of his strength and power.

But his hands were moving too. He held her head cradled in one large palm as the other slid down the side of her neck, stroking, finding the dips and hollows of her collarbones, tracing them. Then down further still over the cotton of her T-shirt to the swell of her breast. She trembled as he traced that lightly as well and then jerked, a lightning strike of pure pleasure arrowing through her as his fingertips brushed over one hard, aching nipple.

"Yes," she gasped. "Oh yes…"

But maddeningly his hand moved away, going down to the curve of her hip, caressing her.

His continued to kiss her slowly, as if he had all the time in the world, nipping her bottom lip and then licking her, exploring her until she felt dizzy. Then his hand was at her waist, finding the tie of her wraparound skirt and tugging at it so that it came undone.

She shuddered, her nails digging into the hard

muscle of his shoulders as his fingers pulled away the fabric before finding her bare thigh. His touch sent chills through her as he stroked, and she shifted beneath him, unable to keep still.

He kept on kissing her, gentler somehow as his hand caressed the sensitive skin of her inner thigh, moving further, brushing over the front of her panties. She gasped, pleasure arcing through her, and he made another of those deep, masculine sounds as his fingertips found the most sensitive part of her and stroked lightly over it.

Indigo gasped again, her hips lifting.

It felt so good. So unbelievably good. She'd experimented a few times with touching herself and that had felt nice, but it had been nothing like this. Nothing like Levi touching her, caressing her as if she were a precious work of art.

"Levi…" His name slipped out of her helplessly, like a plea or a prayer. "Oh, please…"

"I know." His voice was deep and gravelly. "Patience, hedgehog."

She twisted as he slipped his fingers beneath the elastic of her panties, overwhelmed by pleasure and need, trembling with anticipation. "I…d-don't want to wait."

His laugh was soft, like rough velvet. "But you feel so good." His fingers eased through the damp curls between her thighs, stroking gently. "All silky and soft and slippery."

Lights burst behind her lids, making her realize she'd closed her eyes. "I-Is that good?" The way he was touching her made it hard to think, even speak.

"Oh yeah, it's very good." His mouth nuzzled beneath her ear and then moved along her jaw, even as his finger stroked over her slick flesh. "Very, very good. I could touch you all day."

She twisted again as he touched that sensitive little bud between her thighs, his fingertips grazing over it gently, inciting her, teasing her.

She couldn't keep still. If he didn't stroke her harder and right *there*, she was going to explode or fall into pieces or…something.

"Levi," she moaned again. "Please…oh, please…"

His mouth found hers once more, his kiss deep and hot and slow, and he kept on kissing her as the touch of his fingers became fire, and she pressed herself into his hand, pleasure cascading everywhere and yet somehow not enough.

Then his finger shifted and pressed down, and her whole body stiffened as the orgasm swept over her in a great wave of ecstasy that made her cry out against his mouth, leaving her trembling and unable to move.

She felt dizzy, aftershocks pulsing through her, listening to the sound of her own ragged breathing.

Levi stroked her gently, and then his hand pulled away and he shifted. He knelt upright between her spread thighs, grabbing something from the back pocket of his jeans. His wallet. He flipped it open, took something out before discarding the wallet. Then his hands dropped to the buttons of his jeans, and he was undoing them.

Oh, right. Protection. She hadn't even thought of that.

Indigo wanted to help but she couldn't move. She could only lie there as he opened his jeans, dealt with the protection, and then he was back, his heavy weight settling on her, pinning her to the floor.

Heat surrounded her and the musky scent of aroused male, and she was trembling again. Not from fear, but from desire and anticipation and the sudden sense that this might end up being too good. Too intense. And she might not be able to cope.

She put her hands on his hot bare chest, whether to give herself a break and some breathing room, or just to touch him, feel his heat and his strength, the hard muscle that spoke of long hours of hard work in the outdoors, she wasn't sure.

"It's okay," he said huskily. "We can stop whenever you want."

Her eyes had adjusted to the dark now and she could see his face better. There was concern in his expression, but it wasn't the concern that reassured her. It was the gleam of heat in his eyes that burned even in the darkness, and the tension in his jaw, the husk in his voice. Signs of desire. Signs that he wanted her as badly as she wanted him and that this was intense for him too.

She swallowed. "Would you be d-disappointed if I told you to stop?"

"Yes." There was no hesitation, none at all.

"Would you…find it difficult to stop?"

"Yes. But I would." He shifted and she could feel him, hard and long, pressing against her thigh. "You don't have to be scared."

She spread her fingers out on his chest, pressing to feel how solid he was. "I'm not scared. I just…want to know that you want me as badly as I want you."

He said nothing, the look on his face unreadable. Then he bent and his mouth was on hers in a kiss that was very different from the ones he'd given her before. This one held hunger and demand and just a hint of desperation.

Oh yes. He wanted her. He wanted her very much.

Her heart caught and all her trepidation left her. She slid her hands up his magnificent chest to his shoulders and gripped him, kissing him back the way he was showing her, so he'd know that she wanted him that much too.

Then he shifted again, one hand reaching down between them, and she felt him press against her, press into her, sliding inside her. There was pain, but not a lot, and between one sharp breath and the next, it was gone. There was discomfort too, and for a second it felt like she couldn't breathe, as if there wasn't enough room for him and her as well. It made her pant for a second, but then that was gone too, and there was only him and the feeling of him settling deep inside her, unfamiliar and yet wonderful. A closeness with another person she'd never dreamed possible.

"Indigo." He said her name like a prayer, and even in the dark, she could see how his eyes gleamed with gold as he looked down at her. He was deep inside her now, yet he didn't move, leaning on his forearms positioned on either side of her head. Studying her as if he'd never seen anything as interesting as she was.

In the silence she could hear the sound of his breathing, and it was ragged. His muscles were tense. "Are you okay?"

She liked that he asked, but she didn't need him to be concerned. "Yes," she said hoarsely. "In fact, I don't think I've ever been more okay in my entire life."

He dipped his head then and kissed her once more, and then he began to move, a slow, gliding rhythm that made her break out into a sweat.

God, this was good. Even better than the touch of his fingers.

And this time some deep instinct told her exactly what to do. It felt natural to lift her hips, to move with him, creating pleasure together, building it and spreading it out, making it climb higher and higher.

There was something wonderful about this, something wordless and magical and deep. More than bodies joining, she knew that deep in her bones. As if her soul recognized his and welcomed it, making him a part of her.

Her arms wound around his neck, and she kissed him deeply and hungrily, feeling him respond in kind. Desperation crept in then, and he moved faster, taking control of the rhythm, and all she could do was follow his lead, clinging to him as the pleasure reached a fever pitch.

He murmured something hoarse and raw against her mouth, and then she felt his hand push between them, stroking her, and abruptly the whole world felt as if it was shattering, exploding into glittering sparks that fell everywhere around her like fireworks.

And all she could do was hold on to him as he groaned her name and joined her in the flames.

Chapter 11

LEVI COULDN'T REMEMBER THE LAST TIME HE'D been so stunned by an orgasm. Most of the time, they were a pleasurable blur for maybe five seconds before it was either time to say goodbye or begin the process all over again. He hardly ever lay there feeling like he'd been hit over the back of the head with a cricket bat, his brain empty, almost crushing the poor woman he was having sex with.

Speaking of, you should probably move.

Shit, he probably should.

His heartbeat was out of control, his breathing was fast, and the aftershocks were killing him. He could barely pull himself together enough to shift to give her some room, but he managed.

She was a...revelation. He didn't really know how to process that.

Sex was a pleasurable experience, a nice way to pass the time, let off some steam. It scratched an itch. It was not supposed to be...shattering.

It was not supposed to be life-changing.

Yet, somehow, it seemed as if sex with Indigo was both of those things, and he didn't know why.

You do. She's special.

God, no, that wasn't supposed to happen. She wasn't supposed to be special to him. Special as a friend, sure, but not…not anything else.

Her arms were wrapped around his neck, her breath warm against the side of his throat, and the feel of her body beneath his, soft and hot…

Bloody hell, he was getting hard again.

Touching her had been a delight, the sounds she'd made and the way she'd trembled making him feel like a god. Then sinking inside her, so slick and tight and like every goddamn fantasy…

But you weren't supposed to be doing this, remember?

He shut his eyes, took a breath, and made another attempt to pull himself together. No, he'd meant to be honest with her, tell her that he couldn't be around her anymore. Then he was going to walk away.

Except she'd been angry, had wrapped that damn shawl around him, and he…hadn't been able to do it. He didn't want to hurt her, yet he didn't want to keep his distance either, which had left him with only one option.

He shouldn't have kissed her, but he had. And he shouldn't have agreed to sex in the gallery, but he had.

And it had been fantastic. No, more than that. It had been life-altering, and worse, he now couldn't keep telling himself that good old familiar, comforting lie that it was only sex, no big deal.

This was a big deal.

It was a major fucking deal.

And he needed a minute to figure out where the hell they went from here.

He reached up to pull her arms from around his neck, but she held on.

"Don't go," she whispered. "Please, Levi. Don't."

As if he'd go now. As if leaving her was even possible. Because she wasn't some one-night stand who didn't care what he did. He couldn't give her a thank-you kiss, slip out of the bed, and walk away without a backward glance.

She was Indigo and she wasn't used to this, and while she might have said she didn't want more, he couldn't give her his usual one-night-stand behavior either.

She deserved more from him than that.

"Don't worry," he murmured. "I'm just going to deal with the condom. I'll be back in a sec."

"Okay." She sounded reluctant, but she let him go.

He eased himself away, pulling up his jeans and getting to his feet. Then he went out the back and into the little bathroom that led off the gallery.

There was a wastebasket in the corner, so he got rid of the condom before standing there a second, trying to get his heart rate under control. Then he moved over to the sink, and even though his hair was still damp and so were his jeans, he splashed some water onto his face anyway. The aftershocks of that orgasm were still pulsing through him, clouding his thinking, and he had to figure out what to do next with a clear head.

He knew what he should do, which was to take her back to the farmhouse, make sure she was okay, then head back to HQ for the night. Except...he didn't want to do that. What he wanted was to stay at the farmhouse, take her upstairs into her bedroom, and switch on all the lights so he could see her. Then he'd undress her carefully, stroke and caress and kiss every part of her, then feed that insatiable curiosity of hers by getting her to touch him. Teach her how he liked to be touched and where, though he hadn't been lying to her. Pretty much anywhere she touched him, he'd like.

Then perhaps he'd flip onto his back and hold her on top of him, get her to ride him. She'd like that and so would he. He'd love to watch as he made her lose her mind...

"Levi?"

Indigo's voice was soft and came from behind him.

He turned.

She was standing in the doorway, her hair in a wild tangle around her shoulders, the look on her face such a mixture of anxiety and hope that it tugged at his heart.

This is why all of it was such a bad idea...

Yeah, but he was in it now. He was the one with experience, the one who knew how these things went, and he'd made the decision to act on their attraction. He had to take responsibility, and that was something his foster mum Linda had taught him. How important it was to understand that every decision he made had consequences and he'd better be prepared for those consequences. Taking responsibility for them was the right thing to do.

So, he came over to where Indigo stood and reached for her, settling his hands on her hips and drawing her in close, making it very clear what his feelings were.

"I say we take a trip to the farmhouse." He looked down into her eyes. "And you can show me around."

Her forehead creased, her hands settling over his on her hips, as if she was keeping them there. "But you've seen the farmhouse."

"I haven't seen your bedroom though." He gave her a look from underneath his lashes, not hiding the hunger building steadily inside him. "And I'd particularly like to see that. Especially if you're giving a personal tour."

She blushed and he lifted a hand to push one dark curl behind her ear.

"Unless, of course," he went on, "you don't want that. In which case I'd be happy to drop you at the farmhouse, and I'll go back to—"

"No." She moved forward slightly, so she was pressed up against him, the blue of her eyes as deep and dark as he'd ever seen it. "I don't want you to go back to HQ. Will you stay with me? Will you stay the night?"

He wanted to, he badly wanted to, but that meant he shouldn't. So, he shook his head. "Probably best that I don't. Keep this on the down-low, okay?"

There was disappointment in her gaze, and he felt it settle inside him too, but he'd already screwed up badly here. There was no point in making things worse.

Yet all she said was, "Okay."

He bent and kissed her. "Come on then," he murmured. "I'm tired of imagining you naked. I want to actually see you naked."

Five minutes later, they were in his truck, and he was driving hell for leather back up the road that wound up the valley to the farmhouse.

She didn't speak and neither did he, the air between them too charged for words. And when he finally pulled up outside the farmhouse and the two of them got out, Indigo leading the way to the front door, all he could feel was glad.

Glad that he'd made the decision to kiss her.

Glad that he'd made love to her in the gallery.

Glad that he was her first. The first man to kiss her lovely mouth and stroke her silky skin. The first man to hear her cries of pleasure. The first man to know what it was like to be inside her, to feel her thighs wrap around him and bring him home. The first man to make her come.

The first man to show her how amazing her body was and how good it could make her feel if it was touched in the right way.

He wouldn't be her last, it was true, but at least he was her first, using his experience to show her that sex was something wonderful that she could have again with another man.

But that thought made him feel oddly violent, so he shoved it away.

When she opened the front door, he pushed her gently inside and kicked it shut. Then he swept her into his arms and carried her straight up the stairs to her bedroom.

It was small, tucked up under the eaves of the house, a big queen-sized bed covered in quilts and pillows and a knit blanket taking up most of the space. There was a dresser against one wall and everything on it was very neat. In fact, the whole room was neat.

Not that he was taking any notice when he had Indigo in his arms and he was about to finally get her naked.

He'd been desperate before in the darkness of the gallery, but that was nothing to the desperation he felt now at the thought of stripped her bare.

He set her on her feet and pulled the tie of her

skirt, allowing it to fall off her completely. She gave a little intake of breath but made no move to grab it, and it was just as well, because he was already tugging up her T-shirt, uncovering those perfect, rounded breasts, cupped in a demure lace bra.

He got rid of the T-shirt and the bra, so she stood only in her panties, and she gasped as he cupped her, his thumbs gently teasing her hardening nipples.

She'd gone pink, and he knew he should restrain himself, lock down the hunger he felt for her, but he couldn't seem to do it. He was so hungry, he could hardly stand it. He backed her over to the bed, then pushed her onto it so she was sitting on the edge. Then he went down on his knees in front of her, between her spread thighs. He pulled her hips to the edge of the mattress and bent his head, kissing his way down her chest and over the swell of her breasts, his tongue finding her nipples and licking, teasing. She groaned, and when he sucked one nipple into his mouth, she groaned again, arching her back, clearly loving what he was doing.

That sharpened his hunger, and he pushed her again so she was lying on her back on the mattress, and he tugged on her panties, pulling them off completely. Then he leaned over her, kissing her stomach, teasing the hollow of her navel with his tongue before moving down, parting her legs with his hands. She moaned his name, and her hands were in his hair as he put his head between her soft thighs. Using his hands to spread her open and then his tongue to explore. She was so hot and wet for him, and she tasted delicious. He couldn't get enough.

She made no move to stop him or to protest, writhing as he tasted her and teased her, giving her as much pleasure as she could handle.

If he was her first, he was going to be her first in *everything*.

And for once he was glad of his experience, that he could give this to her, make it good for her, make her gasp and cry out his name. Her fingers tightened in his hair, her hips lifting, but he held them down, holding her still so he could taste her deeper.

He drew it out as long as possible, until she was shaking like a leaf, whispering his name incoherently over and over again. And only then did he give her what she was begging for, loving how she convulsed in his hands as the climax took her.

She was still gasping, still trembling as he got rid of his jeans and found another condom—he always carried at least four for "just in case." And when he climbed onto the bed and made sure she was laid out beneath him, her eyes were almost black with desire.

He spread her thighs, positioning himself between them, then he looked down into her eyes as he slid slowly inside her, his whole body drawn tight with need.

She felt so good, so hot and wet and tight. Everything he'd fantasized about. Everything he wanted.

"Indigo," he murmured, purely for the pleasure of saying her name, of seeing her deep-blue gaze widen as he pushed into her and then gleam with heat.

She moaned, lifting her hips, her hands stroking his shoulders and back, her touch incendiary.

He began to move, slowly at first and then faster, because he couldn't hold himself back. The pleasure was indescribable. She left fire on his skin wherever she touched, and as much as he wanted to watch her face as he moved inside her, he couldn't stop from bending to take her mouth, because the feel of her lips on his was a pleasure he couldn't resist.

He tasted her deeply, fully, as he moved inside her, wanting her flavor and her heat all over him, the scent of her body, lavender and feminine musk, driving him out of his mind.

He said her name again, moving faster, harder, reaching down to pull her legs up and around his waist, so he could move deeper. She cried out, her nails digging into his shoulders, and he loved the feel of it. Loved how desperate she was for him, because he was desperate too.

She was nearing the edge though, her face deeply flushed, perspiration on her forehead and tears gathering in the corners of her eyes. He kissed the tears away, tasting salt, and then found her mouth again and kissed that too.

"Levi, oh my God…" Her voice was hoarse.

But it was okay because he was there. He'd make it better.

He moved faster, the bed shaking beneath them as he changed the angle of his thrusts, giving her more friction where she needed it most. Then he shifted his attention from her mouth to her breasts, teasing her nipple once more with his tongue and then sucking gently on it.

Her back arched, her head going back on the pillow, and he felt her convulse around him for a third time, her cry of ecstasy echoing in his ears. And then he was moving, fast and hard, losing every sense of where he was, losing himself as the pleasure came for him and finally, at last, making him see stars.

Chapter 12

A WEEK LATER, INDIGO STOOD IN BILL'S GENERAL store, waiting with Beth while Bill bustled around out the back, preparing to restock the cabinet where he displayed his pastries. Beth, of course, was angling for a sausage roll, while Indigo was hoping for a scone.

Izzy was already back in the gallery, happily eating an eclair Chase had managed to snag for her. Finn was out on a trek. Otherwise he would have gotten her a sausage roll, or so Beth said. It was very lowering having to get her own, apparently.

Indigo couldn't rely on anyone to get her a scone, which was why she had to wait in line like everyone else. Not that she was feeling particularly hungry, even for one of Bill's scones.

A combination of nervousness and trepidation sat in her gut, making her wonder if a scone really was the best idea. She was going into Queenstown with Levi today, and yes, she was on edge.

It had been a week since that magical, life-changing night. A week since she'd woken up the next morning feeling heavy and sated, with unfamiliar aches in all kinds of places. He'd been as good as his word and hadn't stayed the night, but he'd waited until after she'd fallen asleep, which she was grateful for.

She'd tried to tell herself she wasn't disappointed to wake up alone or, in the days following, that Levi treated her exactly the same as he always did. He was friendly, slightly teasing, and casual. As if he hadn't changed completely the axis on which her word turned and altered her life.

But she didn't want to think about that. Because admitting that sleeping with him had changed everything for her would be to admit that she'd been a silly, sheltered, naive virgin who hadn't realized what she'd been getting herself into until she was neck deep.

He'd told her what he could give her, which was a night. It wasn't his fault she'd thought she'd be okay with that.

After all, it isn't the first time you've let yourself get dazzled by someone.

That was different. That had been her father and he'd lied to her. But Levi had never lied. He'd been nothing but honest.

Isn't that worse in some ways?

No, how could it be? At least she knew where she stood with him.

So, she pushed away her disappointment and the inexplicable hurt, tried to go on as normal. But it was difficult. She wasn't used to pretending, and her body wouldn't do what it was told whenever he was around. She only had to get near him, and she'd start to salivate like Pavlov's dog.

Luckily no one else seemed to notice any change in her behavior, though Beth had asked her a couple of times why she'd been so quiet, and Izzy had sent one or two worried glances in her direction.

She'd told them both she was tired and maybe suffering from a bug. That was all. Nothing whatsoever to do with having her life completely changed after one night with Levi King.

"Hey, so you're going into Queenstown with Levi, right?" Beth leaned against the counter, shooting a wary look at Cait from the Rose, who was in line behind them and who also loved Bill's sausage rolls.

"Yes." Indigo swallowed and hoped she didn't look nervous.

It was the first time they'd be alone together since that night, and thinking about how on earth she could be normal around him was making her palms sweaty. He'd come into the gallery a couple of times to show her the plans he'd been working on, but Beth or Izzy had been there too and had been interested to see how they were coming along.

Beautifully, as it turned out. Though Indigo could hardly concentrate on the plans when Levi was standing close enough so she could feel the heat of his body, smell his delicious cinnamon scent.

It was a worry.

"Oh, good. Can you get me a few things?" Beth dug into the pocket of her jeans and pulled out a piece of paper. "Here's a shopping list. Oh, and how's that mosquito bite doing?"

Indigo stilled. "What mosquito bite?"

Beth's green gaze was very level. "That mark on your neck that was there last week. The one you said was a mosquito bite."

Oh, hell. It wasn't a mosquito bite. Levi had left a mark. That morning, she'd seen it in the mirror and had gotten a little thrill. It meant the night before had really happened, and she hadn't been imagining it.

She'd wrapped a scarf around her neck to hide it but Beth had seen it and so had Izzy. She'd muttered something about mosquitoes and the other two had seemed to accept that.

Clearly not.

"Oh, it's fine." She resisted the urge to run her fingers over the tiny fading bruise.

"Must have been a big mosquito," Beth said casually. "A man-sized mosquito, some might say."

Indigo opened her mouth to tell her it was no such thing, when Bill came bustling out from the back, carrying a couple of trays of his famous pastries.

They all waited decorously while he put the pastries in the cabinet, and then there was an undignified rush as everyone raced to get their favorite.

Beth was triumphant with her sausage roll and made sure everyone knew it as she paid for the delicacy while Bill placed it ceremonially in a paper bag.

Indigo was just about to grab a scone when Levi walked in.

Her appetite fled, nerves leaping around in her stomach.

Men that hot should be illegal. Not that he was wearing anything different from what he normally wore—jeans and the green Pure Adventure NZ tee that set off his eyes and his hair to perfection—it was just… She knew now what he looked like under his clothes. Hard. Muscular. Powerful. His skin was smooth and hot, and when he was inside her, his eyes glowed pure gold.

They were glowing pure gold now as his gaze came to hers and the rest of the world melted away, and there was only the two of them in the general store. The expression on his face flickered, the muscle in the side of his strong jaw flexing. She knew what that jaw felt like too, again hot and with the slight prickling of stubble. She'd felt it brush her mouth and her throat and her breast and her inner thighs…

"And of course, some sunscreen. And then could you go on the dark web and order me a couple of Gs of coke? I feel the baby could use a little pick-me-up."

Indigo tore her gaze from Levi's. "Coke? What?"

Beth sighed. "You're staring at that fool again. I wanted to make sure you were paying attention."

"Fool? What fool?" Levi approached, a charming smile plastered all over his handsome face. "I hope you don't mean me, Bethany Grant."

"Of course I mean you." She gave him a severe stare. "You look after my girl today. Hear me? No funny business in that helicopter."

Levi raised his hands. "Hey, the only business that will be happening in the helicopter is serious house business." His gaze settled on Indigo, and all the breath squeezed from her lungs. "Right, Indy?"

"Yes." Her voice sounded weird, not like her usual self at all.

Beth's eyes narrowed, but then Levi said, "I was here to get you a scone. Or did you get one already?"

Oh. Indigo's heart fluttered behind her ribs. He'd thought of her.

Girl, you are so gone.

"No, I didn't." Her cheeks felt like they were on fire, and suddenly she wanted to get out of the store in case people noticed them. "But I've decided I'm not hungry. Come on, let's go."

He frowned. "Are you sure you don't want one for the road? I can handle a few scone crumbs in the heli."

But she shook her head and walked

determinedly past him and out the door into the brilliant sunlight.

It was a beautiful day—one of the last perfect summer days according to Bill, who'd waxed lyrical about how great Central Otago was in late summer before he'd gone out the back for the pastries—the sun warm, the sky a deep, endless sapphire.

The mountains were white and jagged and lovely against the sky, making it the perfect day for a helicopter flight.

Indigo wished she didn't have to go, that she could go back up to the farmhouse and lose herself in the dye pots for a whole week, or maybe even forever. Anything so she didn't have to be around Levi and eventually have him tell her gently that he'd only promised her a night, remember? And also, "I told you so."

Yeah, she especially didn't want to have him tell her that.

Mystery, the mystery dog, was sitting right outside Bill's doorway and gave Indigo a happy doggy grin. To distract herself, she put out a hand, and the dog allowed her to pet his silky head.

"What are you waiting for, hmm?" she asked him. "I don't have any treats for you."

"No, but I do." Levi came out of the store behind her, and instantly Mystery got to his feet, trotting over and nosing first at the paper bag in Levi's hand and then at his pocket. "You can't have that, boy."

Levi lifted the paper bag out of reach. "But I do have something else for you." Except he didn't give the dog anything immediately, striding on toward HQ. "Come on, Indy, let's get going." Then he gave a sharp, piercing whistle, and the dog took off after him like a shot.

Indigo hurried after the pair of them, nerves still leaping around inside her. "Wow," she said. "How did you know he'd obey a whistle?"

"I didn't." Levi reached into his pocket for a treat, then held it down at his side. Mystery grabbed it and ate it as he trotted along beside Levi. "It's a whistle the old shepherd up the valley taught me for commanding dogs. Thought it might work with Mystery, especially if he used to be a farm dog. Looks like he was."

The subject of the dog was a safe one, so Indigo asked, "You still want to adopt him, don't you?"

He flashed her a grin. "Yeah, and I think he's into it. But obviously I'm not going to rush him. I'll wait until he's ready."

Perhaps the dog wasn't a safe topic after all, because all it made her think of was how he hadn't rushed her. He'd waited until she was ready. Until she trusted him and then…

It's not his fault that you want more. But then you always do, don't you?

She swallowed yet again, shoving that thought out of her head. "So," she said more briskly. "What's the plan? I'll look around for suppliers while you get council sign-off on the drawings?"

He'd suggested that she come with him and do a reconnaissance of any of the demolition yards so she could find recycled building materials. She had a few addresses already, and Levi said he'd drive her around to see them after he'd visited his friend at the city council.

She should have been excited that things were moving forward so fast. But she wasn't excited. She felt…unsure and disappointed and even a bit upset. Ugh.

"Yep, that's the deal." He veered off around the side of HQ in the direction of the hangar and open field where the helicopter was. "We could have lunch at one of the restaurants there too, if you like. I know a great place near the wharf." He shot her a glance from beneath his lashes. "Doesn't have scones but they do great sandwiches and the best chips, plus they have a fine selection of tea."

She should smile at him; she really should. He was being so nice to her. She should pretend that she was fine and that nothing was wrong, that her heart wasn't racing and she didn't want to reach for him. That she didn't want to touch him.

He warned you sex would change things and you didn't listen.

Yeah, but she couldn't regret her decision. All she could do was live with the consequences and hope that one day her attraction to him would fade and he'd become like any other man.

He'll never be like any other man. You've fallen for him, you idiot.

Indigo ignored that thought completely. "Sounds great," she said with forced brightness.

He shot her a slightly doubtful glance but said nothing.

Once the preflight checks were done and Indigo had climbed into the machine, they took off, soaring up and over the lake, heading for the mountains.

She'd been in his helicopter before, and while that first trip had terrified her since she hated heights, she'd gotten used to it. She'd even enjoyed the last couple of trips.

But everything was different now.

The interior of the helicopter was small, and it felt as if Levi took up every part of it. One powerful thigh was close to hers in the cockpit, and she could smell his familiar scent, feel the heat of his body so near. She was absolutely mesmerized by how he held the joystick in one long-fingered hand, flying the machine with a casual competence that was so sexy she could hardly stand it.

Her mouth was dry and her heart beat furiously, and all she could think about was how he'd touched her that night and the pleasure he'd given her. How close she'd felt to him. Closer than she'd ever thought it was possible to get with another person.

Just sex, she'd always thought. No big deal.

But it was a big deal. It was a major deal and now she didn't know what to do with herself.

She turned her head away and stared out the mountains passing beneath them, bright and capped with snow. She should say something, break the awkward, thick silence filling the cockpit, but she didn't know what to say.

"Are you okay?" Levi asked after a moment, his voice sounding even closer and more intimate than normal through her headphones. "You're very quiet."

"I'm fine." She kept her gaze on the mountains.

"Right. Just mesmerized by the beauty of the landscape?"

"Yes. Exactly."

Another awkward silence fell.

"Indy—" Levi began.

"It's okay," she said before he could go on in that horrible, gentle tone. "I'm fine. You don't need to say anything."

He glanced at her, the look in his hazel eyes unreadable. "Not even thank you?"

"Thank you? Thank you for what?"

He didn't look away. "For an amazing night."

Her throat closed and she had to force herself to keep looking at him, even though she didn't want to. "No problem," she said, hoping she sounded casual and breezy.

But he wasn't a stupid man, and his gaze was far too perceptive. "You're upset."

"No. I'm not."

"Yes, you are. Don't think I haven't noticed."

This time she didn't bother pretending, looking away and fixing her gaze pointedly on the mountains beneath them. "I don't want to talk about this right now."

He said nothing, which was a relief. And continued to say nothing for the rest of the twenty-minute flight to Queenstown, the silence broken only by his communications with a couple of other pilots checking their position before landing the helicopter in a private airfield not too far away from Queenstown airport.

After they'd landed, Levi drove Indigo and himself into Queenstown itself in the truck he kept in town for that very purpose.

Queenstown was a picturesque little town, situated on the shores of beautiful Lake Wakatipu and ringed around with jagged mountains. Indigo found it lovely but very touristy, all its shops geared toward mountain sports and adventure activities. It did possess a fabulous yarn store though, and she'd already made friends with the ladies who owned it and who were very enamored of Indigo's hand-dyed yarn. She'd dyed some skeins specifically for them, and the yarn had sold so well that they wanted more.

Levi dropped her off near the yarn store so she could take in the bag of yarn she'd dyed for them, then gave her a place to meet, since he was going to the council to get the sign-off on his drawings.

It was balm to Indigo's wounded soul to be in a yarn store and have people ooh and aah over her yarn, then chat about all things fiber related. By the time she'd finished and come out again, she was feeling a bit better.

She wandered around town, trying to find some of the things on Beth's list and doing a bit of window-shopping for herself, though she wasn't feeling up to it.

What she should be doing was taking advantage of some free Wi-Fi to do a few searches on building materials, since she couldn't do that in Brightwater, but she felt listless about doing that too.

It annoyed her. She didn't understand how one amazing night could turn her mood so completely, because it had been wonderful. She'd lost her virginity in the best way possible with the most wonderful man…

He is a wonderful man. That's why it's painful. You always put your trust in the wrong people…

But no, that wasn't true. It wasn't him she shouldn't have trusted; it was herself. She knew what she was like deep down. What she'd always been like, ever since her parents had walked out that door and never looked back.

Her feelings were powerful things, and she'd wanted so much the life her father had promised her. She'd wanted so much to be his little girl. He'd given her gifts and told her she was special and paid her attention in a way her mother never had.

But all she'd been to him was part of his seduction plan to get to her mother. He hadn't cared about her, not one single iota. And she'd always wondered what it was about her that he hadn't wanted. The only reason that made any sense was that she wanted too much, and he hadn't liked it.

Perhaps Levi didn't like it either.

Indigo could hardly bear the thought, so she walked down to the lakefront and tried to distract herself by looking at the scenery instead.

Then something vibrated in the pocket of her jeans, and it took her a moment to realize it was her phone. She hardly used it in Brightwater, since there was no cell-phone service. In fact, she barely used it period. There had been patchy service in Deep River, and none at all where she lived with her grandmother, so she wasn't used to having a phone.

She pulled it out and glanced down at a message from Levi telling her he was ready to pick her up.

She texted back an okay, then waited on the street he'd suggested.

Five minutes later, she was climbing into his truck.

"Weren't we going to have lunch or something?" she asked as he pulled away from the curb.

"Change of plans." He accelerated into the traffic, and soon they were driving along beside the lake. In the opposite direction from the airfield. "I thought we needed some privacy."

Every part of her tightened. "Privacy? For what?"

"For the discussion we need to have." His handsome face was unreadable as he turned the truck off the main road and onto another, narrower road that wound up into the hills behind the town.

"What discussion?" she asked, even though she suspected she knew already.

"You know what I'm talking about," he said, making her scowl. "And no," he went on before she could answer. "You can't just not talk about it."

A few minutes later, they were pulling up outside a clearly architecturally designed log-cabin-style house, perched high on the hill with views over Lake Wakatipu and to the jagged edges of the Remarkables mountain range beyond. The house was surrounded by tall pines and other alpine shrubs and had wide decks. It was large, expensive-looking, and obviously Levi's.

Indigo stared in surprise as they pulled up into the wide gravel driveway and Levi parked the truck. Then he got out and strode to the front door, with her following along behind him. He didn't get out a key, putting a finger to the keypad on the door instead and using his fingerprint to unlock it.

Then he held open the door for her, gesturing her courteously inside. "After you," he said.

She didn't miss the slight edge of command in his tone, and part of her bridled at it. She didn't want to have this discussion, and she certainly didn't want him ordering her around, but it seemed that she wasn't going to have a choice in the matter.

She went in and stopped.

The hallway stretched the length of the house and was bright and airy and open. On one side were doorways that led into a big living area with massive glass doors that opened out onto the wide decks outside, making the most of the incredible views over the mountains and the lake.

It was a big space with an open-plan kitchen down one end, then a dining table, and then couches arranged around a big stone fireplace. The walls were white, the floor warm wood, apart from the lounge area, which was covered in dark, thick carpet. There were other doorways down the hall that presumably led to bathrooms and bedrooms, but for the moment, Indigo was mesmerized by the views.

Levi gestured for her to go into the lounge area, so she wandered over to the big glass doors and stared out through them. There was a big gas barbecue standing on the deck and also a hot tub.

Beth had talked at rapturous length about the

outdoor bath at Finn's, and Indigo had privately thought it sounded wonderful. And now she could imagine sitting in Levi's hot tub at night on this amazing deck, sipping nice wine while looking at the brilliant stars above and the sharp mountains across the lake.

And him beside you, holding you.

No, God, she shouldn't be thinking things like that and constructing little fantasies in her head. She knew all about how that went, and she was an idiot to torture herself.

She tore her gaze from the hot tub as Levi came over and stood beside her.

He had his hands in the pockets of his jeans, and there was a certain tension in his broad shoulders and jaw.

"You were fast at the council," she said after a moment. "Was everything okay?"

"Yeah, got everything signed off, no problem. Helps that Liz, my contact, likes me. Makes everything go smoothly."

Oh, so his contact was a woman. No wonder it had all gone smoothly. All he'd have to do was bat those thick dark lashes and give her one of his warm, wicked smiles, and she'd be putty in his hands.

The cold flick of jealousy caught at Indigo, though she tried to ignore it. "Great," she said. "So, about this discussion—"

"It changed things, didn't it?" He turned to face

her, his usual, teasing levity gone from his face. "Having sex changed things."

Her cheeks got hot, and she very much wanted to deny it, pretend that everything was fine. But she knew already that he wouldn't believe her. She wasn't a good liar, and anyway, she hated lies.

She knew too, with a sinking sensation, that she couldn't avoid this conversation. He was determined to have it and she couldn't be a coward. She was going to have to handle herself.

So, she scraped together some courage and lifted her chin. "It's fine, Levi. You told me what you could give me, and I agreed. It's all good."

"But it's not good." He searched her face. "You've been tense with me all week."

She very badly wanted to put some distance between them because being in his vicinity was hard. But doing so would give away far too much, and she didn't want to do that. She didn't want to admit she'd made a mistake, that her feelings were a lot more complicated than she'd expected them to be, and that she didn't know what to do.

"It's all right," she said, trying to sound firm. "I can deal with it."

But his level gaze didn't miss a thing. "No, you can't."

Indigo turned away, suddenly finding it all too much, only for his fingers to wrap around her upper arm, holding her in place. She was only wearing a T-shirt, and the warmth of his touch stole her breath.

"Hey," he murmured. "What is it, hedgehog?"

She trembled helplessly at the warmth in his voice. How had it come to this? That she should feel so many things about a man who was so out of reach? That she should want more of his touch and his kisses, and lying in his arms—and not only that. She wanted more than just physical closeness; she wanted his company. She wanted more conversations about bears and wētās and silly things that made her laugh. She was lonely. She'd always been lonely. That's why she always put herself in his way, why she'd never been able to leave him alone. Because when she was with him, she never felt that loneliness.

That's why sleeping with him had been a mistake. Because he didn't want those things and he wasn't lonely the way she was, and he'd been upfront about all of it.

"Just let me deal with it," she said huskily, staring hard out the windows and not at him. It didn't matter, her loneliness. She'd been dealing with it on her own for years after all, and she'd keep on doing it. And there were Beth and Izzy now. She wasn't alone in the same way she had been back in Deep River.

It's not enough though. None of it is.

Her throat closed, but she forced the thought away.

There was a moment of silence, then his fingers

tightened and she was pulled relentlessly back until the heat of his body was right up against her spine.

"No." His breath was warm against the side of her neck. "Tell me what's wrong. Was it the sex? Did it upset you? Did I hurt you?"

She didn't want to admit anything, yet she couldn't bear for him to think that he'd hurt her. That wasn't fair to him when she was the problem.

"You didn't." She held herself rigid to stop from melting against him. "And the sex didn't upset me. It was…amazing."

"So, what's up?"

Indigo shut her eyes. Telling him the truth was the last thing on earth she wanted to do, but she couldn't lie. After a night like that, he deserved her honesty.

"What's up is that you were right," she forced out. "Sex did change things and I didn't realize how much, but it did. And I…want more, Levi." She swallowed. "I'm sorry, but I do. So, feel free to tell me, 'I told you so.' I deserve it."

Chapter 13

INDIGO WAS TREMBLING. LEVI COULD FEEL THE faint vibration of it beneath his fingers where they curled around her upper arm, and her distress made his heart squeeze tight in his chest.

He didn't feel good that he'd been right about sex changing things. It didn't make him feel smug. It only hurt. Yet at the same time, a very male part of him was savagely glad.

Because she wasn't the only one who was suffering. He was too. He'd found the whole week a bloody nightmare, and the only way he'd gotten through it was a long experience of pretending everything was fine and liberal fantasies at night where his right hand was his best friend.

Working on her drawings, making them the best they could be, had been one of his only outlets, as had taking as many tours as he could handle at Pure Adventure NZ. If the other two had noticed his sudden workaholic tendencies, they hadn't mentioned it. They were pretty busy with their own crap, so they were probably glad he was willing to take on a few extra shifts.

But none of it had helped. He would have been

fine if Indigo had seemed happy with the way things had gone, but she hadn't seemed happy. She'd been quiet, not grumpy or prickly the way she normally was, and what smiles she'd given him had been forced.

He hadn't needed to bring her to Queenstown with him. They weren't yet at the stage of looking for materials, but he'd thought it would be a good opportunity to find out what the problem was and see if he could fix it.

He needed to know if she regretted what they'd done, and he really had to know if he'd hurt her somehow. It hadn't seemed so at the time, but you never knew. He could be thoughtless sometimes.

"I would never tell you that," he said, not liking the self-blame he could hear in her voice. "You didn't know you'd feel differently."

"You warned me though. It wasn't as if I wasn't told."

He could still feel that fine vibration running through her. He was standing too close, and he knew he should let her go, yet he didn't.

She smelled good, her dark silky hair was loose down her back, and she was wearing a sky-blue T-shirt the same color as her eyes and worn blue jeans. He liked her in those pretty dresses and skirts she sometimes wore, but he liked her in jeans too. He liked her in everything, and he particularly liked her in nothing at all.

He shouldn't prolong this. He should tell her that he'd given her all he could and there wasn't anything more.

But she was hurting, and he hated that he was the cause. He had to give her something.

"Maybe I should have told myself too," he said quietly. "Because you're not the only one who found this week hell."

She was still a second. Then she turned around, her eyes going wide as they met his. And he let her see the heat that went through him in response to her nearness, let her see the hunger that gripped him and had been nagging at him all this week.

Then he let go of her arm, slid his hand along her delicate jaw and into her hair. And he bent and kissed her because in that moment he simply couldn't do anything else.

She responded as if all she'd been doing had been waiting for the moment he kissed her. Her arms came up, winding around his neck as she went up on her toes, kissing him back as if she was starving, her mouth hot and eager.

All rational thought vanished from his head.

The couch was right there so he walked her back and pushed her onto it, following her down. There were a frantic few seconds as she clawed at his clothing, while he tried to pull hers off at the same time. He might have found it amusing and teased her about it if he'd had any amusement in him, but he didn't.

He was only desperate, and the one saving grace was that she was desperate too.

It seemed to take forever to get her naked, and then there was the hurried fumble for contraception. But his wallet saved him. He protected them both with shaking hands and then finally, he was pushing her back on the cushions, and she was hot and silky and hungry beneath him.

He reached down, sliding his fingers between her thighs to find her wet and ready, so he didn't hesitate, pushing in and sliding deep, making them both gasp as the pleasure of it swamped them.

Her eyes were so dark and so blue, he couldn't look away.

"Put your legs around my waist," he murmured. "Hold me."

She shuddered, then obeyed him, wrapping her lovely thighs around him, letting him push deeper, and he could feel the flexing of her inner muscles gripping him tight.

"God, you feel so good." He brushed his mouth over hers. "I don't think I want to stop."

"Then don't," she whispered back and pressed her lips to his, silencing him.

Then there was only the slick feel of her body and the pleasure that rose relentlessly inside him as he began to move, the exquisite friction making them both groan.

He'd never been so desperate that his hands were

shaking. Never been so overwhelmed by desire that he'd cast every good intention he had to the winds. He might tell himself all he liked that he couldn't resist temptation, but the fact was, when he lost it, it was by choice.

And he was choosing her.

He didn't think of the consequences. All that mattered was that he was inside her and she was holding him.

It didn't take long.

A couple of hard thrusts and he was at the limit, and he could tell by the way she trembled that she was too. So, he grabbed her hand and guided it between them, holding her fingers down on her own slippery flesh as he moved, until she cried out in pleasure, her body convulsing.

Then he was following her, thrusting hard and deep until the orgasm exploded in his head like a bomb.

Afterward he lay there like he had that first night, both of them stunned and panting, shaking with the aftershocks.

When he'd gotten himself together, he shifted, propping himself up on one elbow so he could look down into her flushed face. Her eyes were still dark, a shadowed azure that he found stunningly beautiful.

"You okay?" he asked, far too late. "And just so you know, no, I didn't plan on taking you like an animal on my couch."

Her cheeks were red, a pink flush extending all the way down her throat and over her pretty breasts. "Yes, very okay." A crease appeared between her dark winged brows. "Were you? I kind of…threw myself at you."

"Oh no, I absolutely hate having a beautiful woman throw herself at me, then force me to ravage her on the couch."

She hit him on the arm. "I was being serious."

A curious warmth burst through him, fizzing in his blood like champagne.

This was a bad move, buddy. Not a good one.

Except he didn't want to think about that. He'd crossed a line, he knew, and he'd dragged her with him, and now that they'd crossed it, there wasn't any crossing back.

Now they were here in his house alone, no town to watch them and no one to make any judgments. And he had the whole afternoon with her…

He couldn't push her away. He didn't want to. He'd tried very hard over the years not to want anything for himself too much because he knew how life insisted on kicking you in the face. He kept his desires easy—a cold beer after a hard day's work, a good steak, sex when he could manage it. Nothing difficult and always mostly physical.

But this wasn't only physical and there was nothing about it that was easy, and yet he wanted her. He wanted her more than he'd wanted anything for years, and he'd come to the end of his resistance.

He wanted this, he wanted her, and to hell with everything else.

"Okay," he said. "I'll be serious. If I didn't want this, I wouldn't have kissed you. And I kissed you because I couldn't stand *not* kissing you."

"Oh." But the crease between her brows didn't disappear. "I don't know where this leaves us."

"How about we leave that question for later?" He pushed a curl off her forehead. "Right now, there's just you and me and a whole afternoon to fill, and as it happens, I have a few ideas of how we could fill it."

Her hand came to rest on his chest. "Oh?"

He smiled. "Shall I show you?"

Indigo's mouth turned up, the crease between her brows finally disappearing. "Yes," she said. "Please do."

So, he did, indulging his personal fantasy of having her on top, so he could stroke her and watch her fall apart as she rode him. Then he let her touch him, indulging her curiosity and showing her what he particularly liked and how to do it.

A couple of hours later, both of them sated for the moment, they went into his kitchen to see what there was to eat. Not much since he didn't cook and didn't use the house so there wasn't anything in the fridge.

Indigo sat at the kitchen counter, perched on a barstool wearing his T-shirt and nothing else. It suited her and it made him feel unreasonably satisfied to see her wearing something of his. He wasn't a possessive guy, but there was something about her that turned him into a complete Neanderthal.

"I was going to teach you how to cook," she said as he peered into the fridge.

"That's true. You were." He closed the door and straightened. "Well, you could teach me now. Except we'll have to do a supermarket run since there's no food in the house."

She wrinkled her nose. "That means I'll have to get dressed though."

"Which is a crime against nature." He went over to the counter she was sitting at and leaned across it on his elbows so they were nose to nose. "I think it should be illegal for you to wear clothes. Only nakedness for Indigo."

"As long as you have to be naked too." She gave him a look from beneath her lashes. "I could use a nice view."

He grinned. She was adorable when she flirted with him. "Well now, I have no problems with that. But the food situation is kind of serious. Or we could go to one of the places on the waterfront."

"No, I think I can manage a supermarket run. And then I can show you how to cook." She paused. "Do you really not know?"

"No." He lifted a shoulder. "I had no opportunity to learn. I mean, I can do bacon and eggs, but that's about it."

"But what do you eat?"

"Bacon and eggs. Takeout. Sometimes a ready-made meal from the freezer section. And whatever it is that you want to teach me to cook."

But there was a serious look in her eyes now. "Did you have anyone, Levi? When you were growing up. Did you have anyone at all?"

He wasn't sure why she wanted to talk about this now, because he didn't. Yet…she'd told him about her isolated, lonely upbringing, so it didn't seem fair not tell her about his.

"No," he said. "Well, not entirely. I had one foster mum who was good to me. Linda. She made sure I went to school, did my homework, brushed my teeth, all those kinds of things."

"Was she the only one?"

"Yeah, pretty much. All the rest…weren't great. But I liked her a lot."

"Did you get to stay with her?"

He let out a breath and pushed himself up from the counter, needing some distance, because she saw too much, and Linda was a sore spot. "No. I didn't."

She must have sensed it, because she said suddenly, "We don't have to talk about this if you don't want to."

"It's okay. It was years ago." And it had been. He

didn't know why the thought of Linda still made him ache. "I'd been living with her for about six months when her father had a stroke. She was his only kid, and he didn't have anyone else, so she had to look after him. But she couldn't take me as well."

Indigo's blue eyes had suddenly gone soft and dark. "Oh no."

"Yeah. She told me that I'd have to go back into the system. She wasn't a demonstrative woman. She had all these rules, but they were because she cared." He paused a second. "Some rules are there to control you, but some rules are there to keep you safe and to teach you things, and that's what Linda's were. I was pretty angry she couldn't keep me, but it wasn't her fault."

He'd been so mad at the time, only fifteen and not thinking about the fact that perhaps her father was more important than some foster kid. He'd shouted at her, been a total dick about it, which had not reflected well on him. Hell, maybe in the end she'd been glad to get rid of him.

They were always glad to get rid of you.

He shoved that thought away.

"Oh, Levi." The concern in Indigo's gaze caught on a raw place inside him, making it sting.

He forced a smile, because smiling was easier, and if you smiled, it meant you were over it. "It's okay. Like I said, it was years ago, and now I've got Chase and Finn and a home in Brightwater. It's all good."

Is it though? You don't have a house you actually live in, and you're not really brothers with Chase and Finn, no matter how often you tell yourself you are. You had to force everyone there to accept you, and even now you don't feel as if you belong. How is that home?

No, that was ridiculous. Of course, he belonged. Yes, he'd had to work to earn his place there, but you had to work to earn your place anywhere. That was life, wasn't it?

Levi smiled. "Let's go get this food then."

———————

Indigo couldn't stop thinking about what Levi had told her as they did the supermarket run, bought some food to cook, and then went back to Levi's house again. That there had been only one person in his awful-sounding childhood who'd cared about him, and he'd lost her. The way she'd lost her grandmother.

She didn't like to think about that. About her grandmother's stroke and slow decline. Her refusal to go to a doctor or even leave the house. She hadn't liked Indigo leaving the house either. She'd get angry and talk about the "danger" of the "outside world" and how one day Indigo would walk out of the house and never come back. The way Indigo's mother had walked out and never come back.

Tilly Jameson had never gotten over her daughter's abandonment of her and Indigo, and neither had Indigo.

But at least the person who'd cared about Indigo had been there for most of her life. Poor Levi had lost the only person who'd cared about him, and he'd only had that for six months.

It didn't seem fair.

She couldn't get it out of her head even as she taught him how to make an omelet. He teased her as she did so, flirted with her, delivered inappropriate kisses, even more inappropriate caresses, and generally made a pest of himself.

She loved it. She told him off, scowled, slapped his hand with a spatula, and she loved it.

Then he showed her that for all his teasing, being a pest, and not paying attention, he'd been listening to her instructions, because he flipped the omelet like a pro, which apparently made him a "tin arse." *Beginner's luck* in Kiwi, as he explained.

They sat to eat at the dining table while Levi told her funny army stories that involved Chase, and then a few more stories about his guiding experiences. Indigo liked hearing them, but they were about other people, and she was hungry for more stories about him.

"Something's been puzzling me," she said after he'd finished his latest guiding anecdote. "Why didn't you build anything for yourself on that site?"

He was sitting opposite, having already finished his omelet, and was now casting a few glances at hers. "What site? Oh, you mean behind the gallery?"

"Yes. Jim would have let you build a house on it if you'd wanted to, you know."

Levi glanced down at the beer he held in one long-fingered hand. He was in jeans and a T-shirt, which she thought was a pity since he was so beautiful naked. Then again, as she'd told him sternly after he tried to take his clothes off so she had "something to look at," cooking while naked could be a health hazard.

"I thought about it," he said after a moment. "But the time didn't seem right. Finn's wife, Sheri, passed away not long after I arrived, and then we were putting money into Pure Adventure. It didn't seem like a good time to build."

Indigo waved a hand at the room around them. "But you bought this place."

He shrugged one powerful shoulder. "Yeah, well, I wanted a base in Queenstown, and it was a good investment property."

Investment property...interesting that he should call it that and not home. Then again, as lovely as it was, it didn't feel like a home. There was nothing personal in the house that Indigo could see. No photos or knickknacks or cheerful clutter. There was a sterility to it, like a hotel room or a house that had been home-staged with nice but bland furniture.

"You don't use it very often, do you?"

"Not very." He lifted his beer and took a sip. "I use it to crash in or when I'm doing some work that needs the internet. Most of the time I rent it out on Airbnb like everyone else in this town." He grinned. "It can be very lucrative."

Clearly it was.

"So where did you get your money?" It was kind of a personal question, and she'd probably overstepped the mark. But she was so curious. He was such a man of contrasts. Easygoing and flirtatious, yet he could also be very intense and serious. She'd wondered before whether he had substance beneath his slick surface, and he really did. Solid substance in the form of his care for the town and its inhabitants. For Chase and Finn. He was a man of deep passions—she could see that—yet he kept those passions well hidden.

Rather like you, don't you think?

Yes, they were similar in that.

"Why do you want to know?" His eyes glinted. "Digging for some gold, hmmm?"

He was teasing and she suspected he did that when a subject bothered him. He deflected with his beautiful smile and his wit, turning the focus away from himself.

She pushed her plate across the table in his

direction and leaned her elbows on the tabletop. "Maybe. I'm kicking myself now I didn't let you pay for everything with the house."

He glanced down at the plate. "Is that for me?"

"Yes. Come on, rich boy, tell me."

He grinned, put down his beer, and pulled the plate toward him. "It's no mystery. A couple of mates of mine had gotten in with a bad crowd, and I was heading down the same path. Then a social worker told me in no uncertain terms that I could do better than that, and had I considered the army? I hadn't. But then she told me I could live in a barracks and get food regularly, so that decided me and I enlisted."

She folded her arms on the table and leaned her chin on them, watching him. "Did you like it?"

"Oh, I loved it. It gave me structure and discipline, which I hadn't had before, plus lots of dangerous activities."

She smiled. "Wow, Levi, heaven."

"Hedgehog, you've got no idea. Anyway, I finished my education there too. Got a business degree after figuring out I had a gift for numbers. I played around on the stock market a bit, made some money, made some good investments." The memories were obviously good ones for him, judging by the reminiscent smile on his face. "Though it wasn't the money that was important," he went on. "That was just a happy by-product. It was the risk that I liked, and I took a lot of risks."

Her heart tightened at the look of delight on his face. He was so hot when he talked about the things that made him happy, that gave him joy.

You want to make him happy like that. You want to give him joy.

She tried not to pay any attention to the thought. "How surprising you like risks," she said dryly instead. "You're such an adrenaline junkie."

He lifted an eyebrow. "Ever had sex in a helicopter?"

"No, of course not."

He grinned. "Neither have I. Want to try it?"

She gave him a stern look. "Levi."

"Okay, okay." He forked up another mouthful of omelet and chewed thoughtfully. "So yeah, I made quite a bit of money and I didn't spend any of it. I stashed some of it away in some high-interest-earning accounts and played with the rest. Had a shitload when I got out of the army eventually, so when I got to Brightwater, I had enough to buy Jim's land. I offered to lend him the money to repair the Rose, but he wasn't having it. He didn't want me to go shares with him either. He'd only let me buy the land with those caveats on it, which was fine by me." After finishing up the rest of the omelet, he pushed the plate to one side. "I also have a charity I manage, and a lot of my money goes there. It's for helping homeless teenagers."

Somehow the fact that he managed a charity didn't come as a surprise to her. It was just the kind of thing a man who cared very deeply would do.

"Oh," she said faintly. "You keep that all very secret. Just like you didn't tell us you owned the gallery building."

"I didn't want to make it a big deal. And I didn't want to make the gallery thing into a big deal either."

"It kind of is though," she said. "Lots of people with money wouldn't do that."

"Yeah, well…" He glanced away. "It's important to give back. To help people."

"It is." She couldn't tear her gaze from his handsome profile. "You're a hero, you know that?"

Some expression she couldn't name flickered over his face and he glanced back at her, pinning her in place with his hazel gaze. "I'm not, hedgehog. I'm just a guy who wants to help people. That's it. I'm no different to anyone else."

But…he *was* different. At least, he was different to her. And while it was true that she didn't have a wide experience with people, she felt deep in her heart that he was one of the good ones. One of the ones she could trust.

She wanted to tell him that, but there was a curious tension hanging heavy in the air between them, and she didn't want to push.

She wasn't sure what this morning in his house was, but she didn't want to upset the little bubble of warmth and sensuality and closeness they'd created between them. She wanted to stay in it, to keep it for as long as she could.

So, all she said was, "Okay, just a guy. Would you like coffee?"

Later that afternoon, he drove her around some of the demolition yards because she still needed her house to be built and had to find some materials to build it with. And indeed, she found a few great things. A wonderful window frame and an old door. Some beautiful boards in a honey-gold wood that Levi told her was kauri. He suggested using them in the little kitchen, which she thought was a wonderful idea, and then he unearthed some amazing wooden shutters, which she adored and wanted to get there and then.

She haggled with the yard owner, much to Levi's amusement, driving a hard bargain and managing to knock off a hundred bucks at least. Triumphant, she insisted they stop and get a bottle of champagne to celebrate, which Levi duly did, spending far too much money on a bottle of some expensive French brand.

Then they went back to his house, and she helped him unload the shutters so he could store them in his garage for the time being.

It was early evening by then, which meant it was time to start heading back to Brightwater, and that put a dampener on things for Indigo.

She didn't want to go. She wanted to stay here with Levi, talking and laughing with him. Teaching him to cook and having him tease her. Having him steal kisses that morphed into more, that led to hot and desperate on the couch, or slow and even hotter on the floor.

He must have sensed her sudden mood change, because after he'd locked up the garage, he came across the gravel to her and pulled her into his arms. "You know," he murmured, bending to brush his mouth over hers. "I just got word that the weather over the ranges is turning crappy. Might be a problem for our trip home."

She leaned against him, her heart beating very fast. "Might be or will be?"

"That depends. I'm okay with flying in crap weather, though it's not ideal." The look in his eyes smoldered. "If you wanted to be on the safe side though, it might be better to stay the night here since the weather is looking to improve in the morning."

The tightness in her chest eased, leaving behind warmth and a delicious ache. "Oh," she said breathlessly. "I think I want to be on the safe side."

"Good. I was hoping you'd say that." He bent and kissed her again. "Because I have evil plans that involve you naked in my hot tub and some French champagne."

Oh, she liked the sound of that. She liked it very much.

Indigo spread her hands out on his chest. "Are you sure? We didn't bring anything with us…"

"I'm sure." He nuzzled beneath her ear, his breath warm on her skin. "And I have everything I need right here."

You're a goner for him. You know that, don't you?

The voice whispered in her head, but she didn't want to think about that. About what it would mean or whether this was a bad idea, or what would happen when morning came and they had to go back to Brightwater. She didn't want to think how much it would hurt to let him go.

She just wanted to have the here and now, thank you very much.

"Me too," she murmured, then rose on her toes and kissed him back.

It was the most perfect night.

Since he'd never had anyone cook for him, she decided she wanted to. It wasn't anything fancy— only good steak, potatoes, and some salad—and she made him sit down at the counter with a beer while she bustled around in the kitchen. They had one of their silly conversations that ended up with him relating some long story about why all wētās were named Wally. It made her laugh, which then involved him kissing her, so they got a little sidetracked.

The meal was good though, and afterward she got to sit with him in the hot tub, sipping French champagne as they watched the sun go down and the stars come out. The view was spectacular, but then that got a little sidetracked too because he kept insisting on stroking her underneath the water.

After the hot tub, they made it to the bedroom, where after a couple of long sensual hours, she fell asleep in his arms.

But she was disappointed when she woke the next morning to find the sun streaming through the windows and the other side of the bed empty.

She pulled a face at the brilliant weather, her chest feeling as if some heavy weight was sitting on it, though she tried to ignore it. Because of course they had to get home. They couldn't stay in Queenstown forever, no matter how much she might want to.

Indigo dragged herself out of bed, wishing Levi was there so they could have a couple more minutes to themselves, but clearly he had other plans since he wasn't here.

She pulled on her clothes from the day before, and as she was hunting around for her jeans, saw a bag sitting on the floor at the end of the bed. The bedroom was only minimally furnished, and she hadn't noticed the bag the night before. Levi certainly hadn't bought it with him.

Curious, she bent and unzipped it. Inside were some clothes and a couple of pairs of shoes, and a toilet bag. Everything neatly packed as if in preparation for a holiday, though there were price tags on some of the clothing. All of it was brand new and unworn.

Puzzled, she left the bag where it was and came out into the kitchen.

Levi was already there, making breakfast. He looked freshly showered, his dark hair damp. "Omelets." He gestured to the pan he had on the stove. "See? Oh, and also, there's a pot of Earl Grey for you." He smiled, but the smile didn't quite reach his eyes.

Her throat closed, the weight on her chest getting heavier. Was he disappointed about leaving too?

"Thanks," she murmured, coming to sit at the counter. "Why have you got a bag of clothes in the bedroom? Are you going somewhere?"

His hesitation was so brief that she wouldn't have caught it if she hadn't been looking right at him. "Oh, that? It's a bag I keep in case I need to take off anywhere at short notice." He flipped the omelet with what she felt was unfair expertise, given the amount of time he'd actually been cooking omelets. "It's an army thing."

An army thing… She didn't know why, but she thought he might be lying. She didn't have the heart to push it though. "So, when are we leaving?" she asked instead.

"How does half an hour sound?" He picked up a plate, slid the omelet onto it, and turned, coming over to the counter where she sat and putting it down in front of her. His gaze met hers, but she already knew what he was going to say.

"That's good," she said before he could. "And I know. Once we get back to Brightwater, we'll go back to being just friends, right?"

"Yeah." He didn't smile, which she was grateful for.

Her heart clenched painfully, but she ignored that too. "I know. You said you could only do a couple of nights. It's okay."

"Is it?" His eyes were more green now than gold and shadowed.

She should smile and pretend that everything was fine to make sure things weren't awkward between them, to show him that she wasn't a silly virgin, falling for the first man who took her virginity.

Except she couldn't do that. He'd see through her immediately. And besides, while he might not want it, he deserved her honesty. After all, he had asked.

"No," she said. "It's not okay. But I understand."

"Indigo," he murmured. "I—"

"I know. You told me. It was my decision to stay here with you. I could have refused, and I didn't."

A muscle flicked in his hard jaw. "It's not you. You know that, don't you?"

Isn't it though? You weren't enough for your parents. Why would you be enough for him?

The thought whispered in her head, turning

tightness in her heart painful. "Please don't give me the 'It's not you, it's me' speech."

He looked like he might say something to that, but then he glanced away and gave a nod. "Yeah, okay." He pushed himself away from the counter. "It's all good."

But they both knew it wasn't.

Chapter 14

Chase and Finn asked a couple of pertinent questions when Levi and Indigo arrived back after their night in Queenstown, but Levi wasn't in the mood to answer them. He lied to their faces about how he'd booked himself a night in a hotel so Indigo could have the house to herself, which they seemed to believe.

Or at least they didn't ask him any more questions about it. Which was good because he didn't want to talk about it.

He didn't want to talk about Indigo teaching him how to cook an omelet, a crease between her brows as she watched him nearly burn it. Indigo, her blue eyes darkening with sympathy as he'd told her about Linda. Indigo, naked and wet and slippery, leaning back in his arms as they watched the sunset together in his hot tub, her damp hair across his chest. Indigo, murmuring his name as he made love to her. Indigo, laughing at something he said…

Indigo, and the disappointment he'd seen in her eyes when she'd realized their night together was a one-off.

No, he didn't want to talk about any of that.

He didn't even want to think about it. What he wanted was for everything to go back to normal and for the ache he felt in his chest every time he thought of her to be nothing at all.

He threw himself into preparations for building her house instead, since tours were starting to drop off as the summer waned and the weather got colder and rainier.

His drawings got the sign-off, as did the permits he needed, and then there was preparation for the site to do. Clearing bush and digging and then laying the foundations. It was a lot of work and much of it physical, and he relished it.

Unfortunately, building Indigo's house meant he had to see a lot of Indigo, and as much as he wanted to spare her too much contact, he couldn't. He had to ask her opinion on a whole lot of things, especially when it came to materials, since she was the one who'd wanted to use recycled stuff.

She didn't avoid him, though every time he went to see her, he could see by the way her eyes darkened that it was difficult for her. And he could understand, because he was finding it difficult too. Unexpectedly so. He'd thought the ache and the strange longing that crept through him at night would lessen. That she wouldn't be the first thing he thought of every morning and the last thing before he fell asleep.

But it didn't lessen and he didn't know why. He

didn't know why she should be so different from every other woman he'd been with, and it didn't seem to matter how many times he tried to put her in that box, because she wouldn't stay.

Beneath those little prickles of hers lay a warm, sweet, passionate woman. Generous and giving and so painfully honest.

Indigo Jameson was special and every part of him knew it.

A couple of weeks after their Queenstown trip, Levi went into the Rose to talk to Jim. A town barbecue was coming up, which they held on the last day of summer every year, but the weather was looking crap for the day and he wanted to see what Jim thought about having the barbecue in the pub instead.

But when Levi stepped inside, Jim wasn't where he usually was, which was behind the bar. Frowning, Levi gave a cursory look around, but couldn't see him, so he went back out into hallway.

Voices drifted from the direction of the library, mostly female. Izzy's distinctive Texan drawl and then Beth's hard Rs. Shirley was saying something slightly disapproving and then laughter…

He could hear Indigo's bubbly laugh quite distinctly, and it made him go hot all over.

It was her knitting circle, which he hadn't joined since that first day, and which he kept not joining even though her teaching him to knit had been one of things she'd insisted on in payment for the house.

He almost took a step down the hallway to where she was, drawn helplessly to her by the sound of her laughter, but then stopped himself.

He couldn't do that to her, not when he knew what would happen then. He wouldn't be able to drag himself away, because that's what always happened when he was in her presence. Their chemistry went deeper than merely physical, and he couldn't resist it. He didn't want to resist it.

You were supposed to be protecting her, and now you're not. Now, you're making things worse for her. Now you're hurting her.

His muscles tightened and his jaw ached as the truth settled down into him. He'd thought it would be better this way, that she'd soon forget him and move on, but she hadn't. And neither had he. And it was making their lives a misery.

It's not about protecting her, you bloody idiot. You're protecting yourself. So, you don't have to think about all the shit you pretend you're fine with but aren't.

That "shit" being the fact he'd never built anything on the land he'd bought from Jim. Never bought a house here, not anything permanent.

The fact that he had a bag at the foot of the bed in his house in Queenstown, just as he had a similar bag stashed away in HQ. A ready bag in case he needed to go.

It was a habit he'd gotten into as a kid, whenever he was hauled out of a place, sometimes unexpectedly and sometimes with speed, which meant he left things behind. Sometimes he'd be dropped at a new home and there wouldn't be anything ready for him. It took time, for example, to even get a toothbrush. So, he'd taken to packing away a few things in a bag that he could grab and know he had everything he needed wherever he might land.

Remnants of a past he tried not to think about. A past that had taught him he didn't belong, not anywhere, and that at any moment the things he wanted, the things that were important to him, might be ripped away. So, it was better not to have things that were important. Better not to put down roots, not to get too attached, in case…

Indigo laughed again, the sound liquid sunshine falling all over him.

He'd made her laugh like that in Queenstown and it had been magic, so why was he making her eyes darken with hurt now? Why was he now insisting on a distance neither of them wanted, when it was himself he was protecting, not her?

Mate, you're afraid. That's the problem.

Yeah, he was. Afraid to get attached, afraid that it might all turn to crap, because mostly everything had.

But he wasn't that abandoned foster kid any longer. Hell, he was a goddamn daredevil. He was supposed to not to know the meaning of fear. So why was he afraid of this feeling inside him? The one that wanted to be close to Indigo all the time, everywhere?

Oh, there was the town to consider and what they'd think of him if he and Indigo got together, but seriously, did he care about that? He loved this place and the people mattered, but he couldn't tell himself that their opinion mattered more than hurting Indigo, because it didn't.

A new certainty filled him, and he took a step down the hallway, ready to storm into that room and tell everyone to go away, so he could talk to her and tell her his thoughts right now.

But no. He wasn't going to approach this the way he normally did, with pure adrenaline rushes, without a thought or a plan. Indigo was special and he needed to act accordingly. Which meant he needed to think about how he was going to approach it.

Chase would help. Chase would have some ideas.

He strode out of the Rose and went down the steps, heading toward HQ, and was almost there when he realized a black shape was trotting along beside him. He stopped and Mystery stopped too, looking up at him questioningly.

How can you have a dog when you don't even have a home?

It was true. Even if Mystery decided he wanted

Levi to be his person, Levi didn't have anywhere to keep him. He didn't have a home here, only HQ, and he didn't think Chase or Finn would be impressed if the dog stayed there. And he couldn't take him to his house in Queenstown, because he wasn't there often enough.

He hadn't thought that through. He'd wanted Mystery because the dog was a stray and he knew what that felt like, but he'd had no plan about what to do with him once he'd adopted him.

He'd just thought… Actually, he hadn't thought. And well, shit. That ended now. Here.

Maybe he'd get himself a damn house, and not just for investment purposes. Maybe he'd get himself a house here in Brightwater, and he'd live in it. And Mystery could be his dog, and they'd both have a home.

And maybe he'd invite Indigo to visit, and he'd go into his own kitchen and cook her the most perfect omelet she'd ever seen. Get her a pot of her fancy Earl Grey tea. And they'd sit as *his* dining table in *his* house, and they'd talk, and then he'd take her up to *his* bedroom and make love to her in *his* bed.

Yeah, that's right. It was time to admit that there were things he wanted for himself. And it was time to go out and get them.

"I'm sorry, boy," he said firmly. "I haven't got anything for you today. But I will soon, I promise."

Mystery cocked his head, dark eyes quizzical.

"I'd love to take you with me, but there are no dogs allowed in HQ." Levi pointed at the Rose. "Go see Jim. He'll give you a sausage if you play your cards right."

Jim wouldn't, but that was beside the point.

Mystery ignored this, and when Levi continued on to HQ, the idiot dog followed. Levi sighed, but couldn't face scaring him away, and when he stepped into HQ, the dog did too.

Chase was behind the counter, looking at the laptop on top of it, probably going over schedules. He glanced up as Levi came in, then frowned. "No dogs in HQ," he said flatly.

Levi lifted his hands. "Nothing to do with me. He followed me home."

"Bullshit. You've been feeding him treats for months now."

Yeah, he had. He'd lured poor Mystery into thinking he could have a home with Levi, when Levi had nothing of the sort to give. Just like he'd been stringing poor Indigo along too.

No. That ended now. Today.

He turned and looked down at the dog. "Outside," he ordered. "Go on."

Mystery looked at him and then Chase, then obviously deciding discretion was the better part of valor, slunk out the door.

Levi shut it behind him.

"Good thing you're here," Chase said before Levi could speak. "I need to talk to you."

"What about?"

Chase's gunmetal gray eyes met his. "I think you know. You've always been a pain in the ass, but it's gotten worse these past couple of weeks. Ever since... Oh yeah, that's right." His gaze turned sharp. "Ever since you got back from Queenstown."

Levi opened his mouth to speak, but Chase, in Chase fashion, went on without waiting. "And my point, before you ask, is you're being a dick and I'm tired of it. I don't know what your problem is, but you've fallen for Indigo Jameson like a ton of bricks, and she's got it bad for you." He pushed the laptop closed with a snap.

"Hey, I know—"

"And what really pisses me off," Chase went on over the top of him, "is that your current behavior is hurting her, which in turn hurts Izzy, and I'm not having a bar of that. You like her, you want her, which means you need to lock her down hard and stop this pissing-around, brooding bullshit."

"But I—"

"You're a man in your prime. You've got a good job, shitloads of money, and you own property. You've got all your own teeth. What the hell is your problem?"

"I've been—"

"If this is about your shitty past, I get it. We've all

got baggage. But you don't have to let that get in the way of being happy."

"I'm just—"

"And another thing—"

"Chase, for Christ's sake!" Levi finally broke in, exasperated. "Can you shut the hell up for one bloody second?"

Chase, predictably, scowled. But he shut the hell up.

"I know," Levi went on. "I know I've been a dick. I've been a dick to everyone else, but most important of all, I've been a dick to Indigo. And that's not right."

"Damn straight it's not."

"Yeah, which is why I'm going to do something about it." He met his friend's sharp gaze head-on. "I want to try a relationship. I want to see if I can be with her. Not just a night or two here and there, but seeing her every day and being with her every night."

Surprise flickered over Chase's face. "Shit, you've really fallen for her, haven't you? Bloody hell, I knew it."

Levi didn't look away or deny it, not this time. Because yeah, he had fallen for her. Certainly, none of his one-night stands had ever given him the same burst of realization, where he suddenly wanted to change the way he'd been living his whole life just because of them.

But then none of them had been Indigo.

"She's special," Levi said. "And yeah, I have."

Abruptly, a grin spread over Chase's hard features. He folded his arms and leaned on the counter. "So, what are we talking about here? Marriage? Do we need to get a ring?"

Levi shook his head. "Uh no. Let's not get carried away. Like I said, I want to try…you know…a relationship."

"So, what does that look like?"

"Well…" Levi blew out a breath. "That's why I'm here. I want to talk to you about it. Because I've never had anything long-term before. I mean, one or two nights is the longest I'm talking about."

"Oh, believe me, I'm well aware," Chase said dryly.

"Anyway, so that's where I'm at." He lifted a hand and shoved it through his hair, feeling weirdly uncertain and off-balance. "Mate, I don't know… anything about this relationship stuff. I don't even know where to start."

Chase eyed him for some moments. Then he said, "I would imagine talking to her is where you start."

"I will. I just wanted to get some idea of how to approach this." He began to pace in front of the counter, feeling restless and antsy, his brain throwing a million and one ideas at him. "Like, I don't want to begin with having no thought at all.

I want to show her that I've thought about it, that I'm serious."

Chase watched him. "Right."

"I mean, how do you start off? Do you have a date? Go out and dinner and things? Talk about life?" He reached one side of the room, turned, and paced back. "And then do you just keep doing dinners? And buying flowers and nice things? I can do that, I definitely can. But then do you make plans? Go on holiday? And if you want to see her every day, do you just sit around and talk? Or can you have sex first and then talk?"

"Levi."

"And what do you talk about? Look, we were in Queenstown for a night, and yeah, there was no bad weather over the ranges; I lied about that so no one would know we had the night together." He reached the other end of the room, turned once again, paced back. "So, do I keep doing that? I can't keep bringing her to Queenstown. That's not going to work. But I don't have a house here, which means I need to fix that situation."

"Levi."

"What about Kev's old place?" Levi, oblivious, stopped, suddenly struck by the most perfect idea. "You know, that piece of land near Evan's. There's nothing on it at the moment, but I could build something really cool. Big, yeah, it's got to be big. With a hot tub, because Indy loves a hot tub. And

Mystery could come and live there with me. There's space for him and some chickens if Indy wants. We could even get a horse. Would she like a horse?"

"Levi."

Levi blinked, aware suddenly that this was the third time Chase had said his name. "What?"

His friend was giving him a steady look from underneath his dark brows. "Mate, you're not reinventing the wheel here. You're good with women, come on."

With a supreme effort of will, Levi got his frantically spinning brain under control and shoved the issue of horses and land to the back of his mind.

"I'm good at flirting and sex," he said. "And that's not a relationship. I know that much at least."

"Sure, but you're a good guy and Indigo's into you. You'll figure it out as you go along."

But Levi shook his head, his newfound determination solidifying into certainty. "This is the problem. I've been figuring it out as I've gone along so far, and it hasn't worked. And I don't want to keep doing it that way. Indigo deserves better." He took a breath. "It's not just an affair. It's important. *She's* important."

"I get that. Believe me, I do. But all the relationship stuff happens with the both of you, together. You can't just decide how things are going to go on your own." He gave Levi a wry look. "Or so I've been told."

Clearly, he was talking about his relationship with Izzy, which now that Levi thought about it, was exactly the kind of relationship he was hoping to have with Indigo. Same with Finn and Beth.

Both his friends had been through some tough times, yet they'd come out the other side and with two wonderful women who made them both incredibly happy.

He didn't know if that was something he and Indigo could have; they'd both had rough pasts after all, but why not? Why couldn't they be happy too?

Levi shoved his hands in his pockets and fixed Chase with a determined stare. "That's what I want. What you and Izzy have. What Beth and Finn have. Perhaps without the kid aspect though."

Then again, why not have kids? Having a family of his own had never crossed his mind before because he'd been too busy sorting his life out to think about including anyone else in it, but…there was no reason he couldn't have a family.

A family of your own. At last.

The thought and the deep, powerful emotion that came along with it, swept his breath away like a king tide, and he had to glance down at his feet so Chase wouldn't notice.

Yeah, maybe not the family part just yet. Baby steps.

"Okay," Chase said slowly. "It's not easy though. Just warning you. You got to work at it."

"Sure." Levi glanced at him. "But when have I ever been afraid of a little hard work?"

Chase grinned. "Never, mate. Maybe there's hope for you yet." He pushed himself away from the counter and straightened. "So, when are you going to talk to Indigo?"

Levi thought.

Right now, she was doing her knitting thing and he didn't want to interrupt. Plus, despite what Chase had told him, he wanted to get a plan together, think about what he really wanted so he could be clear when he talked to her, and that might take some time.

There was the town barbecue tomorrow evening, the last barbecue of the summer, and everyone liked to make a big deal of it. The whole town would turn out, and there would be a grill on the grassy bank above the lake's foreshore. Cait would bring out sausages and steak, and breads and salads, and Jim would provide and serve beer. There would be deck chairs happening. The Granges might bring a couple of bottles of their latest vintage. There would be talk about the summer just gone and how eventful it was, and about the winter to come and the plans—if any—people had made for it.

It would also be a celebration for the three women who'd come halfway across the world to inject new life into Brightwater Valley with their gallery, and they had. Three months initially had been the plan, and that three months was up. And all of them were staying, having built new lives here.

The weather wasn't looking great, but you never could tell. It was, however, the perfect time to talk to Indigo, ask her what she wanted, and whether that new life might include him.

"Think I might do it tomorrow night," he said. "At the barbecue."

"Right, the celebration." Chase nodded approvingly. "Good timing."

Levi grinned, feeling smug. "I thought so."

"Food." Chase pointed a finger at him. "Make sure you feed her something she likes; that'll get her in a receptive mood."

"Will do, chief."

"Excellent. Now that's sorted out, when are you available to take another climb? The last one you took was a terrific success, and some of their friends want one too."

Levi wasn't thinking about another climb. He was too busy thinking about Indigo instead. "Sure, sure. Whenever."

―――――

The last town barbecue of summer was in full swing. The weather had turned out to be unexpectedly beautiful despite the forecast, and everyone in Brightwater had come down to the lake to catch up, have a sausage and a beer, and maybe complain a bit about the number of tourists there had been over summer or what was really needed was a decent bit of rain. But mainly they were all here to congratulate the Deep River contingent on a job well done. Brightwater Dreams had proved to be a hit, and while everyone wasn't exactly enamored of the tourists, they were all very pleased the three newcomers had decided to stay.

But Indigo didn't feel much like celebrating.

Beth and Izzy had been very careful with her for the past week, treating her like she was a fragile glass sculpture that needed delicate handling, and while she appreciated their care, it didn't help her mood.

It had been weeks since her and Levi's night in Queenstown, and while she'd accepted that they wouldn't be revisiting it, she felt wretched about it.

She'd only seen him when it was time to discuss the house and they only talked about that. He still gave her smiles, but they were distant, and he never talked to her alone. He only ever talked to her in the gallery, or the Rose, or where there were other people.

She knew why. He was very firmly putting their night together into the "been there, done that" basket and probably thought he was doing the right thing by giving her space to get over it. Certainly, he showed no signs of finding the distance he'd put between them difficult.

Except, no matter how hard she tried, she couldn't get over it. For a night he'd given her a connection, a deeper connection than she'd ever had with another person, and now she missed him. She missed that connection with him. And that wasn't even taking into consideration the way her body burned for his touch. He was like a drug she'd been given a taste of, and all she could think about was having more.

But she couldn't. He'd been clear about what he could and couldn't give her, had set out his boundaries, and she couldn't cross them. She couldn't ask for more than he was willing to give. Because if he said no…

It would be your parents all over again.

She'd been so sure she wouldn't let herself get in that position again, where her happiness was dependent on other people. But somehow that's exactly what had happened. She was such an idiot.

She'd debated briefly telling Beth and Izzy about Levi and what had happened between them in Queenstown, but she didn't want to involve them in her own drama. They'd each been through their own version of this, and hers wasn't any different or special. She could deal with it on her own.

Beth, standing at her elbow, was currently in deep discussion with Teddy Grange and Cait about kids. Cait didn't have children, but she had a niece and a nephew in Christchurch and used to look after them when they were small, and from the hair-raising story she was in the middle of, Indigo thought they both sounded like little horrors.

Teddy had a daughter and was laughing at Cait's story and then adding her own about the terrible twos, much to Beth's obvious disquiet.

Not far from where they stood, in another little knot of people, Teddy's now adult daughter was laughing and tossing her pretty blond hair with a tall man who was also laughing.

The sunset had found the brilliant threads of gold in the man's dark hair and had scattered the rest of him in gold dust, making him look like a god come down from Olympus to grace the poor mortals with his presence.

Levi.

Certainly, Teddy Grange's daughter, Iris, thought her mortal existence had been graced by his presence. She was madly flirting with him, and he was flirting back, Indigo could tell. He had that charming smile on his face and his attention was focused explicitly on her, as if she was the only woman in the world.

Indigo couldn't blame Iris for being thoroughly charmed; when Levi King looked at you that way, the rest of the world didn't exist.

He's moved on already.

She dragged her gaze away from the pair of them. Yep, certainly seemed like he had, and that should be fine. She shouldn't be jealous. He wasn't her boyfriend. They weren't together in any way. And Teddy's poor daughter didn't know she was flirting with a complete man whore who broke women's hearts at the drop of a hat.

What did you expect? That he'd change his mind just for you?

No, of course she didn't expect that. No one ever had before, after all.

Indigo angrily turned away from the crowd. There was a little path that led down to the lake beach, and no one seemed to be paying any attention to her, so she took the opportunity to slip away to the beach.

Slipping her sandals off, she walked slowly down the gravelly foreshore and came to a stop at the water, letting it flood over her bare toes.

The lake was fed by snowmelt from the mountains and underground streams, and even in high summer it was freezing. Tourists who didn't know any better and the hardier of the locals did swim in the lake, but Indigo had never done so. Chase, probably trying to be informative, had told her about all the eels that lived in it, and on a different occasion, Finn had told her about the taniwha, a Māori sea monster who was reputed to live at the bottom. She'd lost the taste for swimming after that. Not so much because of the taniwha, but because she didn't like the thought of eels nibbling on her.

She shivered slightly as tiny waves lapped around her bare feet. Her toes were by now small ice cubes, but she didn't move.

It was evening, the last of the long twilight lying over the valley, painting everything in brilliant pinks, oranges, and crimsons. The colors were amazing, and she'd already planned a fabulous series of colorways around the sunsets here. Izzy and Beth had been hugely excited, Izzy especially since she loved all kinds of pinks.

Yeah, it was good all three of them were going to stay here. Izzy and Beth had landed on their feet despite their past difficulties and were in the process of building new lives and new families.

Indigo had no plans to return to the States herself, and she too was building a new life for herself, yet…it didn't feel like as much of a triumph as it should have.

She'd gotten away from Deep River. She'd grabbed her courage in both hands and had crossed the world to come and start up her own business, to live among strangers, and no matter how afraid she'd been when she'd first gotten here, she had emerged from her fear victorious.

The community had welcomed her despite her quirks and anxieties and had taken her under their wing, and she would always be eternally grateful for that.

But…she was still lonely, and now, having had

a taste of what it was like to have someone of her own, she felt even lonelier.

She wanted someone special to belong to, and someone special to belong to her.

But when have you ever been special to anyone? Special and not a burden that was dumped on them?

Her eyes prickled, but she hated such self-pitying thoughts so she ignored them, turning away from the mountains and resuming her paddle along the beach, concentrating on the icy water around her toes and not the persistent ache in her heart.

"Indigo," someone called from behind her.

No, not just "someone." A man. Deep voice, warm as melted honey…

Levi.

Her entire being gathered tight.

She was very tempted to keep on walking, but she didn't like what that would reveal to him, plus whatever it was that he wanted, it might be something to do with the house. So, she plastered on the fake smile she'd been wearing for weeks now and stopped, turning to face him.

He stood not far away from her, his hands thrust in the pockets of his jeans, a curiously intent look on his handsome face. The late evening sunlight made his hair and skin gleam and caught the gold in his eyes… He was so beautiful. He made her heart stop.

"Oh, hey," she said far too huskily. "Something up?"

He didn't say anything, his gaze roaming over her as if hungry for the sight of her. Which couldn't be right since she hadn't been anywhere. She'd been right here in Brightwater, where she'd been for the past three months, and they'd been in contact with each other. So, there shouldn't be any reason for him to be looking at her the way he was right now.

"Yeah, something's up." He paused, his gaze pinning her where she stood. "I want to talk to you."

Something shivered deep inside her, and it wasn't to do with the cold.

"Oh?" She tried to sound casual, as if she wasn't at all dying inside. "About the house?"

"No, not about the house."

"Then what?"

He didn't reply immediately. His gaze traveled down her figure slowly, but not in a flirtatious way, more as if he was…assessing her. She was wearing her favorite blue dress, the loose, tiered cotton one, though quite honestly it was getting a bit light to wear without a jacket, because she was now cold.

"Your dress is wet." He frowned. "And your toes have gone blue."

Indigo looked down, and indeed, the hem of her dress had gotten wet from her paddle in the lake. The water was so clear that she could see her toes, and yes, they were a little blue. She couldn't feel them anymore.

Levi made a tutting sound. "Honestly, hedgehog.

What are were you thinking?" And before she could protest, he'd closed the distance between them and had picked her up and out of the water, gathering her into his arms. "You're freezing," he muttered. "What are you doing wandering around here without a jacket on?"

"Hey," she said indignantly, going rigid. "What are you doing? Put me down."

He looked down at her and raised one dark brow. "You really want me to?"

Yes, she did. She didn't want to be close to him, didn't want his warmth seeping into her and his delicious scent making her heartache worse.

Yet…he was so warm, and she was so cold and so lonely, and a hungry part of her just wanted his nearness however she could get it.

"I'm Alaskan," she said stiffly, ignoring his question. "I don't feel the cold."

He gave her the oddest smile, all warm and almost…tender. "Sure, sure." Turning, he carried her over to the gravelly, pebbly beach and up onto the grassy bank, putting her down in one of the last patches of sunlight. Then he sat next to her and, much to her surprise, quickly pulled off his sweatshirt.

"Lift your arms," he ordered.

"I don't need your—"

"You're cold, hedgehog. Come on, don't be an idiot."

Her arms lifted without her conscious control, and then he was quickly dressing her in the soft black cotton that was the Pure Adventure NZ sweatshirt.

It was far too big for her, the arms completely covering her hands and the hem reaching almost to her knees. But Levi rolled up the sleeves for her, then before she could protest further, put his arms around her, settling her against his warm, powerful body.

Indigo caught her breath. Half of her desperately wanted to pull away, while the other half of her desperately wanted to stay put. To lean in to him, turn her face into his neck, and inhale him. There was danger in his warmth, in the strength of his arms and the hard feel of his body, in his scent. Everything about him was dangerous and she shouldn't be sitting here with him.

"Relax," he murmured. "I've been thinking about a few things. About us. About that night in Queenstown. Specifically, I've been thinking about what a complete dick I've been to you the past few weeks and how that has to change."

She tensed, her heart missing a beat.

"Hey, didn't I tell you to relax?" His voice was so full of warmth and affection that her eyes prickled.

Oh God, was she *that* far gone that a gentle tease could make her cry?

Her throat closed and she had to swallow hard to even make her voice work. "Levi," she said hoarsely. "What are you doing?"

He tucked her more firmly against him.

"Warming you up. Oh yes, and I also need to get your thoughts on whether you'd like to have a relationship with me."

"A relationship," she echoed blankly, too shocked to fully process what he was saying.

"Yep. As in you and me officially together."

She was cold—she could feel it now and she began to shiver—but Levi didn't move, continuing to hold her, and soon the shivers went away and she was just warm. Except her throat ached and her heart was raw, and she felt like an addict being given another dose of her favorite drug.

"I don't…understand," she said. "I thought one night was all—"

"I know what I said," he interrupted gently. "And I was wrong."

Indigo swallowed and turned her head to look up at him to find him gazing back. His hazel eyes were very clear, flecks of gold sparkling in all that green.

"My life is…complicated," he went on. "I've had a crappy past and I've got baggage from that, not going to lie. Literal baggage as it turns out. But… you're special, hedgehog. These past couple of weeks I've been the biggest asshole in the world, and it's because I can't stop thinking about you. I can't stop thinking about that night we had and I-I've decided I want more. I want a relationship. I mean, if you want that too."

Indigo could feel her heart racing, as if it wanted

to beat its way out of her chest and throw itself into his hands. Which was utterly and completely ridiculous.

A relationship. With her.

"Why?" she burst out, part of her furious, part of her ecstatic. "You said we could only have one night. You were very clear about it. And now you've changed your mind? I don't get it."

He sighed and glanced away, looking as uncertain as she'd ever seen him. "Look...I don't blame you for being angry. You've got every right to be. I was trying to put you behind me, but you just won't stay there, and it's driving me bloody crazy." He glanced back, a fierce light glittering in his eyes. "I hurt you and I hate that I did, especially when it's my baggage getting in the way. I want to stop letting my past make my decisions for me, and I want to try to work something out with you." His arm around her waist tightened, the look in his eyes becoming even fiercer. "Indy, I want what Chase and Finn have. I want a home and a family, and I want that with you. And I know we're not at that stage yet, but full disclosure. That's the direction I want to head. I want to build a home here and have a proper life here, and kids one day and—"

"Whoa, stop," Indigo interrupted, shaky and off-balance. "That's zero to a hundred in, like, five seconds, and I need a minute."

He nodded, but the fierce expression in his eyes

didn't fade and he didn't look away. He wasn't lying about any of this, it was clear. It was all genuine.

Is this really a good idea? After the past couple of weeks?

Maybe it wasn't. Maybe she was crazy for even thinking about it. But what did she have to lose? She'd been lonely and miserable without him, and even though she'd been trying to forget him for the past couple of weeks, it hadn't worked. Which meant there was only one solution.

"Are you sure about this?" she asked carefully. "I mean, you looked like you were having a great time with Teddy's daughter."

"Teddy's daughter..." Levi frowned. "Oh. You thought I was into her?"

"No, of course I didn't—"

"Hedgehog." The gold in his eyes glittered. "Were you jealous?"

Indigo tried not to bristle, since bristling would only give away the fact that yes, she was jealous. Very, *very* jealous and she didn't like it. Didn't like it at all. "I only want to you to be sure," she insisted.

Levi reached out and took her chin between his fingers, holding her in a firm grip, absolutely no hesitation at all in his gaze. "I'm sure," he said with such quiet certainty that Indigo's heart leapt. "I'm very sure. And while Teddy's daughter is a nice enough woman, I bet she doesn't have pajamas with hedgehogs on them, or dye-stained fingertips, or eyes like a summer sky."

Indigo's breath caught. Such little things and yet he'd noticed them about her. And remembered. "I should wear gloves," she said thickly, because obviously her brain had disengaged. "But I get too impatient sometimes."

Levi smiled and it felt as if summer had come to all the cold and lonely places in her heart. Warming them all the way through. "Is that a 'Yes, I'd love to be your girlfriend,' hedgehog?"

Chapter 15

INDIGO'S STUBBORN LITTLE CHIN WAS WARM beneath his fingers and her eyes were wide. There was mistrust in them and flickers of anger, and she had a right to them. He couldn't deny that. He also knew he had no one to blame for it but himself.

He'd make it up to her though. He'd take away that mistrust, calm her anger. He'd treat her like the queen she damn well was, and he'd never hurt her again.

"I don't know," she said, her voice gone husky.

He searched her pretty face, his chest tight, uncertainty twisting inside him. He'd screwed up these past two weeks, and all the determination in the world to make it up to her wouldn't be worth a damn if she wasn't into it.

He should have talked to her earlier, should have drawn her aside the moment he'd seen her and Izzy and Beth arrive at the barbecue, but Chase had roped him into getting the grill set up, and then Jim had needed help with the beer. Then Teddy's daughter had cornered him, and he hadn't wanted to be rude. He'd watched Indigo take herself off from everyone, walking alone by the lake, looking like a piece of the sky that had somehow escaped and fallen to earth in her pretty blue dress.

She had seemed so small against the backdrop of the lake and the mountains, and more, very alone. And he was more conscious than he ever had been that she had no one. Izzy and Beth were great friends; he knew that. But Beth was talking animatedly with Teddy, and Izzy was laughing about something with Gus, and Indigo...

She was apart somehow. He'd sensed it before, but it hadn't fully sunk in, just how separate she was. She kept a piece of herself locked away, that she kept secret, that she didn't want anyone to know about. A piece that she guarded jealously.

A piece she'd shown to him that night in Queenstown, laughing and teasing him, looking at him with concern and compassion. Smiling up at him, running her hands through his hair...

He wanted that secret part of her. He wanted her to give it to him. So as soon as he could politely get away from Teddy's daughter, he had. And had gone after his little hedgehog.

Except even though she was now in his arms, warm and soft against him, he could see her defenses were up and her prickles were out. Guarding that little piece of her soul.

He couldn't demand she hand it to him yet, and he would never take it. If he wanted it, he was going to have to work hard to gain her trust so she would give it to him willingly.

Well, he was nothing if not determined.

"What can I do?" he asked. "What can I do to get a yes?"

Emotions chased themselves across her face, gone so fast he couldn't tell what they were. But then her gaze dropped to his mouth. "Well," she murmured, "I suppose you could start with a kiss."

A surge of relief swept through him along with a heat that he already knew was going to become desperate very soon. So, he didn't hesitate, lowering his head and brushing his mouth over hers very lightly.

She gave a little shiver. "Hmmm. Perhaps again, just to be sure."

So, he gripped her chin tighter and held her there as he kissed her again, this time with a more pressure. Then he gently traced the outline of her bottom lip with his tongue before giving her a nip and then a lick, and then her mouth was opening for him and letting him inside.

He deepened the kiss, the relief inside him becoming more intense, as if he'd been away on a long journey and finally he was home.

She tasted sweet, like lemonade, and when her hands lifted and cupped his face, something in his soul echoed. Her fingers slid into his hair and gripped him tight, and she began to kiss him back with all of that shy hunger that had delighted him so very much right from the first. Except it wasn't so shy now. She knew what she wanted, and it was clear she wanted him.

"Is that a yes?" he murmured against the softness of her mouth. "I need a yes, hedgehog." Because he was at the edge of his control already and if she changed her mind, he was going to be in some pain.

The sounds of the barbecue drifted on the air, and because there were a few trees that came down to the water's edge, they were hidden from view of the townspeople.

A good thing. He didn't want anyone to see them just yet. Not when he wasn't sure how this was going to go.

Indigo pulled away slightly. Her eyes had darkened, and her cheeks were flushed. She was so beautiful he ached.

"Yes," she said, her sweet voice husky. "It's a yes."

Instantly he leaned down to kiss her again, because he couldn't stand not touching her a second longer, but then she put a hand on his chest, keeping him at bay.

He stilled. "There's a *but*, isn't there?"

"No, no *buts*." A crease appeared between her brows. "I only want to know what being your girlfriend means. Is this like…a one-night thing? Or a week, or what?"

"It's not a one-night thing." He kept his gaze on hers so she could see the determination in his gaze. "Or a week. Or even two. It's a 'for as long as we both want it' thing."

She gave a cautious nod. "That sounds good. But I don't want you to do that hot and cold thing, Levi. I don't want you to spend the night with me and then the next morning put me at a distance, telling me you're protecting me or some other crap that doesn't make any sense."

You really did hurt her.

His heart squeezed inside his chest. "I get it, believe me. But I'm in, hedgehog. I'm all in, okay?"

The serious look in her eyes flickered and then faded. "Okay." Her rosebud mouth curved in one of her shy smiles that felt like a gift every time she gave them. "I want you too. And maybe...I was a bit jealous."

These were gifts as well, these small confessions of hers. He could tell by the slightly hesitant way she said them, as if she wasn't sure whether to reveal them or not.

She shouldn't. You're going to break her heart. The way you always do.

No, he wasn't. He would never do anything to hurt her again.

He grinned. "Is it wrong that I like you being jealous?"

Her hand firmed on his chest, and she gave him a

little push. "Maybe I should go and flirt with Evan. Give you a taste of your own medicine."

Levi imagined her trying to flirt with the stoic, reclusive painter and failed. "Are you sure? Because even I would have difficulty flirting with Evan."

Her fingers curled into the fabric of his T-shirt suddenly, and he found himself being pulled closer, her sweet mouth brushing his. "You underestimate me at your peril, Levi King," she murmured.

"Apparently," he breathed. "Your kiss could tempt the pope. You want to go back to the farmhouse? Because I sure as hell do."

She was gazing at his mouth, the look in her eyes slightly dazed. "Oh yes, I think so. But…what about everyone else? Do we tell people?"

"Yes," he said without hesitation. "Yes, we're going to tell everyone in the whole damn town, because I want everyone to know you're mine. The real question is, do we let them know now or later?"

Indigo pursed her lips, obviously thinking about it. "Later. I want to have you all to myself tonight."

Oh yeah, he was *all* about that.

"Okay. If we leave together, people might talk. Or you could get Beth or Izzy to give you a ride back to the farmhouse?"

She wrinkled her nose. "I want you to take me back. I'll tell people I have a headache. Yes, they'll talk but that's okay. Tomorrow they'll know."

He was rapidly finding it difficult to think about

anything but getting her back to the farmhouse as quickly as possible so he could get her naked as quickly as possible.

"Okay," he muttered, taking her hand. "Let's get out of here then."

They didn't walk back down the beach. Instead, Levi led her up the bank above the lakefront and through some scrubby bush to the road beyond. His truck was parked out the front of HQ, which could be seen from the barbecue area, and he debated simply getting in and driving off, but he didn't want anyone to worry about her. So, he got her into the truck, then went to find either Finn or Chase to let them know she had a "headache" and he was taking her home.

Chase was in the middle of a crowd of people, chatting up a storm, so Levi cast around for Finn, eventually finding him standing with Evan near the drinks table.

He caught Finn's eye and jerked his head. Instantly, Finn muttered something to Evan and came over to where Levi was standing.

"What's up?" he asked.

Levi gave him a direct look. "I'm taking Indigo home. She has a headache."

Finn raised a brow. "So…does she actually have a headache?"

"No, of course not, you idiot." Perhaps the "idiot" was out of line, but hey, he was impatient. "We're going back to the farmhouse to have sex."

Finn blinked at him a moment, then frowned. "Do I need to remind you that—?"

"We're going to try being together," Levi said. "I'm surprised Chase hasn't told you yet, since he tried to give me the same lecture yesterday, and that's what I told him. Anyway, Indy and I will sort it out ourselves. She didn't want anyone to know right now. And I'm only telling you because I don't want anyone to worry when they can't find her."

Finn's mouth relaxed slightly. "Okay, mate. I hear you. If she's good with that, then go forth with my blessing."

"Not that I need it."

"Not that you need it." His hard features lightened. "You want me to give Chase the heads-up?"

"Yeah, do it." Levi paused. "I know I gave you the hard word about Beth, but—"

"You were right. So, keep that in mind when it comes to Indigo. But hey, if you need some advice, you know where to come."

There was no judgment in Finn's eyes, no doubt about Levi's intentions, and his offer of advice was serious and totally genuine. Levi's first instinct was to make a joke out of it, but he resisted, because there was nothing trivial or funny about this. It *was* serious.

"Thank you," he said, and he meant it. "I don't know if I can do it, but I want to try."

"I get it," Finn said. "All you can do is give it your best effort."

This time Levi did grin. "It's almost like you were in the army."

Finn shook his head, his mouth turning up in a smile. "Go on. Indigo's probably impatient."

Levi didn't need to be told twice and went.

———

Indigo sighed and rolled over.

Or at least she tried to. There appeared to be a heavy, muscular arm circling her waist, and when she moved, the arm tightened, drawing her in close to the hard and very hot male body at her back.

She tensed initially because the sensation of having someone else in her bed was unfamiliar. But then memories of the night before came flooding back and the tension melted away, her heart inflating with happiness and pressing painfully against her ribs.

It felt dangerous, that happiness, though she wasn't sure why. Levi had told her he wanted to try a relationship and she'd said yes, because that's what she wanted too, so what was dangerous about it?

Sure, he'd been blowing hot and cold these past couple of weeks, but he'd been genuine the day before. She'd seen how fierce and serious he was about this relationship thing. He was really prepared to try it and so was she.

They had to start somewhere. Sometimes the only way to know whether something was right or not was to do it. That's how she'd ended up here, after all, by ignoring her anxieties and just... doing it.

That had worked out, so she might as well keep on heading in that direction.

She turned in his arms, and his mouth, hot and insistent, covered hers.

He liked morning sex apparently, and well, so did she.

Afterward, she lay against him, her hands folded on his bare chest, her chin resting on her hands, and gave him a direct look. "So. How are we going to do this?"

Levi's smile was lazy and warm as he reached out to wind one of her curls around his finger. "This being us?"

"Yes, this being us."

"So, okay. Again, full disclosure, I talked to Chase about you."

Indigo blushed. "Chase? Really?"

"He wanted to know my intentions since Izzy was worried about you."

Oh, great. Well, she hadn't been wrong about Beth and Izzy picking up on her mood. She wasn't sure whether to feel embarrassed or pleased, but she liked that her friend cared. That was a nice feeling.

"I see," she said, trying for neutral. "Your intentions."

"Yeah." Levi tugged gently on her curl. "I told him that I was serious about you and was intending to have a relationship with you. And he said that we'd have to figure it out together."

"That makes sense."

"I'm new at this, hedgehog. I'll probably need some guidance." His attention was on his finger, the remains of the heat they'd generated just before glittering in his eyes like a banked fire. He was like a big lazy cat curled up beside her on the bed, or no, not a cat. More like a lion or a tiger, because there was still so much power in him, even lying at rest.

"I'm new at this too," she reminded him, not for the first time, wishing she had more experience so she knew what to say. Because how was this supposed to go now? What did being together look like? "So…are we dating? Is that how you start off?"

Dating sounded like a good starting point. Safe. Nothing too crazy.

Safe? Haven't you had enough of safe?

Sure. But she'd been pushing herself out of her comfort zone for past three months and she was tired. This was so new and so different that safe felt like all she could manage.

"I've got some plans." He lifted his gaze to hers, the banked fire in it glowing hot. "And they're big ones. But I'm happy to start slow if that's what you want."

Did she want that? Slow? Last night he'd

mentioned a home and a family, what Chase and Izzy and Finn and Beth had, but she wasn't sure she was ready for that. She was still getting used to being in another country and new people and a new job. A new relationship. Making the leap into living together, marriage, and kids felt like one leap too far.

Wanting more might frighten him off too.

That was true. She didn't want to do that.

"Slow is good," she said carefully. "Coming here, starting a new business, being in a new place… It's a lot of 'new' for me."

"I know." He tugged gently on her curl again, warmth in his eyes. The sensation was weirdly satisfying. "I get it. You were isolated for a long time, and all of this must be pretty full-on. And then me being a tool for the past few weeks…"

"Months," she said, only partly teasing. "You've been a tool for months."

He laughed. "Okay, months. But I'm happy to take it at whatever speed you want. If dating is what you want to start with, then that's what we'll start with."

A nagging sense of disquiet tugged at her, but since she had no idea why, she ignored it. He was prepared to take things slow for her and she was okay with that.

She grinned. "Yes, that sounds good."

"Great." His gaze caught hers, his mouth curving.

"In that case, tonight do you want to go out on a date with me? A sunset flight over the ranges maybe? It's one of my specialties."

Her heart leapt, the frustration falling away. "Oh yes, I'd love that."

"You're very keen on my helicopter all of a sudden."

Indigo couldn't resist. "Is that what you guys are calling it these days? Your 'helicopter'?"

He laughed. "Yeah, it is. And I think you need another flying lesson."

Then he pulled her beneath him for the second time that morning.

Unfortunately, her "flying lesson" made them both late, so there was only time for a cup of tea and a piece of toast before they were scrambling into Levi's truck for the drive down into Brightwater.

Levi had wanted to come into the gallery with her to declare himself in front of Beth and Izzy, but since he had some day-trippers to take over the lake to Glitter Falls and was already late, he had to go straight to HQ.

Indigo wasn't sure if she was happy about that or not, but she'd been hoping to open up the gallery on her own, wanting some time to think about how she was going to tell her friends about her and Levi, but when she got to the gallery, it was already open, and Izzy and Beth were pottering about inside.

A wave of shyness crept through her, though

she told herself sternly not to be so stupid. She was a modern woman who didn't get flustered about her new relationship with a guy. A relationship the other two probably knew about already, given Levi had said he'd mentioned it to Finn the night before.

What would they think? Especially after she'd been so miserable the previous few weeks. Would they think she was stupid to get involved with Levi? Would they be happy for her? Why did she even care about their opinion?

But that was a silly question. They were her friends, and their opinions were important to her.

"Oh hey, Indy," Beth said as she came in, sounding suspiciously casual.

Izzy gave her a little wave from her place behind the counter, ostentatiously checking something on the laptop.

So, the pair of them were trying to be cool about it, were they?

She felt simultaneously grateful and annoyed. Grateful that they weren't making a big deal of it, and annoyed that they were still being careful with her.

You're not exactly a big sharer and they're being respectful of your feelings.

Indigo gave an inward sigh. This friendship thing was tough, and she was still getting used to it. She'd been so prickly the past couple of weeks, and that really hadn't been fair, not when they'd been such kind and supportive friends.

She let out a little breath and folded her arms. "Okay, yes," she announced. "It's official. Levi and I are seeing each other."

Instantly Beth stopped fiddling with the jewelry display and came over, her face shining. "You are? That's fantastic!" She pulled Indigo into a warm hug. Indigo didn't much care for hugs, but Beth's were different, so she gave her friend a slightly awkward squeeze back.

Beth let her go and smiled hugely. "Come on, I want all the goss."

Izzy had come around from behind the counter, also smiling hugely, and gave her a hug too. "Oh, that's wonderful news. I've been hoping you two might get together. Please tell me Levi is going to live with you in that tiny house."

Indigo's heart gave a hard beat that felt painful for no apparent reason. "Oh no, we're not moving in together or anything," she said hurriedly, since it was clear the pair of them thought something else was going on when it wasn't. "We're dating."

Beth's smile faded, and she and Izzy exchanged a glance that Indigo didn't understand. "You're... dating," she echoed, as if the word was foreign to her.

Izzy's expression too lost some of its brightness, though her smile remained. "That's great, Indigo. I'm so pleased for you."

Beth looked like she wanted to say more, but Indigo didn't miss the short sharp shake of Izzy's head.

The vague unease she'd felt that morning returned. "What?" Defensiveness had crept into her tone before she could stop it. "There's nothing wrong with dating, is there?"

"No, of course, there isn't," Izzy said comfortingly. "That's a great first—"

"Was that his idea?" Beth demanded over the top of her, suddenly sharp.

"No," Indigo snapped, her warm feeling draining away. "It was mine. I wanted to start off slowly."

Beth looked like she was going to say more, then shut her mouth, another expression Indigo didn't recognize flickering over her pretty face. "As long it was your decision," she said somewhat lamely. "And not completely his."

But the unease in Indigo's gut didn't go away, or the nagging ache behind her breastbone. An ache that said this wasn't what she wanted, that while dating and flights over the ranges and great sex were wonderful, that didn't make Levi hers, and that didn't make her his.

That didn't make it special.

That doesn't make it love.

She went hot all over at the thought. Love? Who'd mentioned love? She didn't want that, not at all. Love was empty promises and lies. Love was silence. Love was the slow realization that no one was coming for you, that no one wanted you. That you were nothing but a burden.

No, she didn't want love. Love couldn't be trusted. Friendship was good—Izzy and Beth had taught her what friendship meant—but she'd happily never have anything to do with love ever again.

"It was," she insisted, trying not to pay any attention to how hollow her justifications sounded, even in her own head. "I mean, what did you guys expect? That we were suddenly going to be getting married and moving into together?"

"No, of course not..." Izzy began.

"Actually, I did," Beth said flatly. "You're in love with him, Indigo. You've been in love with him for weeks. Any fool can see that."

It felt as if the floor had suddenly dropped away from underneath her. As if she was falling and there was nothing around her to hold on to.

No, she was *not* in love with Levi. She liked him a lot and liked spending time with him. He was a great guy. And he was super sexy and great in bed, not that she had any comparison, but still.

That wasn't love.

"I'm not in love with him," she said through numb lips. "That's a stupid idea."

Beth's gaze took in her expression and her belligerence faded, replaced by concern. "Do you need to sit down?" she asked quietly. "You look pale."

Then she was surrounded by warm feminine concern, Beth's arm around her waist urging her over to the armchair in the corner that had some rag dolls Shirley had made for sale on it. Beth got rid of the dolls and sat Indigo down, while Izzy disappeared off somewhere.

A couple of moments later, Izzy was back, a steaming mug of tea in her hand. She wrapped Indigo's suddenly icy fingers around the pottery, and the scent of strong black tea hit her. Gumboot tea. Indigo took a reflexive sip and pulled a face at the sharpness of the tannins and the sweetness of the sugar.

Yet after a couple of moments, she felt better. "I'm not in love with him," she insisted. "I'm not. And he isn't in love with me."

"No, no," Beth muttered. "Of course, he isn't."

Izzy patted Indigo on the shoulder. "Dating is fine if that's what you want. It's a fantastic start."

"We're both new at this," Indigo said. "He's never had a relationship before and neither have I. Neither of us know what we're doing."

"Uh-huh." Beth tucked one of the rag dolls into the crook of Indigo's elbow. "It's scary, that's for sure."

"Yes, and we need to take it slow." She took another sip of her tea. "He's had a horrible childhood. He lived on the streets, stole cars, and got into fights. He had nothing." Tears prickled behind her eyes, coming out of nowhere. "He had a foster mother who cared about him, but then she had to go and look after her father. And she couldn't take him with her. He said it wasn't a big deal, but it was a big deal. And he's still upset about it, I can tell." There was a heavy weight on her chest. "He does so much for everyone around here. He fixed Shirley's kitchen after her husband died. He bought Jim's land because Jim needed the money. He's got a charity..." Her voice was becoming hoarse, a deep, sharp pain sitting just behind her breastbone. "No one wanted him. How could anyone not want him?"

The other two murmured comforting things while she sat there, crushed under the weight of a sorrow that seemed to come out of the blue.

For him and the childhood he'd had. Shipped around the foster system, one foster parent after another. No home. No one to take care of him. No one to love him. Oh, he said he was fine, that it was all in the past, but it wasn't.

There was a bag at the end of the bed in the house in Queenstown. A bag he could take if he needed to leave, he'd said. Being prepared. An old army habit. But it wasn't an old army habit. It was a habit a boy had learned after leaving his tenth home in a month and knowing that no one would have thought of what he might need, so he had to bring it himself.

He had to go it alone. Like you.

It was true. They'd both had only themselves to rely on. Only themselves to trust. Because other people had let them down, other people had hurt them. In her case it was the people who were supposed to care about her, and in his, the people who were legally supposed to care. And maybe that was worse. To be constantly shipped around among people who took care of you because they had to. Not because they cared about you specifically.

Then another realization hit her. Were all the things he did to help the people here because he thought he had to earn his place here? That no one would want him simply for who he was?

Her throat hurt, her vision swimming. "He needs someone to make it better for him. He needs someone to care about him. He needs to be special to someone."

Beth let out a gusty-sounding sigh. "Oh, Indy. You do love him, don't you?"

Indigo closed her eyes as a tear ran down her cheek. Maybe it was love. Only love could feel this raw and this painful. Only love could make you feel this alone.

You idiot. When you know how this works out.

She swallowed. "Why is that supposed to be a good thing? It just…hurts."

Izzy patted her shoulder. "I know it does. But it *is* a good thing."

Indigo opened her eyes again and stared at the other two. "Is it? I've never seen anything good about love. My parents used to tell me how important I was and how they couldn't wait for me to join them in Anchorage. But…they never came for me. I

don't know why. I just…wasn't important to them."
She took a shaky breath, all the words she'd been
keeping inside her for so long spilling out. "And my
grandma…she loved me, or at least she said she
did. But I was just kind of dumped on her. She *had*
to look after me because there was nowhere else for
me to go. And then she died…" Another sob collected in her chest. "And I was alone."

Izzy's dark eyes had gotten liquid, and she bent
suddenly beside the chair, wrapping an arm around
Indigo's shoulder. "Oh, Indy. I'm so sorry that happened to you."

"Me too." Beth grabbed Indigo's free hand and
gave it a squeeze. "But you know you're not alone
now, don't you? You've got us." She gave Indigo's
hand another squeeze, harder this time. "You'll
always have us."

And Indigo felt it, truly felt it. The warmth and
support of the other two around her, letting her
know that she didn't have to do this on her own.
That no matter what happened with Levi, she
would have these two women at her side to help.

Beth was right. She wasn't on her own after all.

She squeezed Beth's hand right back and then
glanced at Izzy. "I know. You guys are the best."

"Yes, it's true. We are the best," Beth said. "And
I can tell you that while love is painful and hard,
there are some truly excellent bits that go along
with it. Being with Finn has been…life-changing.

Painful and difficult, yes, but meeting him was the best thing that ever happened to me." Her green eyes were shining.

Izzy was smiling too. "And that goes for me and Chase. He and Gus have made me so unbelievably happy."

Indigo wiped away the tear, her chest still sore. "I don't know. I... Trust is so hard. It's easier to be on your own."

"Well, sure it's easier," Izzy said with some understanding. "But it's also really lonely." She paused a moment. "You don't have to act on your feelings if you don't want to, you know."

"That's true," Beth agreed. "You don't. You can keep dating him if that's what you want for the moment."

Indigo thought about the vague frustration that had lurked inside her earlier that morning, the longing for more. The sense that her feelings were dangerous somehow...

Well, and they were dangerous. She knew that now. But what about Levi? How did he feel about her? He'd said something about wanting a family and building a house, and she thought he probably meant that he wanted her to be part of that, but...was that love? Or had he decided he was going have all the things he'd never had as a child, and it wasn't about her specifically?

You want more than that. You want him to love you too.

No, she was getting ahead of herself. This was new for both of them, and hey, she was still untangling her own feelings, so taking it slowly was the right course of action. Start off small. Show him what it meant to have someone around who was there for him, who would take care of him.

Indigo took a sip of her tea, not caring that it scalded her mouth. "Yes, dating is probably best for now. I think both of us need to take it slowly."

Izzy nodded. "That does sound like a good idea. Men get very skittish when you start throwing words like *love* around."

"They do." Beth had knowing look on her face. "They get *very* skittish. Or at least some men do."

Indigo liked that her friends didn't push or question her instinct. Trust had to be built, and though she and Levi had known each other a couple of months already, they hadn't been seeing each other for very long. And friends was an entirely different relationship—not that they'd ever been friends exactly, but still. He had to trust her, and after the kind of childhood he'd had, that trust might take some time.

And for you too.

Yes, trust was a slight issue for her too, but she was getting there.

"I'm not going to do that," she said. "He's going to need some time."

"Well, make sure you look out for yourself too, okay?" Beth said. "I don't want to see you get hurt."

Indigo smiled at her, appreciating the thought. "I know, but I don't want to push him, Beth."

"Okay. I just want to make sure that you're getting what you need too."

Oh, she would. All she had to do was to figure out exactly what that looked like.

Chapter 16

LEVI WORKED HARD OVER THE NEXT FEW WEEKS. He and Indigo spent a lot of time flying to Queenstown and visiting various places to get materials. Some could be flown over the ranges; some had to be put in a truck and driven.

Indigo was a canny buyer, finding the greatest pieces in the strangest of places before driving hard bargains with the most difficult people. She looked cute, that was the issue, and people under-estimated her.

Levi loved that about her. He loved that she looked so sweet and beautiful and then suddenly there were prickles and a stubbornness that could rival a mule, and a hardheaded practicality that put many a tough Mainlander to shame.

His days were filled with the usual Pure Adventure stuff, which he loved, but he also loved dating Indigo.

He took her to dinner at a fancy restaurant on the wharf at Queenstown, overlooking the lake, and they watched the sun go down as they feasted on crayfish and champagne.

He took her flying to a secret hanging valley high

in the mountains with a pristine blue lake and an alpine forest. It was only accessible by air, so they were completely alone. They went skinny-dipping in the lake, and it was so cold they both nearly froze solid, and then they lay naked in a patch of sunlight, in each other's arms as they warmed up, while she told him stories of life in Alaska.

He took her over the Southern Alps to the wild west coast and showed her the isolated, desolate beaches and the pancake rocks.

He took her down to one of the fjords at the very bottom of the South Island, and it rained and rained, turning all the cliff faces into a hundred cascading waterfalls.

Once they even went up a glacier, and he wrapped her in his parka because she insisted on walking around on the ice even though it was freezing and dangerous.

He took her into the bush one night to see if they could spot a kiwi. They took infrared flashlights so the birds wouldn't be blinded since they were nocturnal, and she was thrilled when she was the first one to spot a little brown bird poking around in the underbrush right where she was standing.

That same night, he took her to a hollowed-out cliff to see the glow worms that lived in the rock, and she exclaimed at the tiny pinpricks of light glowing in the darkness.

He had other plans too, so many other plans, a

trip up north to the Big Smoke, to Auckland. A tour of the volcanoes: Tongariro, Ngauruhoe, Ruapehu. When it got colder, he thought about the skiing trips he could take her on, even heli-skiing.

She was opening up to him like a flower to the sun, telling him more about her childhood and her grandmother, and how she'd coped by herself after her grandma had died. How lonely it had been.

Her trust was a fragile thing, he knew, but she was giving it to him, he could sense it, and it made him even more certain of all the things he wanted to do for her, all the things he wanted to give her.

It wasn't all tourist adventures though.

Some nights she'd invite him back to the farmhouse, and he'd find a home-cooked meal waiting for him and his favorite beer in the fridge. He'd thought it was a one-off at first, just a nice thing she'd done for him, until it had happened again. And again. And then every time she invited him over. She never made a fuss about it. He'd turn up, and she'd tell him to sit down and have dinner. They'd eat together, and then he'd clean up while she sat at the table sipping tea and chatting.

It felt strange to have a meal to come home to at night and to have his favorite beer in the fridge. To have someone smile at him, kiss him, and then ask him about his day.

But this was what happened in a relationship,

wasn't it? You had dinner together at night and you talked, and you relaxed, enjoying their company.

He liked it, but it made him antsy for reasons he couldn't have articulated.

Indigo taught him to purl one morning in bed, and then they both sat in bed, knitting away, naked and chatting about something stupid, which ended up with him teasing her, her pretend-stabbing him with a wooden knitting needle, and then sex that caused her to go off into a rant afterward due to all the dropped stitches.

He also worked hard on the tiny house, taking a great amount of satisfaction in the way it was coming together. His head was full of plans for how he was going to build his own place too—he'd already had a few chats with the owner of the land he'd had his eye on—and how Indigo would come and live with him there, and maybe they could rent out the tiny house eventually.

Because she would come and live with him at some stage; he was quite clear that he wanted that.

In the meantime, he made sure the craftsmanship of the tiny house was perfect so it would be perfect for her.

He wanted *everything* to be perfect for her.

The evening he finished finally putting on the corrugated steel roof—he'd insisted it be made out of new materials because the elements in Brightwater were rough, which meant the roof had to be hard-wearing—he was standing in the small space of the house, listening to the rain coming down on the new roof, when he saw Indigo coming up the track from the gallery.

Nights were getting darker earlier, and it was chilly. It had been raining all day and he was wet through and cold, though he didn't mind since the roof was done and he could relax a little bit. The house was still only timber framing, and getting it closed in was a priority, but he could take a moment to feel some satisfaction that at least it was going to be dry from now on.

"Hey," she said, smiling as she stepped through what would eventually be her front door. "The roof's done!"

He grinned back, the warmth he always felt in her presence growing larger and larger as she came near. "Yeah, all done. Just the interior to do now."

She looked up at the newly installed roof, clearly listening to the patter of the rain, and it made the warmth inside him grow even larger, because he knew she loved that sound, and he was pleased he knew that about her.

In fact, there were a lot of things he knew about her that he hadn't known before. That for all her cautiousness, she had a daredevil streak that sometimes made itself known in the most inappropriate moments. That she was very strict about him washing his hands before dinner. That she would catch her tongue between her teeth in the most adorable way when she was thinking about something. That sometimes she disagreed with him just so she could argue with him, because she loved arguing. That she hated wētās, and it didn't matter how many times he tried to make her like them, she still refused.

That at night she would reach for him and nestle close, her arms around his waist, holding him in a way that made something inside him ache and ache. As if she wasn't going to let him go come hell or high water.

He looked at her now, wrapped up in a bright-yellow rain jacket over the top of a floaty sky-blue dress that was totally inappropriate for the weather and the bush. The hood was back, and her hair was spangled with rain, the damp making her hair curl.

In one hand she had a thermos and in the other a couple of mugs, and her skin was luminous in the growing dusk.

She looked at him, her smile a thing of such beauty he felt his heart stop. "Can you hear the rain? It sounds amazing."

It took Levi a moment to realize that it wasn't only his heart that had stopped; everything had stopped. The whole world pausing.

She turned away, going over to a sawhorse and balancing the mugs and the thermos on it. Words were coming out of her mouth, but he wasn't taking any of it in.

Everything was dark around him. There was only her in her yellow raincoat, glowing like the sun, her smile setting him alight, the blue of her eyes making him believe in heaven, the luminescence of her skin a thing of wonder.

"Levi?" She looked at him, still smiling. In one hand she was holding a small glass bottle and was shaking it playfully at him. "I know it's tradition to have a beer when the roof goes on, but it's too cold for beer. Thought you might like some whiskey in your tea instead."

He liked whiskey. It was his favorite. And he was even coming to like gumboot tea.

All the things he knew about her, she knew about him too.

No one else knew him like that. No one else ever had.

"Indigo," he heard himself say, his voice hoarse. "I think we should get married."

She stopped, her eyes widening. "What?"

And then the world started again, everything seeming to move very fast, his heart, his brain turning over all his plans, his intentions, his dreams for the future, stumbling over itself, because it was coming together, at last, at last, everything he'd ever wanted was right here, within his reach.

He took a step toward her and then another, closing the distance. Then he took the bottle out of her hand and put it down on the sawhorse, gently tugging her against him. "Marry me," he said, his heart beating so fast and hard, he could hardly hear anything else over the sound. "Be my wife, Indy. I'll build us a house, bigger than this one, with room for kids. We'll get some chickens and a horse and, hell, maybe some cows if you want. There'll be a big dye shed out the back for you too, and I'll make it so perfect. Just tell me what you want, and I'll do it for you." He looked down into her lovely face. "We could have a home, hedgehog. A home for us. A place that's ours."

She didn't speak for a long moment, only looked up at him, and for the first time, he couldn't tell what she was thinking. Emotions flickered through her eyes, but they moved too quickly for him to tell what they were. "And that's what you want?" Her voice sounded a bit strange. "A home? A family?"

"Yes." He grinned, excitement flooding through him, his future unrolling in his head. Security and permanence and a wife and kids. A place to call his own. Where he didn't have keep a bag in the closet in case he had to leave. A place he could stay forever, where he belonged. "I'm tired of dating, Indy. I want more than that. I'm ready. I've been ready ever since the last town barbecue."

He didn't know what he'd expected, but the faint smile that turned her mouth now wasn't it. Or the look of…what? Pity? Sympathy? That glittered in her eyes. "We don't need to do this yet," she said patiently. "We don't need to rush. Why don't we finish with the tiny house and see where we get to?"

He frowned, irritated by her calm. "Okay, but I'm not changing my mind. I'm ready, Indy. I told you that. Why wait?" And then a sudden realization hit him. He lifted his hands, took her lovely face between them. "Are you afraid? Don't be. I'm so sure about this. I've never been so sure of anything in my life. You can trust me, hedgehog. I'm not going anywhere, okay?"

She didn't move and she didn't smile. Her gaze met his, a pure, piercing blue.

And a sudden doubt gripped him. "What is it? What's wrong? Do you not want this? Is that the issue?"

"No, I–I do. It's just…" She stopped. "Is it me you want, Levi? Or is it a home? A family? A wife?"

His frown deepened. "What? What do you mean? Yes, of course I want you. Why do you think I asked you to marry me? I want a home and a wife and kids and—"

"Do you want me?" Her gaze was full of an expression he didn't understand. "Or do you only want all the things you never had?"

He blinked, not quite getting it. And then he did.

His gut lurched, the excitement and happiness he'd felt before gradually fading away. He let her go. "Oh, you think this is about my childhood?" He tried not to make it sound defensive. "You think that...what? I'm trying to recreate a family or something?"

She didn't move. "But aren't you? You had a terrible past, Levi. You never had a home, never had anyone who cared about you, never had—"

"No." He cut her off, suddenly angry. Because this wasn't about his past, not at all. This was about him deciding to *move on* from his past. Couldn't she see that? "I know what happened to me. I know it was shit. You don't need to go on about it. And how can I recreate what I never had anyway? No, I'm not recreating anything. I'm building a life. I'm putting my past behind me and deciding on a future, that's all."

Indigo stood there in the growing gloom, the rain pattering on the roof, and it seemed suddenly that there was a distance between them, a distance he hadn't realized until now. The glowing brightness of her retreating, leaving him in the dark.

"You're trying so hard," she said, her voice oddly thick. "You're trying so, *so* hard. Taking me places, doing things. Buying me gifts. But...you don't need to do all of that. You don't need to do anything, don't you see?"

"See?" He didn't know what she was talking about. All he knew was that the happiness and excitement he'd felt earlier had turned into a hard lump of iron sitting in his gut. "See what?"

"That you're enough just as you are." There was

a terrible sympathy in her face, a dreadful kind of compassion that felt like needles against his skin.

But you're never enough and you know it. Nothing you do. Nothing you say. Your entire existence causes nothing but pain, and nothing you do will ever make it better.

Abruptly he couldn't breathe.

He turned away from her and the look on her face, taking a couple of steps so he was standing at the end of the long room that would be the living area, looking out through the timber framing and into the wet darkness of the bush.

"You know that, don't you?" Her voice came from behind him, soft and full of emotion, making his heart ache and ache. "Levi?"

But everything felt as if it were falling away inside him: all his plans, all his hopes, all his dreams. Because he could see it now and it was so obvious.

He had been trying too hard. He'd been trying hard ever since he'd gotten to Brightwater Valley. To be accepted. To be part of the community. To be Chase and Finn's brother. To be an uncle for Gus. To be the best guide for the company.

To be a good man for Indigo.

You can try. But you'll never feel like it's enough. Because it isn't.

How could it be? It had never been enough the entirety of his life. He'd never had a home lasting longer than six months, never had anyone make sure he was okay. He'd never been given one single solitary thing.

He was placed with families, but they didn't choose him.

Linda had looked after him, cared for him, but in the end, she'd given him up like the rest. She hadn't chosen him.

Even his own mother hadn't chosen him.

He'd become friends with Chase because of their experience in the military, and when Chase had left the SAS, he'd followed him to Brightwater because he'd had nowhere else to go.

No one here had chosen him either, but he'd worked hard to be accepted.

He'd never know if that acceptance was because of him, or because of everything he'd done for people. And that *was* acceptance, wasn't it? Nothing came for free. You had to work for it. You had to take it.

So, are you going to take her? Is that what you're doing here? She's right about that. You're taking her on dates and showing her things, building her a house, making her a part of your future, and it's not for her. It's for you. Because you have nothing real to offer her.

He felt cold suddenly. As if he'd fallen into a crevasse and there was nothing but ice and darkness all around him.

"Levi?" She was close. He could feel her warmth. She was right behind him.

Yet it felt as if she were oceans away.

And he knew now that it was all true.

He had nothing real to offer her, nothing of any meaning. Only dates and helicopter rides and picnics. Money. A house. Would that last forever? Would that be enough to last a lifetime?

Oh, but he knew the answer to that already. It wouldn't.

Her hand settled in the middle of his back, a warmth that hit his chilled skin like a lightning bolt. "Levi, talk to me."

She sounded so small, and she deserved so very much. She'd been alone a long time, and he'd been the world's biggest asshole. He'd encouraged her to open up, to give him her trust, and she had.

And he had nothing to give her in return. Nothing at all.

He shut his eyes. "Indy...I'm sorry. This isn't going to work, is it?"

There was a silence behind him, yet her hand didn't move from his back. It made him feel like he was a house in danger of structural collapse and her hand was the main support beam, the only thing holding him up.

"Why not?" she asked quietly.

"You were right. I *have* been trying too hard. I just...want to give you everything. I want everything to be perfect for you. But..." He stopped and turned around.

She was standing behind him, small and delicate in her yellow parka, her face full of a powerful emotion he didn't recognize. "But what?" she asked.

"It's not enough," he said bluntly. "Nothing will ever be enough."

She shook her head. "Didn't you listen when I told you that you don't have to do all these things? That you're enough all on your own?"

He gave a harsh laugh. "I've built you a house, taken you on so many dates. I've made you tea, bought you scones, given you enough orgasms to last you for the next one hundred years. Tell me, would you be standing here if I hadn't done all those things?"

Something cracked in her expression, pain flickering in her eyes. "I don't know. But I—"

"But what? Will you still be standing here in ten years? In twenty? Because helicopter rides and food and money and sex, that's all I've got to give, Indigo. I don't have anything else."

Her chin lifted suddenly, something fierce blazing in her eyes. "Yes, you do. You have *you*, Levi King. That's all I want. Don't you know that? I just want you."

But he felt like he was an island in the middle of space, alone and isolated, just as he always was. Just as he always had been. "You have me, Indigo. And it'll never be enough, will it?"

She blinked, the fierce light in her eyes burning hotter. "You're more than helicopter rides and money, you stupid man. You're kind and generous and funny and warm. You're protective and caring. You're the most interesting, fascinating man I've ever met."

But he only shook his head. "You haven't met very many men, hedgehog."

Anger flickered across her face. "No, don't you dare say that—"

He reached out and laid a finger across her lovely mouth, silencing her. Her lips felt soft and warm against his skin, and he wanted more than anything to take his finger away and put his mouth there instead, but he couldn't.

It wasn't fair. Not to her.

He took his finger away. "Indy, I think it's time—"

"You said you were all in." She took a step toward him, her whole being blazing. "You said you weren't going anywhere."

"I know, but—"

"Don't be a coward, Levi." Her voice was vibrating with anger, but there were tears in her eyes. "Don't you dare walk away. Don't you understand that the only thing you haven't mentioned is love? And that's all I want from you. Love. Because I love you."

———————

His face went blank with shock for a split second, and then abruptly his expression twisted. "Was that before or after the helicopter rides?"

There was a harsh mockery in the words, though she knew it wasn't directed at her. It was all for himself.

It hurt her, made the anger inside her that she'd been vibrating with not even a second before drain away like water from a cracked bucket.

He didn't believe her. He didn't believe she could accept him just as he was, didn't believe she could love him just as he was.

He didn't believe in love at all, did he? That's why he'd never mentioned it when he'd talked about marriage and kids and a family. Not once. He didn't believe in it and why would he? When he'd never had it?

She couldn't be angry with him, she just couldn't. It wasn't his fault his childhood had been rejection after rejection. Hers had been the same, but she'd had her grandma. He'd had no one. He probably didn't even know what love was.

So, all she did was meet his gaze and give him the truth. "I thought you were just like my dad at first, all charm and empty promises. And I didn't want to like you. I certainly didn't want to trust you. And I'm not sure when it was that things started to change. Maybe it was the day you picked up a wētā in your bare hands and called him Wally before putting him outside. Or maybe it was when you gave Mystery a treat and told me you were going to adopt him. Or maybe it was when you tied back my hair with a band you just happened to have in your pocket." She swallowed.

"There are so many occasions that would have made me fall in love with you, but you know what? They don't matter, Levi. What matters is that I love you right now, and I'll love you tomorrow, and probably even the day after that." She was shaking now as the feeling inside her burned outward through her veins, lighting her up from the inside. "And maybe even next week, next month, a year, ten damn years, twenty. Yes, twenty years and I'll still be here, standing in front of you. Telling you that I love you."

Something crossed his face, a flicker of a longing so intense it nearly broke her. Then it was gone, his expression hardening. "It doesn't matter. It doesn't change anything. There was only one person in the entire world who cared whether I lived or died, and even she gave me up when push came to shove."

"But I'm not her, Levi. And I don't want to give you up. I want *you*, whether or not you give me anything. Whether or not there are helicopter rides or sex or money, or whatever." Her eyes filled with tears. "I don't need any of those things. I just need you."

A muscle flicked in his hard jaw, tension radiating from his tall muscular figure. He looked like a man at war with himself, and that's exactly what was going on, wasn't it? He wanted her, she knew it, she'd seen that longing on his face, and he wanted what she was offering him. But he was too afraid to take it.

He was Mystery, the stray. Wanting to be cared for, wanting a home, and yet he'd been hurt too many times before to trust anyone.

Even someone who loved him.

"I'm sorry," he said, his eyes going dark. "I'm sorry, hedgehog. I'll marry you and take care of you. We'll have kids and a house, and all of that. But love… That's not something I can build a future on."

She didn't want to cry. She didn't want him to see her heart breaking in her chest. It would hurt him, and he'd been hurt a lot, and she didn't want to emotionally manipulate him with tears.

"Then where does that leave us?" Her voice was a croak.

"I guess that leaves us nowhere." His gaze roamed over her hungrily, but he didn't move. "I can't hurt you, Indigo. I can't. I won't. And it's not fair of me to demand something of you when I can't give you what you want."

"Levi—"

"It's not going to work, hedgehog. You and me. It's not going to work."

He'd decided, she could see that. He didn't trust love and he didn't trust her, and perhaps he'd never trust anyone. With a past like his, who could blame him?

It wasn't her place to push him. It wasn't her place to tell him that if he truly wanted to move on from his past, he had to stop letting it dictate his own worth. That he was valuable all on his own.

She'd tried telling him, but he hadn't listened. And so he was going to walk away from her like everyone else had walked away from her.

Perhaps her love wasn't enough. It had never been enough before, after all.

"Okay." She stared up at him unflinchingly. "I'm not going to push you. If your mind's made up, then it's made up. But just know, Levi, that my mind's made up too." She lifted her chin. "I love you and I always will. And that's never going to change."

Then she turned away and very carefully laid his fleece over the sawhorse standing next to them.

"Indigo," he said, his voice rougher than gravel. "I'm sorry. I'll finish the house. That won't be a problem, I promise. And I won't make it difficult, I swear."

"I know you won't." Her eyes were prickling, and she felt a tear run down her cheek despite everything, her heart tearing itself apart in her chest. "But…you might want to keep your distance for a bit."

It was clear he wanted to say more, but she couldn't bear it, so she simply turned away and walked out into the rain.

The track down to the gallery was muddy and

slippery, and the raindrops felt like ice on her cold skin and kept getting in her eyes.

But it wasn't until she finally made it back to the gallery, where Izzy and Beth still were, that she realized it wasn't rain in her eyes that made her unable to see.

Izzy and Beth were chatting about something, and they looked up as she came in. And both of them suddenly came around the side of the counter, their expressions full of concern.

"Oh, Indy, what happened?" Beth asked, rushing over.

"Levi and I broke up," Indigo said thickly.

"Oh my God." Izzy's dark eyes flashed like thunderclouds. "If he's done something stupid, I swear to God—"

"No," Indigo interrupted, wiping her eyes. "Please don't. He's just…afraid."

Beth sighed. "Oh, man. I know how that goes. Men afraid of happiness are the worst."

"He's never had anyone love him," she went on, because she had to explain this to them so they understood. It wasn't his fault. It wasn't. "He's never had anyone want him. There was one person he wanted to stay with, but she couldn't take him, and now…he does all these things to earn his place, to prove his worth, and I told him that he didn't have to do any of those things, but…I think he just doesn't trust people."

Izzy rubbed her back, still looking furious. "I know, but still."

"Yeah, but still," Beth agreed. "You want me to slap the idiot upside the head? Because I will."

Indigo shook her head. "No. He's got to come to it in his own time. I told him I loved him though. I told him I'd be here, that I wasn't going anywhere. I want him to know that I'm not leaving just because he's being an ass. He can't push me away."

"Well, good," Beth said firmly and then more comfortingly, "He'll come round. It might take some time, but he will. He's not going to let someone as awesome as you get away."

Indigo felt a sob gather in her chest because while she might not have the man she loved, she had two of the greatest friends in the world.

She had a whole town as well.

She wasn't alone.

She just hoped that one day Levi would understand that he had all those things too.

Chapter 17

LEVI STAYED IN THE HALF-BUILT HOUSE UNTIL the cold drove him to grab his fleece and he couldn't stay there any longer.

He wasn't thinking. All he could do was see was the hurt in Indigo's deep-blue eyes and feel the pain that echoed in his chest in response.

His fault. But then that's what he did, wasn't it? He hurt people.

He had no idea what to do next. Word would get out that they'd broken up, and no one would think particularly highly of him.

They would be right, of course.

He'd face the music—Linda had taught him that actions had consequences—he had no problem with that, but if he could just have one night on his own to get straight in his head what to say that would place the blame squarely on him, that would be a plus.

It was all his fault, and he knew that. He didn't want a whiff of any disapproval in Indigo's direction.

The rain fell in depressing fat drops, making the bush seem gloomy and oppressive, and he knew if he didn't leave Brightwater now, the weather was going to make it impossible. So, he went out of her half-built house and into the rain, walking quickly, hoping like hell he wasn't going to run into anyone.

It felt like he had a great lump of concrete solidifying around his heart, making him feel heavy, like he couldn't breathe.

He tried to ignore the feeling and made his way quickly to HQ.

There was no one upstairs, which made it easy to grab the bag he'd stashed in the bedroom, and luckily, no one saw him leave.

He went quickly out the back to the helicopter hangar and started the preflight checks. It was dumb to fly in this weather, but staying till morning was impossible. He needed to get away and fast.

A black shape appeared as he rolled the helicopter out into the field, Mystery the mystery dog sitting there with his tongue hanging out, watching him with interest.

Another you've let down.

The concrete surrounding Levi's heart felt heavier.

"Go on," he said sharply to the dog. "I've got nothing for you. Go on, get out here!"

Because he did have nothing. Nothing for anyone, not even a dog.

Mystery seemed to hear the fury in his voice and darted away.

Good job.

Levi didn't muck around. Fifteen minutes later he was airborne and flying through shitty weather. He thought the weight in his chest would get lighter, but it didn't. If anything, he felt even heavier.

The flight was uneventful. He landed in Queenstown, and not too long after that, he was finally at his house by the lake. His faux log cabin.

And as soon as he opened the door, he knew he shouldn't have come, because all he could see was Indigo. She was everywhere, memories of her in this house filling him. Her by the stove cooking dinner. Her on the couch with her knitting. Her naked in the shower and shrieking in protest as he joined her even though the shower stall was too small.

Her everywhere.

He felt exhausted suddenly, his head too full, his chest aching with the weight of what he'd done.

You broke her heart and then you ran away.

Sure, he'd broken her heart. That was a fact. He'd seen the moment it had cracked right through as she stood in front of him in the house he'd built for her, telling her he was sorry. That it wasn't going to work.

But what else could he do? Love didn't make a difference, didn't automatically make him any more worthy than he had been right at the start. He was still the same person, the lonely, desperate guy trying to find acceptance and a place to belong. Still dragging around the remains of a past he couldn't escape.

How could he give her that? He couldn't. Not Indigo. Not his gorgeous little hedgehog.

In the kitchen, he got himself a tumbler and carried both it and the bottle of scotch he'd bought on the way from the airport out to the lounge. Then he proceeded to drink his way steadily through it, and somewhere in the middle of it, he fell asleep.

"Levi."

Someone was shaking him by the shoulder.

"Levi, for chrissakes!"

He growled and tried to roll over. His head ached like a bastard, and all he wanted was to go back to sleep because he had a feeling that waking up would be bad.

And he was just drifting off, when suddenly something very cold hit him in the face, sending a shock wave through his system.

He cursed loudly and profusely, pushing himself up and wiping his hands across his face.

Water. Someone had dropped water in his face.

He cracked open his eyes to find both Finn and Chase standing in his living room, both of them looking disapprovingly down at him as he lay on the couch.

"What?" he demanded in a cracked voice. His head ached and he felt like shit, and the concrete around his heart felt like it was never going away. "How did you guys get here?"

"We drove," Chase said flatly.

"Okay, well, if you're going to lecture me, can you do it when I'm more awake?"

Chase ignored him. "What the hell are you doing?" he demanded, every inch of him the SAS officer he'd once been. "You break up with Indigo, take your stuff, and then you leave? Without even a goodbye?" He looked furious. "What the fuck is that all about?"

Agony crawled through him as the memory of the night before filtered through, the ache in his heart burning. "I know," he said hoarsely. "I screwed up. I screwed everything up." He scrubbed a hand through his hair. "I wanted to marry her, build a life with her, and I asked her and..."

"And what?" Finn's voice was also flat. "I don't believe for one second she said no."

Levi dropped his hand. "She didn't. She told me to stop trying so hard."

Both brothers stared at him.

"She told me I didn't need to keep doing things for her," he heard himself say, babbling like a complete idiot. "That she wants me for who I am, not all the things I could do for her." He gave a harsh laugh. "Like that's ever happened to me before."

Neither Chase nor Finn laughed. They didn't smile either.

"Shit," Chase murmured, staring at Levi like he'd never seen him before in his life. "Is that what you believe? That you have to…what? Prove your worth?"

Levi stared back, hating how desperate that sounded. And even now he didn't want to admit it. But it was true, and he knew it. "No one ever asked me to come to Brightwater," he said. "I just turned up and never left. Because I had nowhere else to go. And I'm not proving my worth; I'm earning my place. A community is about people supporting each other—"

"You know Shirley doesn't think you're God's gift just because you built her kitchen, right?" Finn interrupted. "She likes you because you ask her about her husband, and then you flirt a little because you know she likes it. And Jim thinks you're a good guy, not only because you bought his land when he needed the money, but because you promised you wouldn't build on it. Because you knew how he felt about the land and that mattered to you."

Levi couldn't speak.

"And I'm not your bloody friend only because I couldn't get rid of you," Chase added. "I'm your bloody friend because you were loyal and generous, and you were passionate about the same things I was and not afraid to show it." He took a step toward the couch, scowling down at him. "You think I call you my brother for the hell of it? You think everyone in Brightwater calls you a local because of all the things you did for them? No, they call you a local because you *are* one. Because you care about them and the town, and they care about you."

Levi's heart beat hard in his chest, a cold lump of something he hadn't known was frozen suddenly beginning to thaw.

I want you, whether or not you give me anything. Whether or not there are helicopter rides or sex or money, or whatever... I don't need any of those things. I just need you.

Indigo's voice rang loudly in his head, standing in front of him, that last little piece of her soul in her eyes, all there for him to see. And she was giving it to him, her precious heart. Trusting him with it.

And he hadn't listened to her. He'd been too caught up in his own self-pitying bullshit.

She'd *trusted* him with the most precious part of herself, and he'd thrown it back in her face. Demanding marriage and kids and a house, a family without even thinking about the most important thing of all. Love.

Because he was afraid. He could see that now.

Afraid of the love he saw in her face, the love she was giving him. Afraid he wasn't worthy, that he didn't deserve it, because love had never been given to him before. He'd never had love at all.

But she wasn't afraid of it. Guarded Indigo

had given him her truth, despite knowing that he would hurt her, and when he had, she'd only told him that she would be here. That she wasn't going anywhere.

And then you walked away and left her like her parents walked away and left her.

Jesus Christ. He'd been such an idiot.

"I don't know what to do." He stared at both his friends—no, his *brothers*. "I don't know how to make this right."

Chase let out a long breath. "Don't know when I became the default for relationship advice, but here goes. Do you love her?"

And there it was, curled deeply in the cold, lonely spaces of his heart, a little glow of sunshine. Of light and brilliant color and joy.

His hedgehog. His Indy. His Indigo.

He'd had friendship and companionship, and these two men had taught him how, but he'd never had love before. Not like this. Fierce and wild and uncontrollable. The ultimate adrenaline rush.

The feeling that he'd do anything for another person—jump in front of a train, stop a bullet, give his life and gladly.

Unconditional love, no need to earn it. No need to prove it. It just was.

Did she feel this? Was this what had made her stand in front of him and open her heart and soul?

Had this given her the bravery to do it? Because it *was* bravery. She had more courage than him.

Yes, he would do anything for her. He'd walk off a cliff for her.

So? Walk off that cliff, take that leap. For her.

It was scary as hell, and he couldn't remember ever being more afraid. But danger was his middle name, wasn't it? And at least he had somewhere warm and soft to land. Her arms.

"Shit," he said wiping his eyes. "Can anyone give me a lift to the airport?"

It was raining and the gallery was empty of people.

Indigo sat morosely behind the counter. Even knitting wasn't helping. Levi had disappeared the night before, taking the helicopter. Probably gone to do a tour of the bars of Queenstown, everyone said.

Indigo didn't know. She just ached for him, hurt for him.

He would change his mind, wouldn't he? It might take a few months or maybe even years, but he would. She had to trust that he would. And when he did, she would be here.

She wasn't going anywhere.

And then she heard what she thought was thunder, but then no, it was more rhythmic than that.

Helicopter rotors.

It wasn't Levi. No. It couldn't be. Not in this weather surely, because it was still bucketing down. He wasn't coming back, and if even if he did, it wouldn't be for her.

Still, she was curious, and she wasn't doing anything else, so she put down her knitting and went to the door of the gallery.

Someone was striding down the main street of the tiny town, coming in the direction of the gallery. He was soaking wet, the rain plastering his hair to head, and he was carrying a bag.

Levi.

Her heart squeezed tight, and she couldn't breathe, every cell in her body tensing. He was here, he'd come back. But...why? It couldn't be for her. No one ever came back for her.

Several people had come out to stand on the porch of the Rose and were watching him.

He saw her in the doorway of the gallery, and he stopped dead. The bag dropped from his hands. Then he opened his arms.

There was no hesitation. One moment she was standing in the doorway; the next she was running, no thought in her head but to get to him.

Because he had come back. And he was here. He was here for *her*.

Indigo ran through the rain and straight into his arms.

And they closed around her, holding her tight with the all the strength that was part of him, and she could feel the promise he was giving her; he would never let her go.

She lifted her face and his mouth found hers, hot and desperate, and she was kissing him. Tasting his delicious flavor and rain. Kissing him as if she was drowning and he was her last chance of rescue.

He kissed her back with the same desperation, demanding and feverish, the lonely places in her meeting the lonely places in him, filling each other up with light and warmth and the sense that neither of them would ever be alone again.

Then he lifted his head and looked down at her, his eyes pure gold, rain streaming down his hair and his face. "I'm sorry, hedgehog," he said thickly. "I'm sorry about what I said. I'm sorry I left. I don't know if what you said to me still holds true, but...I'm shit scared. I don't know if what I have to give you is enough, and I don't know if I'll ever believe that I don't have to do anything to make you love me. Hell, I don't even know what love is. But...I want to try. Because I think that maybe *you're* love, little hedgehog, and I love you. I love you so much."

Happiness burst like a flood wave inside her, swamping her, and she didn't know whether it was the rain in her eyes or tears, but that wasn't important. What was important was the man in front of her.

The man who loved her and whom she loved with all her heart.

Her special someone just as she was his.

She lifted her hands and took his face between them. "It's okay. You don't have to do anything. I'll show you how."

He smiled, the same deep, fierce happiness glowing in his eyes that she felt herself. "I want a family and a home and kids, and a dog. And maybe a horse. But most of all, I want love. And if I can't have yours, I don't want it all."

Tears and rain both slid down her cheeks. "You have it, Levi. You have all of it." Then she pulled his head down and kissed him again.

Everyone watching on the porch of the Rose applauded.

"We'll have a wētā," Levi murmured against her mouth. "And we'll call him Wally."

"Absolutely not," said Indigo.

Turned out that Grandma Tilly might have been right about a good many things, but she was wrong about one: there were some men you could trust with your heart, and sometimes those men were gorgeous.

Sometimes those men picked up wētās called Wally in their bare hands and took them outside to let them go.

That's what she was going to tell their children—because they would have children, she'd already decided.

You could always trust a man who called a wētā Wally.

You could trust him completely.

Epilogue

THEY HAD AN AUTUMN WEDDING, THOUGH Indigo insisted on calling it fall, which Levi thought she did purely to annoy him.

The bride wore a beautiful lace shawl all the colors of the sky that she'd knit herself, as well as a floaty white silk gown that was far too cold for the weather. She also wore the necklace he'd bought her as an engagement present, a chain with a little silver hedgehog on it that she never took off. He'd commissioned Beth to make it especially for her, along with a pair of tiny dangly wētā earrings.

She was not wearing the earrings, he noted.

He, however, was definitely wearing the small knitted cravat she'd made him out of the same yarn as she'd knitted her shawl with. It didn't really go with his suit, but he wasn't bothered. She'd made it; therefore it was priceless.

The entire town turned out to watch them get married on the Rose's front porch. Jim gave Indigo away, while Beth and Izzy, the bridesmaids, sniffled into their bouquets.

Levi felt a bit sniffly himself as she came to stand beside him in front of the celebrant. She was so heartbreakingly beautiful he couldn't believe she was his.

Behind him were his best men, Chase and Finn. Chase had gotten married only a month earlier in the very same spot, and Finn was currently annoyed that Levi had pipped him at the post, but only because Finn's son had been born three weeks early, surprising everyone.

Mystery, whom Levi had formally adopted, and who was now living with him and Indigo in the tiny house until their larger home was completed, was being very good and sitting at his feet. Indigo had knit him a collar and he was wearing it proudly.

The rest of the town was around Levi, the community he'd stumbled into and, as it turned out, had accepted him long before he'd accepted them.

It had taken him some time to realize that he needed to accept himself too, but he'd gotten there in the end.

And all thanks to his beautiful Indigo.

After the ceremony, there was of course a barbecue on the bank beside the lake, and someone had brought some speakers, and there was music and even dancing.

It was the best night of his life.

And at the end, they sat on the gravelly beach beside the bonfire that someone had lit and watched the sun set.

Chase with Izzy leaning against him and

offering instructions to Gus as she tried to toast a marshmallow.

Finn holding his new son in the crook of one arm, while he held a sleepy Beth in the other.

Indigo put her head on Levi's shoulder and sighed. "Is it time to go? I want to spend some alone time with my husband."

Yes, he had a home, and he had a wife, and they would have a family together, a future.

Everything he'd ever wanted was finally his.

Everything he'd ever wanted being her.

"I think so," he said quietly as a peace he'd never known, a peace he'd always been searching for, settled down inside him. "Let's go home, hedgehog."

Luckily, they didn't have to go far.

They were already home.

Acknowledgments

Many thanks to Deb Werksman, my editor, and the wonderful Sourcebooks team; also my agent Helen Breitwieser, and the beautiful South Island for being the most geographically gorgeous part of New Zealand.

About the Author

Jackie Ashenden has been writing fiction since she was eleven years old. Mild-mannered fantasy/SF/pseudo-literary writer by day, obsessive romance writer by night, she used to balance her writing with the more serious job of librarianship until a chance meeting with another romance writer prompted her to throw off the shackles of her day job and devote herself to the true love of her heart—writing romance. She particularly likes to write dark, emotional stories with alpha heroes who've just gotten the world to their liking only to have it blown wide apart by their kick-ass heroines.

She lives in Auckland, New Zealand, with her husband, the inimitable Dr. Jax, two kids, one dog, and one cat. When she's not torturing alpha males and their obstreperous heroines, she can be found drinking chocolate martinis, reading anything she can lay her hands on, or being forced to go mountain biking with her husband.

Find Jackie online at jackieashenden.com, Instagram @jackie_ashenden, or facebook.com/jackie.ashenden.

Also by Jackie Ashenden

ALASKA HOMECOMING
Come Home to Deep River
Deep River Promise
That Deep River Feeling

SMALL TOWN DREAMS
Find Your Way Home
All Roads Lead to You

The Calendar

A Week

by Patricia J. Murphy

Consulting Editor: Gail Saunders-Smith, PhD

Capstone
press
Mankato, Minnesota

Pebble Books are published by Capstone Press,
1710 Roe Crest Drive, North Mankato, Minnesota 56003.
www.capstonepub.com

Books published by Capstone Press are manufactured with paper
containing at least 10 percent post-consumer waste.

Library of Congress Cataloging-in-Publication Data
Murphy, Patricia J., 1963–
    A week / by Patricia J. Murphy.
    p. cm.—(The calendar)
    Includes bibliographical references and index.
    ISBN 13: 978-0-7368-3627-2 (hardcover)
    ISBN 10: 0-7368-3627-6 (hardcover)
    ISBN 13: 978-0-7368-5076-6 (softcover)
    ISBN 10: 0-7368-5076-2 (softcover)
    1. Week—Juvenile literature. I. Title.
CE13.M87 2005
529'.2—dc22
                                           2004011901

Note to Parents and Teachers

The Calendar set supports national social studies and history standards related to time, place, and change. This book describes and illustrates a week. The images support early readers in understanding the text. The repetition of words and phrases helps early readers learn new words. This book also introduces early readers to subject-specific vocabulary words, which are defined in the Glossary section. Early readers may need assistance to read some words and to use the Table of Contents, Glossary, Read More, Internet Sites, and Index sections of the book.

Printed in the United States of America in North Mankato, Minnesota.
012012   006536CGVMI